Matthew 7:7

In 1380 Wycliffe translated the Bible into English for the first time.

> "Axe ze and it schal be zoun to zou,
> seke ze and ze schuln fynde."

In 1534 Tyndale had to hide from Church authorities while he risked his life to translate the New Testament from Latin into English.

> "Axe and it shal be given you;
> Seke and ye shall fynd."

In 1611 King James authorized a new version.

> "Ask, and it shall be given you;
> seek, and ye shall find."

Recovery of the Lost Sword

L. L. CHAIKIN

BROADMAN PRESS
NASHVILLE, TENNESSEE

© Copyright 1990 ● Broadman Press
All rights reserved
4260-09
ISBN; 0-8054-6009-8
Dewey Decimal Classification: F
Subject Heading: BIBLE - VERSIONS - FICTION
TYNDALE, WILLIAM - FICTION
Library of Congress Catalog Card Number: 89-27119
Printed in the United States of America

Unless otherwise stated, all Scripture quotations are
from the King James Version of the Bible.

**Library of Congress Cataloging-in-Publication
Data**

Chaikin, L. L., 1943-
    Recovery of the lost sword / L.L. Chaikin.
        p. cm.
    ISBN 0-8054-6009-8 : $12.95
    1. Tyndale, William, d. 1536—Fiction. I. Title.
PS3553.H2425R44 1990
813'.54—dc20   89-27119
                                                                CIP

To all those who made
the publication of this book possible—
my deepest gratitude

Glossary of Fictional Characters

Justin Brice, the hero
Lady Regina Redford, the heroine
Lord Marlon, a close friend to Justin
Captain Ewan Brice, father of Justin and Stewert Brice
Felix, a slave
Andrew, the corsair (pirate)
Baron Soleiman, on the Balearic Islands
The giant Nubian, the bodyguard of the baron
The Soothsayer, enemy of the Scriptures
Master of Arts Mirandola, in Rome
Marcus and John, fellow student-priests at the monastery in Rome
The archbishop, uncle of Marcus
The abbot at Saint Athenians in Italy
Lisbeth, the maid
Hicks, the stable boy
Bishop Constantine, who arrested Lady Regina, the heroine
Lord Simon Redford, the father of Regina and Marlon
The young man at Peter Quentel's print shop in Cologne
The scholar from Wittenberg University who brought news of Martin Luther's ninety-five theses
The Masters of Arts and doctors at Cambridge, who debated Luther's work

Glossary of Historical Characters

William Tyndale, translator of the first printed English New Testament. Martyred in 1536.

John Wycliffe, translator of the handwritten English Bible in the fourteenth Century. He is called "The Morning Star' of the Reformation."

John Frith, the able scholar and close friend of Tyndale.

Dean John Colet, Oxford University, Reformer.

Erasmus, Cambridge University, Reformer, and translator of the Greek New Testament.

Martin Luther, Wittenberg University, Reformer.

Philipp Melanchthon, Wittenberg, Reformer.

Henry VIII, king of England.

Catherine, queen of England.

Lady Anne Boleyn. queen of England after Catherine. She was an indirect friend of Tyndale and was responsible for giving *The Obedience of a Christian Man* to King Henry. She also owned a copy of Tyndale's New Testament signed, "W. Tyndale."

Cardinal Thomas Wolsey, persecutor of the Reformers.

Bishop Cuthbert Tunstall, the bishop of London to whom Tyndale went to receive permission to translate the Scriptures into English. He is the bishop who burned the English New Testaments at Saint Paul's Cross.

Bishop Stokesley, bishop after Tunstall. One of the bitterest enemies of the Reformers. He is believed to have financed Henry Phillips, the man who betrayed Tyndale.

Sir Thomas More, lord chancellor to King Henry. He was commissioned by the king and the Church to refute Tyndale, and wrote nine books against him and the English New Testament.

Humphrey Monmouth, a cloth merchant in London who aided Tyndale.

Thomas Poyntze, one of Tyndale's greatest friends among the English merchants at Antwerp.

Sir John and Lady Anne Walsh, Little Sodbury. It was while he served them as tutor to their two small children that he made the famous statement to a priest, "If God grant me life, ere many years pass I will see that the boy behind his plow knows more of the Scripture than thou dost."

Thomas Cromwell, chancellor to the king who succeeded Sir Thomas More. A Protestant, he tried to befriend Tyndale.

Fredrick the elector of Saxony, who defended Martin Luther against the edict calling for his arrest on the charges of heresy.

Miles Coverdale, a friend of Tyndale, and a fellow translator. The English Bible King Henry approved had Coverdale's name on it, but the work was primarily Tyndale's.

Vaughan, a friendly agent of King Henry VIII who tried to bring Tyndale back to England to serve in the palace.

Henry Phillips. He betrayed Tyndale in 1535.

Will (William) Roye (or Roy) was clerk to Tyndale in the first translation of the English New testament at Cologne.

Peter Quentel, the printer in Cologne.

Schoeffer, the printer in Worms.

Patrick Hamilton, the young Scottish martyr.

Mistress Margaret von Emmerson, a friend to Tyndale in Hamburg after the shipwreck which destroyed the translation of the Pentateuch.

Thomas Garrett, the distributor for the English New Testaments in London.

"For the word of God is quick, and powerful, and sharper than any two-edged sword" (Heb. 4:12).

"And the sword of the Spirit, which is the word of God" (Eph. 6:17).

Part I

1

Windsor Castle, London
A.D. 1513

> I rejoice at thy word,
> as one that findeth great spoil
> (Ps. 119:162).

In the distance, Windsor Castle stood a sullen gray against the backdrop of the worsening winter sky, which threatened to overcome the weak sunlight before it had a chance to warm the frosty morning. Galloping hooves of fine royal steeds broke the hush as a group of young squire knights raced down the road toward the stables of King Henry VIII.

On Justin's left, the boundary of land was mostly marsh—the haunt of wildfowl—and the headlong rush of his thoroughbred frightened a raven which gave an irritated shriek and took off down a lane of trees, swooping among the low-hanging branches that held shadows against the light.

A faint patter of rain wet his helmet, swiftly turning into a steady downpour. The spirits of the young men were soon dampened as well as their armor and royal standard.

But Justin Brice felt good this morning. He had won the practice tournament with the young squire knights, who were all sons of lords and earls. He relished his victory because he was not bred of English nobility. His father was from Scotland.

The Brice castle, lands, and Scottish title of Earl of Kendall had been lost in the devastating battle at Flodden Field, when the Scottish king unwisely turned against his brother-in-law, King Henry VIII, and invaded England. Some of the best and most gallant Scottish fathers and sons had been cut down at Flodden. The king himself had been left arrow-pierced and dying on the field.

Justin's father had left Scotland and took to the merchant routes of the sea where he became a famed privateer in search of ways to replenish his lost fortune. Captain Brice had left Justin and his two sisters in the care of his English friend, the head groom at King Henry's stables. Had it not been for Justin's close friendship with Marlon Redford, the son of an English lord, he would have found no acceptance among the sons of the other English nobility. Now, Justin anxiously awaited his father's return to the Port of London.

It was December, 1513. In the spring his father would return, and Justin expected to begin his career as a privateer, joining his older brother Stewert, who was already on the Brice galleon, loading cargo at Genoa for King Henry. Justin dreamed of the sea, the feel of the water lapping against the hull of the ship, and the freedom that sang with the tug of the salty wind against his tunic.

Justin glanced over his shoulder. He was still a length ahead of the others in the race to the stables. He knew a shortcut through the dismal woods and turned his horse out of the road into the thicket where black branches interlaced overhead.

An angry shout reached his ears. The other squires admired his tenacity but dared not follow. Superstition, mingled with erroneous religious beliefs, lurked in the hearts of many, who nurtured old tales of medieval history which declared the woods a habitation of "wicked things," or even worse—"heretics." At times they weren't sure which was the worst, a cloven-hoofed demon or a follower of John Wycliffe. The ecclesiastics said they were the same. To question the difference often meant heresy; Justin had heard of some Wycliffites being put in dungeons and, if they refused to recant, burned at the stake.

But Justin had no time to worry about cloven hooves nor yet to concern himself with the definition of heresy. He was soon going to sea! He would draw swords with the other corsairs and one day join the ranks of the explorers who had discovered the New World. It was enough to attend the services at the village church, rush through his memorized prayers, and attend the school where the determined Dominican monk relentlessly tried to teach him Latin.

The marshy earth was soft beneath the stallion's hooves as the rain fell, and ahead, a field that in summer was overgrown with purple heather was now dark with winter gray.

On the road, the young squire knights reined their steeds to a nervous but proud prance. The son of the Earl of Roxbury threw up his face shield.

"The Scottish knave has won again."

Lord Marlon Redford was especially vexed. He already felt irritated at losing the tournament to his friend, but the race, too?

Lord Marlon gave a disgruntled glance at the earl's son, while he adjusted the angle of his helm and chin strap, then with determination leaned over and grasped the royal standard with his gloved hand. The scarlet banner hung wet but refused to yield its dignity. With that, he dug his heels into the horse's side and galloped after Justin, intent to run him down whatever the cost.

Justin raced the king's black stallion through the field. Ahead the few remaining oak trees stood, reaching their web of dark branches to mingle with the fir, beech, and pine.

The stream ran dark and sullen in the cloud-shrouded land, and the merging clumps of dark woodland thickened. Justin turned in his saddle to see Lord Marlon not far behind. He smiled to himself, for Marlon feared the superstitious marsh as much as the others.

Darkness deepened and lightning flashed as they raced forward and the mizzling rain whispered through the dark fir trees. Suddenly Justin pulled the reins and the horse dug in its front legs and stopped. Lord Marlon was not far behind and was too cautious to drive his charger past, even if it would gain him distance in the race. Instead he rode up beside Justin. At once he understood Justin's reluctance.

They heard the sound of a skirmish ahead and the smell of a campfire hung on the moist air. The sounds of distant alarm set their chargers to prancing with nervous anticipation, and they held them with firm hands. "Easy, boy, easy," Justin whispered leaning forward to stroke the sweating animal.

Marlon tugged apprehensively at his gloved gauntlet, and scowled. "Fighting, here?" He asked softly, surprised. "We'd best turn back."

Justin shook his head, still poised to listen. What reached his ears over the wind was not the sounds of battle but voices and the cries of women and children.

"Trouble," said Justin. "Let's see what is is"

"No, if it is trouble among the peasants, let it be their trouble, not ours." Marlon fretted. "Do you intend to involve yourself in a matter you know nothing about?"

"Shall we not see, at least? It is the cry of women."

Marlon managed a stern look which boasted the superiority of position. "One day your inquisitive nature, surely born of ill Scottish blood, will get you into more trouble than even I can squelch."

Justin ignored him and moved the stallion cautiously ahead. Reluctantly, Marlon followed.

As son of Lord Simon Redford, Marlon had gained permission for Justin to joust with the noble squire knights, but, in fact, neither of them were yet considered knights. If they became involved in a skirmish, Lord Simon would ban them both from training for several months.

Chivalric custom denied the knightly accolade to youths under eighteen, except in unusual circumstances. Meanwhile they remained in subordinate rank as squires.

The jingle of their royal harness and the plod of horse hooves over the wet moss went unnoticed as they threaded their way through the trees. Ahead, Justin began to see the signs of trouble. At a place where a number of trees had fallen in some past windstorm, he saw clustered around a campfire a number of unarmed peasants, men, women, and children. A shouting argument was under way with a Dominican cleric. The cleric was not armed, but several men of civic authority were. They waited for the word to arrest the peasants.

"Wycliffites," breathed Marlon. "Stay far afield if you wish to avoid wrath. Come, let us go back."

The Wycliffites were followers of John Wycliffe who had translated the Scriptures into English in 1382.

"Do something!" Justin demanded. "Use your authority as a lord's son."

Marlon looked at him sharply. "Are you completely out of your mind? Me? Confront a Dominican?"

"Aren't you the son of Lord Simon? The king thinks highly of your father. Demand that the clerics release the people in the name of the king."

"And risk not only the wrath of my father but the bishop? The Wycliffites are heretics. Why else would the clerics arrest them?"

Justin knew nothing of the belief of those who after a century, still followed John Wycliffe, who had been a leading theologian and philosopher at Oxford, Europe's most outstanding university. He was responsible for the first translation of Scripture into English, and the Church had issued bulls, or edicts, against him for heresy. He had questioned the doctrines of the Church and criticized the corruption of the clergy. The worst crime had been to translate the Scripture from the Latin into English. Even though Wycliffe had died peacefully in his home, the Church had exhumed his body years later, burned his bones, then scattered his heretical ashes on the River Swift.

Although his followers had been persecuted and nearly disappeared from England, the theologian's ideas still troubled the Church. And groups still gathered in private cottages or in the woods to hear the Bible read in the English tongue, or to hear sermons translated and simplified from Wycliffe's Latin taught by itinerant preachers. The gatherings were unauthorized and the literature strictly forbidden under the law of 1501 which ordered the burning of any literature questioning the Church's authority.

"Look—they are about to be arrested. Who knows what ill fate they shall meet?" Justin kneed his horse forward as Marlon reached to halt him.

"In the name of the king, stop!"

Surprised, all eyes turned upon the rider on the black stallion. He wore chain mail with a dark tunic over it, and a helmet. They could not see his face and stared, aghast.

Seizing the moment, the Wycliffites broke and ran in all directions. Looking over his shoulder Justin saw the old man who had been in charge of the meeting running through the trees. There was a scroll in his hand and, unnoticed by his opponents, he hid it swiftly under the fallen trees, then ran on, disappearing into the shadows.

Justin stared at the spot where the parchment was hidden until the angry cleric demanded, "Who are you?"

Just then Lord Marlon grudgingly rode up, giving Justin an angry look. He bowed. "Forgive our interruption, my Lord," he said soothingly. "My friend is a mite hasty when it comes to the practice of chivalry. He mistook you for raiders against poor farmers and wished to prove himself worthy of knighthood."

"You dare interfere in the arrest of heretics?"

"We did not know, my Lord, that you were arresting heretics," hastened Marlon.

The priest looked at him askance. "Don't I know you?"

Marlon cleared his throat, reluctant to admit it. "My father is Lord Simon Redford," and he bowed again. "Your servant, my Lord."

The Dominican recognized the esteemed name. Marlon removed his helmet showing his face. As he did so his dark eyes angrily met Justin's. The incident could mean real trouble for both of them.

"Ah? Is his lordship aware that his son keeps company with an obvious Wycliffite?" he challenged, pointing a finger at Justin.

Justin removed his helmet, pushed back the sweat-stained arming cap from damp brown hair tinged with auburn, and scooped back the tendrils with a mailed gauntlet from his forehead. The face was handsome, and the blue-gray eyes did not yield to the priest's glower. He had been called many things since coming to London, and he supposed that being called a "Wycliffite" was only one more insult added to the others.

"What is your name?" the cleric demanded.

"Brice, Justin Brice."

The name meant nothing to the cleric, but the brogue did. He looked at him more closely. "Are you Scottish?"

"Aye."

"H-m, and your father?"

"Sir Ewan Brice," Justin hesitated and added, "the privateer. He is at sea. I now serve His Majesty in the service of the royal horses. And I could not be a Wycliffite, my Lord, for I know not who, or what, they are."

"They are heretics. And you have stupidly intervened in their arrest. I say your intervention was planned."

"Not so," he said simply. "His lordship and I were returning from a joust. We decided—that is, I decided—to race his lordship to the stables."

The priest took in this handsome youth and relented somewhat. He scanned him, taking in the form of a lad who promised fine strength and wit, and found his guilessness almost endearing. Nevertheless, he glowered to think that the heretics had escaped, and his black brows furrowed.

"And what will you do about your transgression?"

Justin shifted uncomfortably in his saddle, trying to remember what he had been taught about "transgression."

"You have just made it possible for a nest of heretical cockleburs to escape. I have been after them for months! Are you also a lad bent on heresy?"

Justin felt his heart pound. *A heretic!* "I could hardly be that. I know not what these fellows read in their forbidden books."

Marlon interrupted, for he felt Justin was not apologetic enough. "My Lord, hearken unto me. The lad," he said of Justin as though he himself were twice his senior, "is, as I explained, merely anxious to win his knighthood by deeds of merit. I confess, Sir," he hastened, "to filling his mind with dreams of knighthood."

Justin turned his head sharply toward Marlon who ignored him and went on speaking to the priest. "Release the stableboy to my care. I vow to see that my father, Lord Simon, rebukes his guardian for not keeping tighter control of the lad. May his transgression be pardoned with an indulgence from the Church, my Lord."

The priest rubbed his chin thoughtfully. His eyes took in the royal black stallion.

21

"He belongs to His Majesty," Justin stated swiftly.

Marlon grew exuberant at the success of his intercession, believing he was making headway, and added, "Let the lad pay twice his indulgence."

"Twice!" Justin turned to him indignantly. "With what, your Lordship, do I pay 'twice'? When but once is beyond my penury?"

"Silence!" the priest demanded with such awesome thunder that even Justin felt the lightning of doom strike his head. For the first time he measured the weight of his error. He grew mute. *How am I going to explain all this to my guardian, Balin York? Twice the indulgence! Where can I get the price to pay?* He began to think of what he might bring to the blacksmith to sell. *My hunting bow, my sword, perhaps my boots—they are made of fine cordovan leather. My father brought them from Cadiz on the coast of Spain. Still—it won't be enough.*

In the silence following, nothing moved but the wind rustling dead leaves overhead, and the drip of rain pelting his armor and running down Justin's neck. The stallion snorted and restlessly pawed the mossy, sodden earth.

"Master Brice," said the cleric. "See that you are at Saint Catherine's in the morning. The set price of your indulgence shall then be decided."

Tiny beads of perspiration broke out on his forehead and he wiped them away with the back of his gauntlet. "I shall be there at dawn, my Lord."

"Be on your way."

Justin turned the stallion and rode off at once, Lord Marlon swiftly behind him. Some distance away at the stream bank, Justin held his mount.

Marlon's face was flushed with exasperation. "Yeoman clod! You have blundered us both into trouble." His dark eyes flashed. "My father will surely hear of this venture."

Justin gave him a dour look then turned his horse in the

direction they had just ridden from. He stood in his stirrups to peer back into the shadows. He could see nothing.

"Now what are you doing?"

"I wonder if the peasants escaped?"

"Do you not know that the Dominican will go posthaste to Lord Simon about this? I doubt if I will be permitted to see you again. And you concern yourself with rabble Wycliffites!"

"The old teacher hid his parchment in the logs."

"Let it rot! I ride to Windsor. Perchance I can head off the Dominican with a worthy gift."

"Go then. I will see the parchment for myself."

Marlon looked at him with incredulity. "If the writing is found on your person, you could easily be put on trial. Your call to be at the church was anything but a light matter."

"Have you no curiosity to see for yourself what these heretics are preaching behind locked doors and in the darkness of the woods?"

"No," Marlon said dryly.

"You are too typically a lord's son."

"Come, Justin! Do not meddle. Let the viper sleep and you will not be enchanted."

"Go then. I will have a look. What can one glimpse do? Surely it will change nothing."

"Why I involve myself with the poor likes of you, I can only guess. Go then, Yeoman, but I will not beg my father this time to help you."

Lord Marlon rode off. Justin watched him disappear among the birches, then turned his stallion in the direction of the little meadow where the followers of Wycliffe had met.

The Dominican had gone and Justin drew up, stopping well back under the trees. The rain had ceased, except for a few last drops falling from the branches.

Justin listened, hearing no sound. The small campfire no longer smoldered for rain had dampened it out, but the smell of smoke lingered in the air. *It was a mistake to have made the fire in the first place,* he thought, associating himself with them in his mind, *and they should have gathered deeper into the forest.*

The horse snorted, shaking his mane as though bidding him to stay, and Justin felt an inward tug-of-war. *Why this curiosity? What does it matter what these Wycliffites think? Let well enough alone,* he told himself. *Perhaps Marlon was right; why risk it? In a few months my father will dock his ship at the Port of London and I will join him for a life at sea. If the Wycliffites are heretics, let them be. And if the Church is disposed by God to destroy them, then let them do their work. What should any of it matter to me?*

Yet, a strange prodding overcame him that urged him forward to the parchment to read it for himself, to understand the motivation which drove men to risk imprisonment and even death in order to read forbidden words. What words were these which held such compelling power over them? What manner of man was this devilish Wycliffe who urged men, women, and children to risk their lives to read his work?

Darting from the shadows to the cluster of fallen logs, Justin removed his glove and ran his hand under the spot where the old teacher had hidden the parchment.

The teachers were called by the Wycliffites "evangelical men" or "apostolic men," and they were both laymen and ordained, who had accepted the call to preach. Wycliffe had prepared tracts, skeletons of sermons, and translations of Scripture portions, all in the English vernacular of the people.

Despite the chill wind he perspired, looking over his shoulder in fear of seeing the cleric with hands on hips, shouting, "Aha! So we have you now!" but there was no one in sight except the king's restless stallion.

His hand touched the parchment. Grasping it, he lifted it free and with trembling hands shoved it inside his tunic. Then from behind him, a soft footfall!

Turning, Justin saw a feminine figure on horseback. She

wore a hooded cloak of dark blue velvet lined with marten fur. Lady Regina Redford, Marlon's younger sister, gave him a smile. "So you have come back for it. I thought so."

Justin was relieved, yet disturbed for her safety. Regina surpassed the adventurous spirit of her brother.

"Trouble surely awaits you at Saint Catherine's tomorrow. What will you do for money?" she asked.

"You too, My Lady, will know trouble if found with me. For your sake, you had best go. Look—a thunderstorm is coming, and you will ruin your garment."

"I fear neither thunder nor lightning. Indeed, such storms remind me of heaven's power over men. I rather enjoy them."

"A worthy description, My Lady, and your zeal of heavenly matters is noteworthy. Nevertheless, Lord Marlon has ridden back to the stables. And you should not be found alone with me."

Justin held the parchment behind him and backed toward his stallion.

Regina was calm but adamant. For weeks now she had been spying on the Wycliffites and was curious to know their condemned beliefs. Her tutor in the palace, Master of Arts Whitfield, knew some of the leaders of the heretical group. With the skill of a fine rider, Regina eased her mount around the treacherous logs and rode up to him.

"I will not leave without a look at the forbidden writing."

"You should not have come, My Lady. It is dangerous to involve yourself."

She smiled. "Yet you do not hesitate."

Regina played with the reins in her gloved hands while she tried to reject her growing feelings for the young man below her horse. She was to marry the Earl's son the following year. The marriage was political, and she was trying every truthful way to avoid it.

"I know something of John Wycliffe," she said cautiously,

glancing about. "My tutor is a friend of the great Erasmus, who teaches the original language at Cambridge, and also of Master John Colet at Oxford. Do you know that Erasmus criticizes the abuses in the Church?"

"You are brave to admit there are any. You know too much for your own safety."

As ever, her intellect, mingled with her feminine graces, impressed him. Lady Regina was not vain, nor was she bragging. He had learned long ago that her interest in serious matters was bred from a sincere desire to know. His own learning at the small Dominican school consisted of simple Latin grammar, reading, writing, and some calculation.

"I confess, My Lady, that the school I attend is not fortunate enough to have your tutor."

"I have asked my father that you might join my classes," she said, looking about indifferently and flapping the reins against her gloved palm, "but he thought your presence would cause talk. And now, let us share the forbidden parchment," she whispered. "If not, I could go directly to my father about your heresy." Her brown eyes teased and challenged him.

Her determination had him trapped. He looked about. Obviously, they couldn't stay there. "There is a stream a few miles from here. I go there to hunt coneys. We shall be safe for awhile."

At the quiet stream they listened to the rustle of the leaves. Convinced they were alone, he took the parchment from his tunic and they smiled in equal excitement. As his eyes fell to the writing, his breath caught. He stared.

Regina couldn't stand the silence. She pushed her head close to his, and at once saw his reason for surprise. This was no paraphrased sermon of Wycliffe, but a translation of Scripture from Latin into the vulgar tongue. Her breath caught and her eyes met his.

"Do you know the penalty for translating any portion of Scripture into the vulgar tongue?" she whispered.

"Yes."

The Church had decreed in 1408 that no one could translate Scripture into English, nor even speak it, except in the sacred tongue of Latin.

"Look! The very holy words are in our own tongue," she breathed, awed. Her brown eyes gleamed. "Doesn't it make you feel strange?"

"Yes, like walking into a holy place where you have not been invited."

She glanced about with a chill of excitement. "Nonetheless," she whispered, "read them."

They settled themselves against the trunk of a great oak, its overspreading branches keeping back much of the rain. Justin's voice read quietly, at times hardly more than a whisper. The pale light of noontide fell across the handwritten page like a light from heaven.

"Holy Scripture is the preeminent authority for every Christian, and the rule of faith of all human perfection . . ."

He paused to consider 'preeminent authority' . . . then went on reading,

"Five Rules for Studying the Bible:"

"Obtain a reliable text . . ."

Now! How do you go about doing that? he wondered. He thought of the old battered Vulgate used in the schoolroom for translating simple verses from Latin.

"understand the logic of Scripture," he began again.

"Compare the parts of Scripture with one another . . .

"maintain an attitude of humble seeking, and receive the instruction of the Spirit."

His eyes dropped further down the page. In clear handwriting the words *The Gospel of Matthew* stared boldly up at him.

"Now the birth of Jesus Christ was on this wise . . ."

As he read through the Gospel of Matthew the midday sun crept lower in the sky. A squirrel had braved their presence to scamper among the fallen leaves.

But thou, when thou prayest, enter into thy closet, and when thou hast shut thy door, pray to thy Father which is in secret; and thy Father which seeth in secret shall reward thee openly. But when ye pray, use not vain repetitions, as the heathen do: for they think that they shall be heard for their much speaking. Be not ye therefore like unto them: for your Father knoweth what things ye have need of, before ye ask him. After this manner therefore pray ye: Our Father which art in heaven, Hallowed be thy name. Thy kingdom come. Thy will be done in earth, as it is in heaven. Give us this day our daily bread. And forgive us our debts, as we forgive our debtors. And lead us not into temptation, but deliver us from evil.

The afternoon wore on, but in their hearts, time had ceased. There was neither anything devilish nor rebellious to be found in the writing. They had never heard such such wondrous words and their souls burned as he read of the crucifixion and the resurrection of Jesus Christ. Regina wiped the tears from her cheeks with the back of her velvet glove.

And Jesus came and spake unto them, saying, All power is given unto me in heaven and in earth. Go ye, therefore, and teach all nations, baptizing them in the name of the Father, and of the Son, and of the Holy Ghost; Teaching them to observe all things whatsoever I have commanded you; and lo, I am with you always, even unto the end of the world. Amen.

They sat there, unable to break the spell. Neither spoke a word. Finally, Regina stirred and rose to her feet. The sun was low in the west. If her maid Lisbeth were not waiting to sneak her into the palace, she would be in trouble. She swallowed hard, easing the cramp in her throat, and wrapped her damp cloak more snugly about her, for it grew colder. She wondered at the new tenderness for Christ which burned like hot coals within her heart. She would know more of this wondrous Person—yea, much more.

She turned her back to Justin and walked slowly to her horse. Her cheeks grew damp, her dark eyes dimmed with moisture, and the wind stung her vision. She stroked the auburn mane of the horse, then mounted without his assistance.

"Truly," breathed Justin, still staring at the parchment, "I do not know what to think." He placed it carefully under his tunic and walked to the stallion. "I cannot see why the Wycliffites are persecuted, or why they cannot meet to read such fine words without being hounded."

"You do know why," she warned quietly. "It is heresy to translate the Scripture into the vernacular, and no less a crime to read it." She shuddered.

His response arose from past indifference to sudden conviction. "It is considered to be so," he corrected. To himself he thought, *But is it? Why should it be?*

"It was awesome to hear the words in English," Regina whispered. "And to hear so much at one time."

"And to read it," marveled Justin. "I tasted the words with my tongue and they were like honey! I confess to being deeply moved."

His eyes sought hers and for the moment they shared the miraculous experience in the oneness of profound silence, their hearts knit together, and he loved her.

"John Wycliffe is certainly no devil," said Justin.

"Yet, to possess his work is strictly forbidden."

They turned their horses to ride, Regina to Windsor Castle; Justin to the humble cottage of his guardian near the stables.

"I will send word to your guardian tomorrow. You are invited to dine," she said.

Regina often invited him to their table. "You must put the

parchment back where the teacher hid it. If they find it on you.
. . ."

Justin shook his head. "Nay, I must surely read it again. There was so much to comprehend. I would go back over the story of the cross and the tomb, for I have never heard it so plain before."

Regina was sure he would contemplate making a copy. "If you do, and they discover it, you will be arrested," she whispered, her eyes troubled.

"I will memorize it. It is better than the other things I am commanded to memorize in school."

She turned again to ride on, then looked back over her shoulder. Her eyes were grave. "Do your best to please the cleric tomorrow. How will you pay?"

He glanced at the sun. It was getting late, but he must still ride over and see the blacksmith. "I will sell my sword." He smiled ruefully. "I shall ride with you to the road; it will be dusk before you reach Windsor."

Justin's guardian, Balin York, paced the flagstone floor, the herbs crunching under his boots, his sun-bronzed forehead furrowed. His large hands rough with work, the nails hopelessly blackened, dangled at his sides clenching and unclenching as his dark mood smoldered with the gathering thunderstorm that threatened the night.

He was a great hulk of man with little patience for the errors of others. *Had the lad no wit? Must he forever meddle in the plights of others?* Only the week before he had intervened to stop a farmer on his way to market from using a tree branch on a donkey pulling the cart. Now, saints forbid, he had intervened to save heretics!

The Dominican had left their cottage and Balin York was frightened. *Wait until the wretched lad shows up! Where is he at this hour? Supper's late!*

Mistress York stirred the blackened pot slung from a winch above the fireplace. Signs of weariness were etched upon her prematurely aging skin. She moved her mouth to keep from crying aloud. Justin's two sisters sat in wide-eyed silence at the scrubbed table.

"I tell you I'm at my wits' end with the lad," Master Balin York growled. "He will have us all burned." He was sorry now that they had agreed to take Justin and the girls into their cottage. Captain Brice would pay them well on his return from the sea, but it was another thing to have a cleric come and question them about heretical beliefs.

"His will is strong," she said. "He is much like his father."

"Yes, and like Ewan Brice he will have a heavy price on his head one day."

"Was it not you who helped him aboard the ship to escape?"

"To save his neck from hanging."

"Hush!" she gave a jerk of her head in the direction of Justin's sisters. The girls knew enough to pretend they didn't understand. Catherine played with the rim of her empty bowl, her eyes downcast, but Mary, only five, stared at them with her mouth open, her eyelids heavy with sleep. She glanced toward the pot simmering over the fireplace wondering how much longer it would be until she could eat, then climb into her blanket in the loft.

"Husband, give him time to explain. The lad will have a worthy reason for his actions. Justin is no troublemaker."

"Bah, and where is he? He deigns to confront the priest, then keeps me from me supper!"

"Captain Brice will return for him this spring," she soothed. "Our days with him will be over. Has he not promised a worthy pay? Let the lad find a little peace here. He serves you well in the stables. You said so yourself only this morning."

"Aye, but we all might be burned before spring."

"Silence, I pray! You will scare us all into bad dreams."

Mistress York made no further comment but vigorously stirred the pot. To relieve her rising emotion she cried, "You, Catherine, don't sit there gawking. Lend a hand. Bring your uncle's plate. Mary! Wake up for prayers!"

Justin opened the cottage door and stepped into the main room that served as both hall and kitchen, bringing a gust of wind and rain with him. He tried to close the door quietly but the gust caught it from his hand and slammed it.

The room went silent as every eye fixed upon him. He had left the helmet and chain mail in the care of the captain at the armory, and was dressed now in a dark tunic, a cloak, and a wide-brimmed hat.

"Well, Lad?" Balin York boomed. "It's about time you showed your face. The priest was here. Tomorrow your wicked debt must be paid!"

So, Justin's hope that the news would not reach them had proved vain.

"You have aided the bloody Wycliffites, and you think that it means no harm? Know that the priest accused us of being followers of John Wycliffe. They searched the cottage for his writings—what have you in your tunic?"

The bright blue eyes seemed to bore a hole through Justin.

Mistress York, alarmed at the turn of events, drew his two sisters away from the table.

"Nothing that will bring harm to your soul."

Balin stepped toward him and held out his hand. "Hand it over," he whispered. "If you refuse to show me respect. . . ."

Justin with tense but calm dignity slowly produced the parchment. "It is a month's work by hand, at least. Treat it carefully, I beg you."

When he saw his worst fears realized, Balin York broke out into a sweat. He turned at once to his wife. "Take the girls and put them to bed."

"But, husband, our supper, . . ." but one look at Balin and the parchment, and her face turned pale. She took hold of the startled girls and ushered them away, promising them they would eat later, and if they were good, a sweet bread sprinkled with sugar and seeds would follow.

"This," he choked, "are you altogether mad? Will you have us all burned with you?" Balin hissed, his eyes blazing. He whirled and in one giant stride was at the door, bolting it. In another stride he was before the hearth. At once he begin ripping the parchment and throwing the pieces into the flames.

Justin was stunned. Then sprang at him, grasping for the parchment. "Will you burn the words of God?"

"I burn the work of the devil's agent!"

Justin had no sooner reached for the parchment when Balin's hand struck like thunder sending him backward, his head striking hard against the stone floor.

Dazed, it took a moment to get on his feet. A trickle of blood ran from his lip. The pages smoldered within the flames. A terrible sense of horror engulfed him.

Justin stumbled to the hearth, and on his knees snatched wildly to retrieve the burning pages, his fingers seared with pain.

With fierce determination Balin held the rest of the parchment to the flame, the perspiration dripping from his furrowed brow. The sparks flew upward and Justin watched the last portion of Scripture turn into feathery ash.

Gone! Dear God, what have I done? I should have left it where it was. Now the old teacher will have nothing. And I? What have I now? A momentary vision of light, forever gone!

"Confess your sin that God might take pity on you!" Balin said hoarsely.

Justin stared at the burning coals.

At dawn, the spiritual dilemma of his soul continued when, in a downpour of rain as the lightning flashed across the still-darkened sky, Justin rode to the monastery located far from houses and farms. He reached the monastery steps, his heart weighted down with burden. In a small bag he carried the coins from the sale of his sword and boots. It would hardly be enough.

The Dominican was waiting behind his desk, a candle burning. The rain beat like small pebbles against the windowpane. The priest had been up all night in a prayer vigil and there were dark circles under his eyes. For the first time Justin noticed how weary he looked, how his brow was furrowed.

The cashbox sat on the desk and a price list of standard fees for indulgences was before him. Justin wrestled with the dilemma. *Why is it a transgression to be responsible for the escape of the Wycliffites, when the words they had met to read are only Scripture? Why are the words forbidden in the vernacular?* He laid the small bag of coins on the desk.

The cleric ignored it. "Go in peace. Your debt has already been paid."

Surprised, Justin stood there. The Dominican said, "A worthy sum arrived last night by the servant of Lady Regina Redford. She has been most generous. A brilliant damsel. One day she will stun the royal palace with her wit and learning. Whereas you had best watch the waywardness of your feet, before they turn you to the gates of hell."

The message of his father's arrival came on a fine June morning and it was with difficulty Justin restrained his excitement as he walked the London wharf to the Brice ship. The clammy chill of the dawn soaked through his cloak and the mist hung heavily on the dock.

The harbor was rich with the masts of ships from East and West.

The poignant aroma of the sea, and the wind that was crisp and tugging at his cloak, called of freedom. He took the steps down to the quay, walking among the bronzed and often bare-foot sailors and dock workers who carried bundles and baskets on their backs.

His hungry eyes took in everything, including the swarthy faces and boldly dangling earrings. His ears rang with the voices shouting in unknown tongues. With the salt air, Justin inhaled the pungent odors of everything from fish to spoiling fruits, tar, and human bodies. In the eerie whitish-gray mist of the Port of London came the slapping of the water against hulls, and a flock of seagulls that screamed and wheeled in search of their breakfast.

Ahead, Justin caught sight of the ship he sought. The familiar gonfalon of his father's clan appeared, boasting the lion of Scotland.

As he neared the ship, all was quiet. The lulling sound of water slapped against the hull and the wood creaked. One of the crew members on watch saw him and scowled down. "What are you looking for, Lad?"

"My father," Justin called up proudly. "Captain Ewan Brice."

The reddish brows under the blue cap rushed together and he raked the fine figure from head to toe. Justin stood there poised and waiting for the rope ladder to be tossed.

The ladder came toward him, hitting the ship's side. He grabbed hold of the rough rope and climbed up and over the side.

The seaman stood staring at him. In startling ways he looked every inch a Brice, but the blue-gray eyes that met his were unlike the captain's, he decided. They lacked the hard brittle-ness of a man who had drawn sword on his opponent and struck with deadly accuracy. There was a disarming quiet to the young face with no spark of Scottish ferocity that often drove his restless, moody captain to fits of emotional despair. And since a storm at sea, and his fear of God's wrath, Captain

Brice had grown worse, declaring that demons were after his soul. His moods were enough to downright spook a man!

"Is my brother Stewert on board?"

"No. He is on leave."

Justin flung his bag over his shoulder and followed the sailor across the deck to the cargo. The man gestured ahead but made no attempt to escort him.

"Captain Brice waits in 'is cabin. Careful, Lad, 'e's a mite troubled tonight."

All at once Justin felt at home. Dreams of exploration surged through his blood. Someday he would sail as Columbus had done!

The captain's cabin was small. A lantern hanging above the rough wooden table cast a glow on the bowed, dark head of the massive man who sat there poring over a chart. Justin's heart pounded. His father. . . .

For a moment he couldn't move, then he drew in a stilted breath and ducked under the small arched doorway. Captain Ewan Brice looked up with shrewd blue eyes that scanned him with slow recognition. He seemed taken aback, as though expecting the boy he had left. Then a smile spread over his bronzed face and he stood, his broad shoulders swelling under the dark woolen tunic. At once he measured his son and was pleased until his eyes fell on the sword in the scabbard at his side. Ewan Brice at once forgot all else. He gestured abruptly. "Where'd you get that, Lad?"

Justin was thunderstruck. After two years, was this his response? Hurt, he answered stiffly. "From his Lordship Marlon."

"His 'lordship,' he says. Do you not know that you yourself be a lord in Scotland? Am not I an earl? Hanging around with English blood!"

Words of defense rushed to Justin's lips, but he held them back. He owed much to Marlon but before he could explain, his father gestured at the sword. "Off with it, me Lad. 'Tis no mark of a scholar, nor yet a holy man."

Scholar? Holy man? Justin ignored the order and reached an arm toward him. "My Father, I. . . ."

"Dinnae ye hear me, Lad?" His eyes sparked. "Off with it!"

Justin stared at him. The determination in Ewan Brice's face was too clear to ignore, but he rebelled. "On board ship I will need a sword, and I use it well." He gestured to his father's scabbard resting on the small cot. "My own father bears a sword, why not his son?"

"Why, indeed, Lad! Because ye will not follow your father's steps. God forbid! Now do as your father bids. D'ye think ye be man enough to withstand a good whipping?"

"Father!" His eyes burned with exasperation at the thought of being treated like a child.

Ewan Brice started from behind the desk. One sweep of his growing son, convinced him that it might be his last opportunity.

Angry, embarrassed, Justin loosed the sheath and flung it aside with a clatter. Their eyes met evenly and seeing his temper, Captain Brice smiled.

" 'Tis better. Now come here." He gripped him firmly about the shoulders looking him over proudly. "Ye look like ye mother, may she rest in peace. Ye will not bear a sword while I yet live to stop you, and ye will not take one step within my footprints. I have got your good future all settled, my Lad, and proud I am of it." He gestured his head toward the desk where a letter was waiting. He beamed. "From the good bishop in London, no less."

Justin tensed. "Bishop?"

"Who else is good enough to guide you while I take again to the sea? No more of wretched yeomen like Balin. And your sisters, too, shall be sent to a better place. You are too good for such waste. T'was a mistake I din' see to this sooner. But me mind is made up now, Lad. Your destiny lies not with me but in the Church."

Justin did not want to believe what he was hearing. He stared at his beaming father as if he had surely gone mad. The Church! He remembered the dank, stifled monastery. He wanted no part of it. He wanted the sea, the ship, his father, cantankerous though he be. The Church?

"A monastery, no less," said Ewan Brice with satisfaction. "My son shall be a saint. And ye shall make me proud."

"A monastery!" Justin stepped back as if his father had struck him across the face. Stunned at the turn of events his frustration poured forth in angry resentment. "I will choose my own path, even as you did chose yours as a lad. I have done what you asked! I have excelled with the sword, the horse. . . ."

"And nearly broke your neck in a reckless race in the marsh, so Balin sent word. And nearly mixed with heretics!"

Justin stiffened. So he had already been in touch with Balin York!

"It will not happen again because ye will be safe in the robe of scholar and priest."

"A fate worse than death. No! Never!"

"Silence!"

Justin could not be silent. "I learned to read and write as you wished. Is that not enough to demand of me? I will not accept the life of celibacy. I want the sea! A ship of my own!" His eyes flamed with a sudden surge of rebellion. "What of my training as a knight? Ask the baron, he will tell you. I handle the sword and Great Horse better than Lord Marlon."

Ewan Brice was adamant. "That is what I fear. As my younger son it is your right—yea, your responsibility to serve the Church."

"Then it is time for custom to change, if my heart is right."

"Tsk', tsk', me lad. A man's heart has nothing to do with it.

'Tis your duty. I have delayed your journey to Rome long enough."

Rome!

"I have no wish to enter the cloister! Father! Please! Be reasonable, I would even become a barrister if it is education that will make you proud of me, I could go to Magdalen College, then to Oxford University, if I must. But a monastery!"

" 'Tis not a barrister I want, but a holy son, a priest, one to intercede for me."

Intercede? Justin was so overwrought that he nearly laughed —a fatal mistake. He, Justin Brice, to intercede for his father?

Justin's desperation mounted. "And if I refuse?"

"Refuse, says he! You have no choice. You are my gift to God. Surely the Almighty will be pleased and my transgressions lessened in His sight by this act. I vowed you in a storm, my Lad, only months ago. I cannot go back on it, nay," and he shook his large head vigorously, "not if it means me very life. I have already pledged ye, my Son."

Justin went cold. So young, and already his future plans had met a black end. "Pledged me? When?"

"At sea in the storm. And this good morning, I have visited Saint Catherine's and made it official. This letter is yours to bring to the abbot in Rome. 'Tis a good monastery, the best, and full of wealthy and religious sons. 'Tis called Saint Athenians. And there is mention of a great university nearby."

Justin tried to hold back his anger by clenching his jaw. His voice came cold and brittle. "Then you have consigned me to a living death. A dungeon of darkness is no better. Why not simply thrust me through with your own sword? I would show that much mercy for a wounded animal."

"Hold your wicked tongue! God wills it."

His father, a great hulk of a man with fierce Scottish blood, then grinned as his moods swung from high to low. The smile was broad and affable as he tried to console Justin, throwing an arm about his shoulder with a strong surge of power.

"Try to understand, Justin. Should death strike me, my soul will know rest for this worthy deed. My enemies would see me dead. Know ye not my head is hunted this very moment by corsairs on Crete? They wait like vultures for a moment of weakness."

"All the more reason why I should return with you to the sea. I am good with a sword, Father. As good as my brother Stewert. I have been jousting for years."

"Nay. 'Tis ye father's sin to wield a sword; 'tis your fortune to seek a better road." He sloshed his goblet full of brew and drank deeply, wiping his beard on the back of his arm. His eyes scanned the handsome young man with swelling pride. " 'Twas no mistake of ye dear mother to name ye 'Justin.' A wise dove she was, gentle, praying," he drank again. "Ye have always enjoyed mingling with the booksellers and philosophers. The knowledge of a scholar will do thee far more good than a sword ever will. You are not vain and proud—like me and ye brother Stewert." He scowled. "Aye, Lad, ye are like your mother. You look like her," he said wistfully. "When she was alive, she had eyes as blue as yours, yet as stormy as the sea when she blustered at me. Yea," he sighed, "just like ye. She will know peace in her grave now that I have vowed ye to the Church. I will go there where she is buried on the cliff overlooking the sea and tell her so." He smiled tenderly to himself. "She will rest in peace as ye give yerself to prayers for us both."

"What good is my sacrifice? It is vain, my Father. I will not do it—no, not even if I take to a stranger's ship to man the galley oars!"

In a rage his father smashed his goblet against the desk. "The words of a rebel? A mere lad born of my loins who dare contest the will of his father? D'ye not know I could have ye beaten to an inch of ye life."

"Being my father has nothing to do with this. It is not you I reject but. . . ."

"It has everything to do with it. Obedience is demanded. I am your father," he bellowed, "and 'tis your duty to obey. D'ye you think it is a light thing to contest me authority? You? A mere stripling?" He grabbed him roughly by the shoulder and banged him backward against the side of the cabin. "Ye are *my* son, have ye forgotten?"

"No, I have not forgotten, but no man should vow for another. Not the king, not even a father. I have a right to my own vows, my own life."

"Who told ye so? Speak! Who told ye so? You have no rights but those I give you! It so happens I now give thee none. Hear?" He leaned toward him. "*None.* If ye wish to contest me," he stopped for emphasis and stepped back, "then draw your sword now." He swept up the scabbard Justin had thrown aside and tossed it to him. Justin caught it. Captain Brice scowled. "We will see who is master and who is servant!"

The great Scotchman drew his prized blade from his sheath. He drew it often. His temper was as unmastered as the race he had come from, and it seemed sensible to him to draw it now. He stepped toward Justin who remained leaning against the cabin wall, completely frustrated. With a warning flick of the blade Captain Brice boasted his skill by flicking open the doublet Justin wore. Justin threw the scabbard down in disgust. "Reason, Father, reason. Would I raise a sword against you?"

No. His father knew he would not. Never. So he pressed his son further.

"What good a son who brings me shame?" Ewan Brice sent a vessel flying across the small cabin. "He wishes battle, and scorns the garb of a holy man!"

"Holy? Do you think I am fit for the priesthood?" He made

a pleading movement toward his towering father. "Give me time, training at sea, then a merchant ship. Give me the navigation chart found on the Persian captain and I shall bring back to London such treasure and fame as the merchants have never seen. You speak of shame? I shall make you proud."

"If merchant ships sail, it will be left to me to fight the sea. Ye shall fight the devil. Would ye see my soul burn in hell, Lad? Is that how you deem the fate of your poor father? Know ye not the devil has me by the scruff of the neck? Yea! At night in my dreams I see the cavernous pit with leaping fire."

Justin stared at him, wondering at the stark fear on the rugged face.

"If I give ye to the Church, I shall be pardoned. Heaven is mine, do you understand?"

His father's reasoning so frustrated him that he turned his back, leaning his shoulder to the cabin wall. The monastery. . . .

Ewan Brice anticipated gaining the upper hand in their debate. His son was now reacting as expected, bridling his anger in a way that he could not. *I have always admired him,* he thought. *He is not like me. He has the strength, but he also has self-control. Yes, I have won.* He could always depend on Justin's respect, even when he disagreed with his rantings. He sighed, satisfied, and his loud voice slowly ebbed. He sheathed his sword and sloshed another goblet to overflowing. "I have seen to it that you will go to the best monastery in Italy."

Justin refused to reply.

"Do ye not see? I have done ye well, my Son. Dinnae ye know ye mean more to me than anyone else in this life? More than your sisters, bless their souls, and more than even your fair mother, may she rest in peace. And certainly more than me bloody son, Stewert, the bloke!"

"Father," he gritted, "please!"

"Be pleased with what I have done! It was no easy task to send thee to Rome, of all blessed cities."

Rome . . . the monastery. . . . And what of his friends Marlon and Lady Regina? Regina! Though there was little hope to own the heart of a damsel with royal blood, he could not get her out of his mind. Regina with her dark hair and eyes. . . .

"At the monastery ye will do wonderful works of mortification. And ye will pray! Ye will serve the Church."

Slowly, Justin could feel the bars closing about him.

"When thy father speaks, answer! Do ye understand?"

"Perfectly."

"Good. I will be proud of thee. We will all be proud of thee, my Son." He drank from the goblet he had stolen from a pirated ship from Persia, finishing the contents in one breath. He sighed, wiping his mouth on the back of his hand. Justin heard the goblet bang against the table. It reminded him of a dull bell ringing out of tune. Monks. . . .

"Christ will be pleased with us both," his father stated. He was satisfied with himself and his religious decision. "Now, surely peace shall come to me wretched soul." He sank wearily into the chair.

Justin continued moving the map about the desk with his hand. *It's meaningless. Doesn't he know that?* He looked into the scowling face of his father. The words, *Christ will be pleased* repeated themselves in his mind.

"He shall not be pleased," Justin told him tonelessly.

His father was startled. For a moment they only looked at each other. Then his father leaned forward. There was a flicker of anger in the stark blue eyes. "Have you been reading heretical literature? What do ye mean!"

Justin held out his hands palms up. "There is blood on them."

"Thou speakest like a fool. I see nothing."

"There is not only blood but other things that I have done."

"Forget it, me Son. Your religious duty for the Church will make them into the hands of a sweet child. They shall not only purify with service, but they will lift me from earth to heaven."

Distraught, Justin searched his face. No words would come to his mouth. His father's confident gaze left him speechless. His father believed it!

Lord, thought Justin. For the first time the Name was a genuine call. *Lord God, what am I to do?*

They bowed before the abbot at Saint Catherine's. The bell chimed and the Latin chant monotonously came to Justin's ears.

"As vowed," his father murmured, "I give my younger son to God for the penance of my soul. He will follow the monastic life from this day on. Neither will he remove his neck from the yoke of his service. Neither I, Ewan Brice his father, nor any family member, wilt tempt him to leave, and thereby sin against Christ. Amen."

2

A Monastery in Rome

> Mine eyes fail for thy salvation,
> and for the word of thy righteousness
> (Ps. 119:123).

Justin arrived in Rome feeling more like a conquered slave brought in chains for a triumphant Caesar than a willing servant dedicated to God. He awoke with a start in the deep, airless dark, and above the sound of heavy breathing heard the bells begin to ring from a convent elsewhere in the city. The first glimmer of dawn had not yet shone on the seven hills of Rome when the call to rise for prayer monotonously repeated itself, echoing down the stone passages like a summons of doom. The other young monks were hastily on their bare feet, blundering about in the icy cold. Someone fumbled for the flint and candle, and the quick commotion of sharp strikes to steel gave way to a tiny spark.

On a winter's morning the darkness of the chamber seemed impenetrable, and the weak illumination of the fluttering candle, a mockery. Soon others rushed by to touch their charred candlewicks to the wavering flame. Justin could see the lanky figures of a dozen young men in monks' robes making swiftly for the door. In a moment they were gone, and Justin realized that he was already late.

Marcus, a nephew of the archbishop himself, was the last to start for the door. He paused and gestured wryly at Justin's bed—a stone bench with a log for a pillow.

"Did you sleep well?" The cynical whisper was the very first that Justin had detected among the other dour faces in the monastery. He was quick to take it up.

"Isn't sleep a transgression?"

"Speech in the vulgar tongue of English is."

With cold numb fingers Justin reached for his robe, finding it strange after wearing chain mail and a sword, but Marcus halted him and shoved a prickly vesture into his hands.

Justin's brow was quizzical.

Marcus smirked. "Where have you come from, pagan, from the Saracen?" He spoke of the Moslem East. "The hair shirt must be worn night and day under your robe. The superior will look to see if you have disobeyed."

"Make haste," Marcus prodded, "the hour strikes."

Quickly Justin dressed, finding the hair shirt a nervous distraction. They flew from the chamber, hurrying down the passage to the hall where the monastic chant in Latin was underway. Kneeling bodies shivered for warmth that was not there. Oddly Justin found himself wondering why the chanting voices did not stammer from the cold.

As they reached the closed door, he heard Marcus groan his apprehension. They were late. He pointed above the door. Justin looked up to see a woven garland of tinkling bells. Each morning after the monks filed into the hall for Mass they were securely fastened in place so the door would strike them. No latecomer could possibly enter unnoticed by the superior.

The bowed heads did not dare turn as they slipped into the hall while Marcus grimaced, helpless to keep the clattering bells silent. They knelt at once and Marcus began the pious chant, but Justin groped in his memory for the appropriate Latin. He had mastered enough of the language at the little

London to be considered far more scholarly than his fellow students, but here in Rome he had proved to be hopelessly dim.

Justin heard the slippered feet and rustle of a robe. The superior stopped beside him and bent his dignified head, cupping his ear toward Justin. All at once his lazy Latin fumbled into silence.

"You . . ." The stick prodded his shoulder. "Louder."

Justin's Latin slowly struggled forward.

"What?" The superior whispered, "will the sun not set before you seek mercy for the morning?"

Justin's chant burst forth into English, larded with the Scottish brogue. He heard a slight groan and caught himself at once.

The superior sighed deeply, then snapped in Latin, "The vulgar tongue is forbidden. Thou shalt neither pray in it, nor quote Scripture in it, nor speak it at all. Understand?"

Justin nodded, not trusting his Latin response.

"You shalt see me in my chamber after you break fast."

When the superior walked on, Marcus ventured to lean toward him. "Now your yoke has begun. The grammar master shows no pity. His love for Latin transcends his love for wine."

In the great vaulted chamber the superior sat behind the large table with both hands clasped peacefully before him. The walls were lined with awesome books, parchments, and stacks of manuscripts, some sealed with an imposing insignia. The robe he wore over his religious garb was patched here and there, and furred for warmth. On his head was a battered velvet hat from which straight silver hair hung limp.

Justin halted as the superior studied his muscled body with unsmiling concentration. The scrutiny was so minute that Justin humorously wondered if he might wish to utter something in Latin and turn him into a toad. But, at last, the lips curved into a smile and the sharp eyes softened.

"Thy name is Justin Brice. Thy father, er . . ." the superior hesitated to search his memory, and sought for the letter on his desk. He held it close to his face, squinting through a single spectacle to read, "is Sir Ewan Brice of London, England."

"The same, my Lord," Justin said in careful Latin.

"He has written a most moving discourse acclaiming thy skills with Latin." He fixed his gaze on Justin, his mouth twitching with wry amusement. Justin remembered the embarrassment of the morning.

"Thy father's parental enthusiasm is, shall we say, exaggerated? For the moment," and the superior offered a grimace, "you may speak English, but softly," he hastened, "oh so softly."

Relieved that his superior was not as unrelenting as he had first thought him to be, Justin apologized. "My Latin, I fear, is born of the grammar school in an English village."

"So I gathered. Your father has wondrous plans for you. Are you in agreement with them?"

Now it was coming. "My Lord," his breath came rapidly and he became aware of the hair shirt, "I am beholden to my father, yet if the choice were mine, I would be far at sea."

"That, too, I gathered."

"I mean no offense to this religious community. It is only that I have not the heart of a monk."

The superior surveyed him through heavy lids. "That is what we intend to change."

Justin felt the chill of the vaulted chamber. The superior then grew businesslike.

"Your father's plans concerning you are noble and to be commended. He wishes, as any good father, for you to become a man of holiness, a man of letters, a scholar of the Latin tongue—and he has sent a most wondrous endowment to the Church in order for his wish to be exercised with all speed. Therefore," and he smiled, "you shalt be given every opportunity to learn Latin as Latin ought to be spoken. You shall speak it with the splendor of those masters who use it as sweetly as their mother tongue."

Justin was aware that his future was taking another turn on the swiftly moving shuttle he had no control over. He had been in Rome only one day and it seemed a lifetime.

"It is your privilege to have classes each day with the learned scholar Mirandola at the university in Rome. Those chosen to attend these classes from our monastery are young men of notable backgrounds. Know, therefore, that this learned privilege is to be revered. However, your daily classes will in no way excuse you from your duties. Prayer vigils and godly endeavors are to continue with devotion."

The superior stood now and came around to him. "I notice your body is handsome of flesh and muscled with strength. You must gain ascendancy over its passions." He pulled back the robe to see if he wore the hair shirt. "So far, well enough. The attained victory of chastity and holiness is not awarded to the sluggard. You must strive! Your body is to be used as a farmer uses his ox. Strokes and burdens lighten the soul, though the rebellious flesh quivers beneath the load. Far better the groan of the chastened flesh than its licentious freedom to bring the soul headlong into the bottomless pit. Enough." He turned away with a wave of his hand. "Go to your vigil and Christ give you grace."

With his every hour controlled by ritual and unending demands, it was startling one morning to notice, as a blind man receiving sight, that the dreary winter had given way to spring blossoms in the meditation garden; then some days later he noticed, as he labored over his grueling schedule of Latin, that there was frost on the ground and his breath was white in the air.

The monastery in Rome had been his prison for three years, but it had not imprisoned his desires nor tamed the storm of doubt growing within his soul. The life of rigorous self-denial had not brought him internally to a higher spiritual state; ritual had not quieted the fires smoldering deep within, nor had it brought him peace with God. He was more troubled now then he had ever been in London.

For three years the ritual varied little. He rose before dawn giving himself to the monastic chant, to devotion and prayers. In spite of the required fastings and watchings, and the hair shirt, he found his body to be most rebellious in response to the unending demands, and no amount of discipline silenced the struggles going on within his heart, or his mind. And when he lay down on the stone bench of his cell, with a log under his head, allotting himself only four hours of sleep, he felt more wretched than ever.

"My body is to be used as an ox," he repeated as taught, but the self-rebuke fell dully upon his senses, neither quickening him to joyous victory nor granting inward strength to overcome.

"If heavy strokes secure chastity, and acts of self-mortification make me holy," he argued with another monk named John one morning on the way to class, "why has Christ not seen fit to give my soul peace?"

John was younger than all the others, a delightful boy with the tenderest brown eyes Justin had ever seen. He was gentle, dedicated, and outraged at such debates, yet he had strangely taken up friendship with Justin and the cynical Marcus.

John scowled at him. "Must you argue with me daily and wear me to the bone? Do you wish to make me into a heretic?"

"To question is heresy? You be truthful with me, as I have been with you. Do you have assurance of acceptance with Christ?"

John quickened his steps over the cobbled way. "More works are needed to please heaven if His smile come upon you."

Justin knew that John was not at peace. Often he heard him sighing. The sigh had become such a habit with him that it reminded Justin of an old yeoman farmer he had once seen in London, tilling his field by hand, for his ox had died of sickness at planting time. As the plow was tied to his shoulders and he sought to till the unyielding earth, he would stop under the grueling heat of the sun and sigh deeply as his body shuddered under the heavy load.

Justin pressed him in Latin. "Then all your striving has brought the benediction of peace between you and your Lord? You are not burdened as I am with the emptiness of ritual?"

John, a slight figure in his worn robe, refused to look at him. "Heaven is not won in a day."

"No? When? When shall I know? Will I know when the day and hour has struck? Will it be morning or evening? Summer or winter? No, perhaps spring?"

"You speak like a fool, Justin Brice!"

Ahead, Marcus and an exceptionally tall young man with red hair followed the superior. He escorted them up the awesome steps of the university and into the cloistered halls of learning.

Having put his mind to it, Latin came far easier than Justin had anticipated. Of the five young men, including John, who were permitted to attend the famous university, Justin had striven to excel, and his progress had reached a high level of pleasure to the Master of Arts.

"Surely you will be chosen to be the abbot's secretary on his journey to visit the bishop at Bologna," sighed John the following year. "My Latin falls behind yours."

Justin had more intense ambitions than to serve the Abbot of Saint Athenians. He ventured now to share with John the hope he had not breathed to anyone else. "I will seek to work in the university library as a translator. I heard Master Mirandola speak of an opening for an assistant yesterday to the superior."

"A lofty goal. If anyone has Latin down well enough to translate lesser volumes, it is you. But Marcus too, wishes the position. Most likely he will prevail since he is nephew to the archbishop."

Justin's schedule began at four in the morning and went well into the night. Even after the candle went out and they sought their sleep, he went over his Latin by memory until his eyes shut on their own. It was not love for the language that drove him but the desire to escape the empty rigor of religious ritual. If he could show himself somewhat of a scholar he might obtain a position in the library doing translation. If his fate was to be cast among those in the Church of Rome, there seemed no better opportunity than to use his mind in the great library where he might have access to important works, especially the Scriptures. So far, among the endless religious activities demanded to sanctify his soul, access to the Scripture was rare, and the few verses that were used, were spoken and not put in writing. Justin remembered the Wycliffe translation of the Gospel of Matthew and longed again to have the written words before him, to see them, to speak them, to meditate over them like a cow lying under the cool shade of a tree chewing her cud.

"Well then, Master Brice, what could be on your mind?"

The great hall of the university was nearly empty. Master Mirandola came toward him dressed in the scholar's gown and academic biretta. The dark eyes were friendly and encouraged him to speak his mind. Speaking his mind to anyone besides Marcus and John seemed a venture too risky. However, he believed that the Master of Arts felt kindly towards him as one of his most promising students.

"I am under no illusion of my abilities as a scholar, being but a junior grammarian when it comes to the language you speak so well, but. . . ."

"You are far more learned than you give yourself credit for, Master Brice. As I have mentioned to the other masters at the University, you have untapped resources."

"I am honored, Learned Sir. You have mentioned the library and the need for an assistant in translation. I could not hope to fill the position, realizing I am but a learner, but I had hoped to begin in that direction. The work of translation holds great interest for me."

"I had hoped your interest would be routed in that esteemed direction, Justin. It may surprise you to know I had you in mind all along."

Justin was astonished.

"I must first speak to the bishop about this," said Master Mirandola, "but he is a congenial man where my requests are concerned. And there is urgent need for copies to be made of certain works in order to send them to the Rector Julius."

The interview had gone so well Justin could hardly accept it. Few matters in his life had gone well recently, so he thought, and why should this? The opportunity to handle precious parchments, including Scripture, nearly drove him to lose control of his grave demeanor; a demeanor he had rigidly practiced to ordered sobriety. He could almost believe that Christ did look upon him with grace.

"I shall know how it will go shortly," Master Mirandola was saying. "The bishop will arrive in a few weeks to meet with Herr Docktor Martin Luther's delegation from Wittenberg. I shall speak to him then."

It was with a lighter heart Justin resumed his arduous schedule. The message arrived during supper one winter evening. The superior, who had taken to Justin with affection, brought the news to the table.

"Well, my Son, your father shall be proud of you. You have

gained position in the university library under the supervision of the renown Master Mirandola."

When he had gone, Marcus, who saw himself becoming a cardinal one day, took to groaning. His family was rich and powerful in Rome and he often mocked them, as well as himself, for the personal use of position.

"Alas! How my uncle the archbishop has failed me in the hour of need. He has promised me a secure position where future wealth and power wait. Yet the position of assistant translator to Master Mirandola goes to a pagan Scot," he teased.

"Master Mirandola looks for scholarship, not a powerful family to bribe him," said John with a twinkle in his eye.

Marcus grimaced a dry smile. "What scandal do you breathe? You who are so blindly dedicated to the Church? Are you so wicked as to even suggest that wealth buys position in Christ's Church?"

John blushed at the obvious. The abuses in the system were offensive enough, but it was shameful to have Marcus unveil them with his irony.

Justin however, took up Marcus's challenge. "In Christ's Church, no. Among those who would use religious means to secure unholy ambitions without inward merit, yes. Where is your burning conviction to resist compromise?" he concluded, goading him in friendly humor.

Marcus winced but was quick with his ready retort. "I prefer as Erasmus, wine to ale, roast meat to a crust of bread, and friends in high places."

"Erasmus has been offered the position of cardinal," John whispered.

"Erasmus?" said Marcus with disbelief. "Ho! What jest is this? My uncle knows him well. I have often been in the same room with him. Erasmus would sooner stand aloof of the Church and ridicule its hypocrisy than wade in and work to cure its ills. This much I will say for Erasmus—his writings are work enough. They are meant, like John Colet, to light a needed spark of renewal."

"When you speak of sparks, let us hope with Erasmus that you do not mean wood and fire," offered John.

"Forbid," said Marcus hastily, suddenly grave. He leaned over to Justin with another whisper. "Speaking of heresy, the great Erasmus has left Cambridge in England where he taught Greek to come to Italy. It seems Cambridge is seeded with new thinkers who plot for reform in the Church. And it is said that a secret few hope that Erasmus will render a translation of Scripture in the English tongue. Cambridge is now laden with floating ideas of heresy, and so Erasmus has wisely come to sunny Italy, leaving what he began to others."

Justin's attention was riveted. He found his heart pounding. "What! Erasmus will translate the Scriptures into English?"

"No. Erasmus will not meddle. He will instigate it but take no part. Instead he has promised a new translation in Greek only and a new Latin without the errors of Jerome's version."

"To admit of errors in the Vulgate brands you, too, as a thinker," said Justin with a wry smile.

"Erasmus distinctly said that the Scriptures should be placed in the tongues of all people. Why do you think Erasmus left Cambridge? It is because, while he believes in the task, he will have nothing to do with the translation. It is left to Colet, or others. Perhaps someone even now stands in the shadows."

"The stirring of the bones of the devil Wycliffe," John said.

Like a slap across the face, Justin turned to them. His compelling gaze struck them into silence.

Justin's mind went with painful clarity back to the woods near King Henry's stables. The Wycliffites were fleeing; men, women, even children. The stirring words of the Gospel of Matthew in English pierced his heart anew, and he relived the gripping agony of Balin York ripping sections from the parchment and throwing them into the fire. He saw again the ashes, and felt his former guardian's knuckles sting his mouth.

He looked from Marcus to John, and his look wiped their faces clean of irony.

"Wycliffe saw what the leaders of the Church have no spiritual enlightenment to see. Or if they do see it, they cower before the cost of such a stand. Does that make Wycliffe a devil? Is he not rather a saint? He was a man before his time, but will the time ever come unless men such as he risk all to do what is necessary? Why shouldn't the common man be entitled to hear and read the Word of God in his own tongue? Is the God we claim to serve Lord only of the religious cloister? Does He dwell only with learned scholars in the halls of the university? Then what of the masses who shall die in their sins before they ever hear all the truth? And what of truth itself if committed only to the few in the cloister? If the trusted few have strayed from the flock to feast alone on the fatted calf, what shall become of the sheep left to starve? What shall they feast on if not the Scriptures? Tradition and ritual, tarnished by the self-seeking of the clerics?"

They stared at him. John feared to speak, and his face flushed, his eyes dropping to the table.

If anyone knew the danger of these words, it was Marcus. He was grave for the first time, his dark eyes glanced about to see if anyone besides the few in their circle had heard.

"If you will be burned as a heretic, such words as you have uttered will surely light the torch to the faggots."

Justin knelt during his prayers in the chamber, but he could not concentrate for thinking of his outburst at the evening meal. As his own convictions began to take shape, he wondered just where they would lead him. He tried to pray and could not. His heart was not in the chant, for the fixed chant did not speak his true feelings.

3

How sweet are thy words unto my taste!
yea, sweeter than honey to my mouth!
(Ps. 119:103).

For Justin, to translate a work was to know it. His memory
was disciplined and he entered his work at the university library in Rome with a sense of destiny.

He glanced about. The various translators were busy at their
own duties. Cautiously, he pushed aside the lesser works he
was to translate for the village rectory and slipped Jerome's
Latin translation from under the stack before him. He viewed
the Old Testament with awe. How would he ever master this
book? He turned to the New Testament. To gain a general
understanding of what it offered he begin to look through the
Gospels, then to The Acts, and the beginning of Paul's epistles.
He intended to move on to what followed, but his attention
was arrested by the word *Rome.*

He read, "To all that be in Rome."

Was he not in Rome? And indeed, a servant in the Church
at Rome? What did Saint Paul have to say to the Church in
Rome? This was the logical place to begin, he told himself, and
with another cautious glance around the silent room, hearing
nothing but the scratch of quills, Justin settled down to read.

The morning light had turned to afternoon shadows. How

long he had been absorbed, he knew not. An hour? Two? Even three? His mind was swollen with the sheer compulsion of the written words, as he struggled to grasp their profound meaning. "Justification by faith . . . faith alone justified . . . apart from works of man's religious endeavors . . . faith in the finished work of Christ justified a sinner before a holy God . . . Christ's righteousness was imparted to the justified believer and Christ himself 'was' his righteousness . . . the believer was 'in' Christ and therefore his position was completely accepted."

The tolling bell marking the close of the day at the university interrupted his concentration. A look around proved the bell was no noisier than usual. The other translators were calmly putting their work aside until the next morning. Justin reluctantly closed the Vulgate, slipped it under the other manuscripts, put his quills aside, and stood. A moment later he had donned his hat and cloak and was out the door. That night in the dining hall he managed to secure a private corner for John and Marcus to join him. At once he shared what he had discovered. John was silent and scowling, but Marcus listened with quick interruptions, pressing hard. "How do you know Saint Paul meant it as you interpret?"

"It is so written."

"But you may have interpreted it erroneously."

"No. The words speak for themselves."

Marcus pointed a finger against his chest. "I would see for myself."

Justin's hesitation was only slight. The decision came as easily as though born from blossoming seed pushing through the earth. "You shall see for yourself. Tomorrow I will make a copy of Romans and bring it here. Where can we meet to debate?"

John looked at them both as if they had gone truly mad. The minor debates they had were one thing, but to debate Scripture within the walls of the monastery? And on a subject strictly forbidden?

John sucked in his breath. "Here?" He looked from one young face to the other. Marcus would not flinch. "In the chapel," he told Justin. "Tomorrow night is my vigil. But remember Justin, if caught, I have the archbishop to turn to; you have no one."

"I have the truth."

At the library the next morning Justin searched immediately to see if his collection of manuscripts had been disturbed. With relief he saw they had not. He slipped the Latin version from under the stack and found his way more easily to the Epistle of Romans. With a vast inkwell and a stand of quills near at hand, he begin to write.

> Paul, a servant of Jesus Christ, called to be an apostle, separated unto the gospel of God, (Which he had promised before by his prophets in the holy scriptures,) Concerning his Son Jesus Christ our Lord, who was made of the seed of David according to the flesh, And declared to be the Son of God with power, according to the spirit of holiness, by the resurrection from the dead.

That night the three of them met in the chapel. The candle flames flickered, casting swaying shadows. They reminded John of spirits. He cast his eyes upward where the chiseled faces of saints and angels stared down upon them from the chapel roof. John drew his robe more closely around him to keep from shivering, but Justin felt nothing but the burning in his heart.

The handwritten epistle sat on the floor between the three of them.

Justin read in whispers but with distinction, pausing now and then to look up and search their faces to see if they understood the profound meaning.

John soon hung on every word, his eyelids fluttering nervously as he sat, his figure as small as a child's lost within his clerical robe. The candle flame made his brown eyes luminous under the dark lashes.

Marcus frowned and raised a hand to cut Justin off. "Slowly, slowly. With rapidity you do sear the page with the flame of your tongue." He then leaned over the page, his forefinger sliding over the Latin text. His finger went back and forth over the same line several times, repeating the words, but he seemed to still miss the emphasis.

Justin made small jabs at the key words in the Scripture passage repeating them for Marcus with emphasis, and then explaining their meaning.

"Therefore"

"Because of what Saint Paul has written previously," Justin insisted.

"being justified"

"Do you see it?"

"by faith,"

"Not by works," Justin pointed out.

"we have"

"That means right now."

"peace with God through"

"By the merit of another."

"our Lord Jesus Christ."

Marcus rubbed his chin. He agreed, slowly nodding his head. "Yes I see it. But let us move on. There is much to read and the night wears on. Who has a vigil tomorrow?"

"I do," said John.

"Then let us meet again. Let us invite a few others to see what their minds will tell us."

"Is it wise?" breathed John. "If word gets out, . . ." his voice trailed.

"Whether it be prudent, I do not know," said Justin, "but it is good that any who have a desire should read for themselves. The more we discuss this doctrine, the more defined it will become. But our arguments must not stray from what the Scripture saith. Let the words speak for themselves."

"They speak more clearly than I thought," said Marcus. "This is the first time I have heard the Epistle of Romans word by word."

John whispered. "I confess the words make my skin crawl. How awesome is the pen of Saint Paul."

"Nay," said Justin quietly, "it is not only the pen of Paul but also that the words are living with the very breath of the Almighty. Agreed?"

"Agreed," they said.

Justin's smile was disarming. "Good. We cannot walk the same path unless we agree."

"But where does this path lead us?" Marcus questioned ruefully.

"We will follow until the path forces a new direction. Only then will we know. But if these words guide us, then we can be sure of going in the right way."

For the next weeks they met until the number of those who risked attendance swelled to a dangerous level. They changed their meeting place nightly and when it was impossible to meet, the word was passed with hand signals. Not all those attending the study agreed with Justin's interpretation of justification by faith apart from religious works, and at times the discussion grew tense and voices rose only to have their emotions bridled by the necessity of whispering once again. But the meeting around the handwritten Epistle of Romans continued.

One night he slept restlessly on the stone floor. The events of the past weeks swirled through his sleep like actors on the stage. He tossed about and saw an image of the superior twice his usual size, yet gaunt, illuminated by the candle he held above his head which made his eyes appear empty sockets of yellow. "Recant!"

Justin awoke in a sweat. He was startled to wakefulness for no apparent cause other than his muscles cramping, but between wakefulness and sleep he imagined someone standing by his feet, or was he really there? He assumed that it was one of the other 100 student-priests who slept with him on the floor. His mind, filled with Romans, formed the words in his memory. It seemed as if Paul stood before him in chains.

"But to him that worketh not, but believeth on him that justifieth the ungodly, his faith is counted for righteousness.

"Therefore, we conclude that a man is justified by faith without the deeds of the law . . ."

Justin cried, "Then I shall not recant! Never! In those words I shall rest my soul!"

He felt John's hand grab his shoulder. "Silence," he hissed in the darkness, "you will have the superior in here. Who were you talking to?"

Justin lay down and in spite of the cold his body was wet with perspiration, yet a peace beyond verbalization wrapped itself with glowing warmth about the inner recesses of his soul. He murmured in Latin, "To my Lord."

John squinted at him in the darkness, then lay down. Try as he might John couldn't go back to sleep. He begin his own rote prayers, then stopped. Timidly he began again with only his lips moving, and spoke from the heart. "If You hear me, Jesus Christ, and do in truth offer justification from all things vile, and this justification lasteth forever in Your holy presence, and this is based alone on Your sufficiency, and not on any merit of my own—then give me boldness to believe. Grant to me the courage to act in an hour of darkness. For I quake with trembling in my bones, O Lord. I sense the prison walls of separation coming between we three friends and the end of our diligent pursuit before it has truly begun. Help me to be true, for I fear greatly the darkness of a dungeon."

The one tree struggling to stay alive near the library wall had leaves of red and gold. The wind blew chill, shaking it to its meager roots, threatening to topple it before it posed a threat of dense shade to the few square feet of ivy now inhabiting the earth and reaching for the university wall. But one tentacle of ivy had already latched hold of the slim trunk and was climbing upward, prepared to swallow up the highest branch which was poised as if in prayer toward the gray sky.

Justin ran up the steps of the University and upon entering the echoing musty halls, he slowed to a walk. The day promised rain and strong winds, but his spirits were light. He had peace, and the joy of his relationship with Christ seemed more blessed and real then it had ever been.

He wanted to whistle as he entered the library, but dared not. As he entered sedately, it waited for him as it had for the past year, and as usual he removed his hat and the drab woolen cloak which had sufficed him for the three years he had been in Rome. It was getting threadbare at the elbows but he scarcely noticed. And, as usual, the odor of musty parchments, ink, old leather, and wood also greeted him inoffensively. He had grown accustomed to the smell and now linked it in some pleasant way with the Latin text and the great teachings of Paul the apostle.

The other translators glanced up sharply. Justin murmured his customary Latin greeting. He was thinking of the promise of Erasmus, and did not notice that one head bent low did not meet his eyes.

Erasmus vowed a better version of the Greek, and a new Latin text to remedy the errors in Jerome's. As of yet Justin had heard nothing and wondered how long the church would need to wait.

Of course, the honored task would be a mighty one and would take time. Marcus had told him that Master Colet had called Erasmus the "finest scholar in Christendom." He had tried to keep Erasmus at Oxford University to teach literature and the Old Testament, but Erasmus did not feel ready to handle the language, and he came to Italy.

Justin sat before the stack of uncataloged manuscripts which filled his table to overflowing. It was his job to bring them to some kind of order before the Christmas holidays.

He began the work at once, the silence made the scratch of his pen seem loud.

He paused, and his mind turned back to the new Greek version promised by Erasmus. It dawned on him that if he were ever to study it for himself he must become proficient in Greek. Thinking of Scripture, he reached under the stack of manuscripts for the Vulgate, expecting it to be there as always. It was gone!

Caution, he dare not draw attention by showing alarm. Affecting unhurried calmness he begin to move the manuscripts about. He might have placed it elsewhere. The Vulgate was a seldom-used copy in the library, and therefore safe to keep at his disposal, but it was not there. It had been removed. The implications caused a rise in his heartbeat. No one would look among his work unless sent to do so. And who would bother unless they suspected the Latin version to be there?

He looked up. Every head was lowered and busy as always. Then he saw a head turn slightly and glance in his direction. The eyes of the scholar meeting Justin's were averted, and the pen scratched quickly.

Had news of the meetings in the monastery reached the abbot? Justin was sure the man across from him knew the answer.

He was right. A moment later the scholar slipped from his seat as if to visit the lavatory down the hall. A message hastily scratched in Latin was dropped at Justin's feet as he walked past. When Justin was sure no one was watching, his foot reached out and brought it closer. He dropped a quill and, stooping to pick it up, grasped the message. "Your secret is known. Be prepared in mind and spirit for arrest."

Aware that some of his fellow monks were glancing in his direction, he resumed his translation work. His arrest would come at any moment. Should he make a run for it? But if he did would he not be admitting transgression? And what would those who had followed his example in the monastery believe of his actions?

He glanced about the library. The other scholars all knew of his situation. He sensed the sympathy of some, and the satisfaction of others who disagreed with his actions.

He looked past the candle to the door. It swung open and the translator reentered from the lavatory. He left the door wide open for a moment to reveal that several guards had entered the outer hall.

It was too late for any recourse. The others knew it as well, and one by one went back to their work, resigned to the outcome. Tomorrow morning they would be one less, and there would be an empty desk.

Justin's internal struggle heightened. Was his newfound conviction worth the danger he was now in? He immediately thought of John and Marcus. Had they been found out, too? But, of course. The superiors would have to know. Whoever reported them would be sure to give the name of every young monk who had attended and how much involved each man was. The leaders were sure to be singled out first.

To his right, lying on the table in a leather envelope, was the handwritten copy of Romans. Cautiously he pushed it to one side, but there was no hope he could keep it. Soon the precious parchment would forever be out of his reach. It had been his intention to commit the entire letter to memory, yet with all his other studies and religious duties he had memorized only the first chapter. He now saw that it would have been wiser to memorize key passages and verses. And he should have hidden the epistle somewhere in the monastery instead of carrying it daily back and forth to the library. He had been overly confident. He might have known, that as the meeting around the Scriptures grew, there would be one individual to turn against them.

Hindsight, they say, is always the best teacher. The hour for better planning had passed. Perhaps his youthful zeal had carried him away, but for the joy of those months of study with his fellows, it was worth the risk. Who knew what new seeds of faith the Word had planted in their hearts? He could only guess the harvest. He waited for the footsteps of his superiors.

Recant? His hand rested briefly on the leather envelope. How could he forget those astounding words written by Saint Paul, when they resounded within his brain like the beat of a drum? The dream of the night before stirred, waking his memory. Recant? No.

The click of sandals on stone brought him back to the moment. He prayed for strength to remain true. Two superiors stopped at either side of his table. "The abbot will see you in his chamber."

Justin scanned the Epistle of Romans. He sensed he would not see it again. The cautious glances of the other monks followed him out the door.

> I have more understanding than all my teachers;
> for thy testimonies are my meditation.
> (Ps. 119:99).

As they walked swiftly and silently back to the monastery along the cobbled streets of Rome, a few drops of rain were falling. They went through the gate of the high wall that encircled the compound, through the cloistered garden where he walked each day, and down the passage to the door of the abbot's chambers.

The door swung open and Justin stepped inside and heard it shut solidly behind him. There would be no turning back now. It was one thing to be brought in question by a superior, but the abbot was a powerful man.

The head of the monastery school sat behind his desk with an open ledger before him, quill in hand. Once he had enjoyed his work at the monastery of Saint Athenians, and had satisfied his interest in scholarship by involving himself within the university, but the favor conferred upon him by the archbishop, and the prospect of an esteemed position within the Vatican Palace, now owned his ambitions. If he distanced himself from unorthodox opinions, both religious and political, his opportunities would blossom into a distinguished career.

He looked at Justin, then reached for the letter on his desk. "Your name is Justin Brice and you are from London. You have been here at Saint Athenians for three years. You have excelled in your scholarship at the University. Master of Arts, Mirandola, writes highly of your use of Latin, and your position in the library." The dark eyes now fixed upon him.

A fire was crackling on the hearth, but in spite of the cold, Justin felt too warm. Tiny beads of perspiration formed on his forehead as he struggled over what he would say. Words now eluded him, and his previous confidence fled. Suppose he could not defend his position? How would he answer the distinguished man before him? That he may have no answer disturbed him more than the thought of punishment. What would he say? His throat suddenly constricted, he felt as though he had been stricken dumb.

The pressure of the strained silence mounted as the abbot stood. He was tall and lean with a shock of silver hair and keen dark eyes. He reminded Justin of a man of military bearing, a handsome Roman with the noble manner of royalty. Instead of a robe, Justin pictured him with a cloak tossed over his shoulder and a laurel wreath about his head.

The abbot scanned him and tossed the parchment onto the desk. "I was told you see yourself as an authority to judge between the original writings and the teachings of the Church."

The dark eyes were satirical, yet not altogether angry. A glimmer of amusement turned his lips into a smile as he took in Justin's youthfulness.

Justin felt the humiliation of his scrutiny.

"Yes? Or no?" asked the abbot.

Justin cleared his throat and bowed his head. "The abbot is a very wise man. Surely he knows that I see myself as a mere humble student? No less than a worm."

The abbot was amused. "I once heard of a humble worm from Wittenberg who came to Rome and kissed the ground. That monk has since sprouted butterfly wings. He now debates heretical teachings on justification by faith. A growing and popular theme, so it seems, among humble worms."

"The monk you speak of I do not know, my Lord Abbot."

The abbot scrutinized him. Was he satisfied? Would he accept this token or would he press him?

"Brice, you are a hypocrite, truly a worm of compromise." The abbot arched his brow. "A 'Latin' scholar who deigns to teach the Epistle of Romans, 'humble'?" he jested, and smiled.

"What a rare find! But for such a humble worm, Young Man, you hold such lofty opinions. Strange ideas that breed conflict and disunity within the monastery of Saint Athenians."

"I have not sought, nor do I wish conflict with you or the Church."

"I am pleased to hear that. Obedience to the will of your superiors will put an end to all conflict."

The silence locked them in. It was an awful stillness to

Justin. As their eyes held, Justin lowered his gaze, for the fire which burned within contradicted his words.

The abbot's voice was toneless. "Questions can be healthy, but, then again, it is no light matter to undermine the foundational teachings of one's own house. The house can come crashing down upon one's head," he warned. "Tell me, I would hear from your own lips and not the lips of any who may be jealous of you."

He then fixed Justin with a grave stare. "To willfully undermine any foundation ordained by Christ is heresy. A wise priest will work to maintain that ordained system." He paused with emphasis. "Do you agree, Justin Brice?"

"The abbot speaks wisely. But, My Lord, what if the foundation is discovered to be newly laid by men, and not by Christ? What if it is contrary to what has already been set forth in the Scriptures? Then, is not change necessary to recover forgotten truth? The questioning of such foundations would then not be heresy, but vigilance."

The moment seemed endless. Under the probing stare of the abbot, Justin felt like a dismembered frog.

"This necessity," the Abbot inquired. "Do you see it as a need for reform in doctrine?"

Justin chose his words cautiously. "I would see it as a necessity to differentiate between written Scripture, and the growing emergence of tradition. Such tradition, if not differentiated from the written words of God, will surely lead the Church into a path of further error."

The eyes of the abbot glinted. "I must be sure I hear you right. Did you say *'further'* error?"

"Yes," he froze.

"Ah, so the Church is smothered with the darkness of tradition?" he suggested mockingly. "Our lamp has gone out? Is that it? The voice of the Church is the voice of men and not of Christ? And so you, a mere 'humble worm,' as you have chosen to describe yourself, have felt inclined to teach your erring brothers."

He held up the parchment. "The writing of Saint Paul," he explained as though Justin had never seen it before. "The Epistle of Romans. I understand you consider yourself familiar with it, and qualified to teach it."

"I never considered myself to be anything. But I would wish both great and small to labor over its awesome truth. Therein we will find light to lead us from darkness."

"Indeed! But who will lead with book in hand? You? Even as I gaze upon its truths, I often find myself a mere child before a fathomless sea. Are you tempted to think you have plumbed its depths? Perish the thought! Where is your humility, your mortification before the feet of teachers better than you? You have but captured in your cup a drop of water! Do you think yourself wise enough to understand what is written without the guidance of your superiors? Do you believe that you can teach the writings of Saint Paul?"

"I confess to be but a learner. Yet, even as a student, I have stumbled upon vast differences between what the writings say, and what I am taught."

"Great minds within the Church have wrestled to understand the high and lofty words of the apostle from the beginning of Christianity—yet you can expound his words with confident authority!" He proceeded to thrust the Epistle of Romans into Justin's hands and sat down quickly, arms folded.

"Will you teach? Will you confuse the young minds of your brethren under cover of darkness? Be so bold now as to teach me. I wait with baited breath."

The ridicule stung and Justin felt himself getting hot.

"Or do you want me to wait for the archbishop? Perhaps I am not audience grand enough for thy scholarship. Perhaps the pope? Shall I hustle you off to the Vatican Palace?"

His mockery provoked Justin to match his satire. And before

he could control his tongue he blurted out, "Surely I have sinned, My Lord Abbot. For in reading the Scriptures and in discussing its contents, I did not know that God gave them in order to hide His truth in a sea of profundity. Nor was I aware that He gave Scripture to frustrate the minds of great scholars for centuries with words that cannot be understood. I did not know, My Lord Abbot, that the words were to be kept under lock with the key given only to the few whose religious position, often bought by temporal wealth, has then authorized them to teach the ignorant multitude—but only in Latin.

"I have grievously erred, My Lord Abbot, for I believed God gave Scripture to reveal, to quicken, and to teach His Church His will on earth. And that of all epistles, the letter written to the church at Rome could be understood by us at Rome. Unworthy though I be, I confess to have learned more truth in one year of studying the Scriptures than all my vigils, fastings, and strivings in prayers have gained me."

The abbot slammed his fist down on the lectern. "You insolent and stupid young fool. You are hereby declared a heretic." He stood. "You shall wait in the dungeon until I bring your case before the archbishop."

"I meant not to be insolent, Sir, but you mocked my sincerity as the babble of a fool."

"Babble aside! You are here to receive just correction, and do you audaciously seek to correct me with your cynical tongue?"

"I will receive correction if I am shown wherein I have erred."

"Shown? Is it not enough that your spiritual superiors by their very position have called your behavior into question? You sin now before me by refusing to accept it. Your obedience to the Church is demanded. I warn you now, Justin Brice, if you do not recant of your errors, your situation will be grave indeed."

"Sir! Since when has reading the Scriptures in Latin become an act of heresy?"

"I would remind thee that Savonarola was tried and put to death on charges of disobedience alone."

Justin recalled the Dominican monk who was assigned to Florence. He tried to reform both state and church in the city, but his cries against the evil life of the leaders in the Church had resulted in his death.

"Answer me. Have you, or have you not copied Holy Scripture without authorization?"

"Yes."

"All or some?"

"The Epistle of Romans only."

"And smuggled it into the holy cloister to teach to your brethren in training?"

"I saw no sin in bringing the Word of God into the cloister, nor meeting about it with those who willingly came to hear and see. I have uttered nothing in the ears of my fellow brethren but what was written in this parchment."

"And is it not also true that you preach the 'need' to translate the Latin into," he spread his hands, "God forbid! English! The language of peasants! And 'herein,' the Church shall be delivered from the darkness of tradition! Answer me, Justin Brice, do you see yourself a man called of God to translate the Scriptures into the vulgar tongue?"

Trapped, thought Justin. *If I do not speak, I will despise myself as a man, and even more as a Christian.*

"Yes, My Lord Abbot."

The silence seemed to thunder. The abbot threw up his hands and turned away. After a moment he said very quietly, his back still turned. "For that you can be burned here in Rome."

Justin stood silently, his emotion now leaving him spent.

The abbot turned. "Don't you see that translating from Latin into the carnal language of peasants and slaves would corrupt the holy words? The original writings must be preserved."

"Preserved, My Lord? Preserved to sit silent in musty rooms in a language few can speak or understand? Should they not be translated and fed to both priest and people?"

"Are there not enough problems trusting student-priests with the Scriptures? Do you expect us to also turn them over to peasants?"

"The Scriptures should be in every man's own tongue."

"Ah."

Justin imagined the clang of the cell door, the key turning. "I have said no more than scholars like Erasmus. Has he not said the Scriptures should be in the common language?"

The abbot took the parchment from him and for a moment stood reading it. "A pity. Your work is quite good. Master of Arts Mirandola was right. He had plans for you. It was the reason he chose you to translate in the university library. He was wrong, however. You cannot be trusted with such an awesome task. If your education proceeds beyond Latin to Greek and Hebrew, you will soon be at the bazaar peddling handwritten portions of Scripture along with the leeks and fish."

He walked to the hearth and tossed it into the coals. Justin watched the writing disintegrate.

"This is a dangerous time for the Church. The winds of heresy are stirring in unlikely places across Europe. I must bring your case before the archbishop. Perhaps a year or so in the dungeon will be enough to bring you to your senses."

Years!

"My Lord Abbot! Since I have not yet earned my ordination, is it not enough to banish me from this diocese and return me to London?"

"So you can sow your seeds elsewhere? I could wish Justin Brice that it were so light a matter." He rang a bell. "The bishop will decide your fate. It is out of my hands. I have no more to say." He turned away.

Justin stood there in resolute silence. It was evident that further argument would be useless. A servant came in. "Put him in confinement until the bishop comes."

4

Trouble and anguish have taken hold on me:
yet thy commandments are my delight
(Ps. 119:143).

His body ached from lying on the cold slab of the damp cell,
and the wind blew rain through the small barred window
above his head. It was black, and he had no idea of the time
or what day it was. He pulled his soiled cloak about his head
and moved across the filthy straw to the other corner, hoping
to get away from the rain. He felt the loathsome movement of
the rats who were so accustomed to his presence that they
brushed against him without fear, and only smelled him in-
quisitively. He moved cautiously in the gross darkness to keep
from being bitten.

How many days had passed? How many weeks? It seemed
months. He never knew, for his questions to the monks who
brought his food were greeted with silence. He had tried to use
his fingernail to scratch a mark for each dawn that lightened
the window but the stone was too hard, and he could find
nothing sharp enough to use on the wall, even his cross had
been ceremoniously removed from around his neck.

Where was the archbishop? When would his trial begin? Or
had they decided to let him remain in the dungeon? What had

been the fate of John, Marcus, and the others? Were they too in dungeons, or had they recanted?

The nights were always the worst with darkness, the cold seeping through his clothes, and the stench of lumbering rats. Again he rebuked himself for not memorizing the epistle. If he had done so, how much comfort would be his.

Instead, he concentrated on prayer and found that the mercy of the Lord knew no bounds or lack of patience. During his endless vigil through the night, the warm peace he remembered so well upon resting in the written Word again came to brighten his mind, and he found his courage strengthened.

"Christ of goodness, give me the faith to rest my case confidently in Your hand and to believe Your will shall prevail. If it is here You wish me to stay, grant me peace. And if it is death, do not let me recant in fear of the hot faggots, let me die knowing my conviction is not in vain."

He took consolation in remembering the sufferings of Christ, and in knowing that his own, however presently miserable, were light in comparison. The One who had suffered and died, now lived to come beside him as Sustainer and Helper, and not even the dungeon could still His sweet presence.

He slept, and when his eyes opened upon a new dawn the rats were out of sight. He stirred. Someone was coming.

At the end of the outer passageway a flight of chiseled steps led up to a smaller door. There was a rattle of keys followed by the sound of footsteps. A torch gave light and a monk came hurriedly down the steps. Even before he came into clear view Justin recognized the form and face. Marcus! He was free! Had he recanted? Or had his uncle, the archbishop, moved on his behalf?

Marcus reached inside his tunic and removed the smuggled apples, bread and cheese, and a flagon of cider. Justin grabbed them through the bars, feeling relieved to see him well, yet faintly disappointed.

"So you have recanted?"

Marcus arched a mocking brow. "Have you no confidence in my integrity? No, say nothing. It is enough that I have the keys, is it not?"

Victoriously, he turned the lock and the cell opened.

Freedom! Justin could hardly believe it. Marcus lit a second torch and passed it to him. With an upward glance toward the steps he hissed, "A friend waits for you in the meditation garden. He masquerades as a priest and calls himself Felix. He has a message, and says a Brice ship is docked in Italy."

Felix! Ewan Brice had first bought the Saracen out of slavery in the Moslem East. Changing his name from Tahir to Felix, the servant had been in the Brice family since Justin was a boy.

"All things have come together for your escape. If we make haste, you will soon be aboard ship sailing for London."

"God be praised, but," Justin felt a twinge of dread. "What of John?"

Marcus stiffened. "He became ill in the dungeon and died. Grieve later. We have no time to linger. There is a passage through the lower dungeons. This way."

Justin fled after Marcus who darted down the passage. They walked for several minutes before Marcus paused at a cross-way to consult a small drawing which he held to the light of the torch. Justin knew better than to ask him where he had gotten the drawing. They stopped before another door, a key rattled, and a dark passage loomed before them. "There is an aqueduct that takes water to the orchard."

"Who told you of the exit?"

"The archbishop."

Understanding the reason for Justin's surprise, Marcus looked him squarely in the eye. "He is not my uncle, but my father. My mother is of the Italian nobility."

Justin begin to understand the reason why Marcus had been able to get himself out of trouble.

"Escape from Rome is your last hope," said Marcus. "The trial would condemn you to death."

Their torches had burned down and Marcus pointed ahead with his flickering flame to the narrow passage. They heard the sound of water and lowered themselves into the cold flood. Their light was gone now, and they edged forward through the tight tunnel, the dark water was waist high.

The long distance seemed endless amid the pitch black, and the rush of water tore at their bodies. Marcus was much lighter than Justin and he grasped hold of him as they moved forward together.

Emerging unexpectedly, the light greeted them and the water echoed ahead. Marcus was shivering, his teeth chattering. "Y-you first. M-my strength . . . is lacking."

Justin grabbed hold of the top of the tunnel and climbed up and over the wall, then bracing himself flat to the rock reached down to Marcus. In a moment he had pulled him up.

They rested against the outer flume of the aqueduct. A gust of cold wind blew the rain on their faces. They listened for voices but the garden was silent. A glance about proved the area deserted. The grove of fig, apricot, and olive trees stretched before them, and still further was the large garden where the monastery grew its own food. Little of the summer harvest remained, except tired squash vines, and the yellow and brown leaves of the abbot's prized grape vines.

In one corner of the grove was a sheltered path that led through an isolated arbor of climbing roses. Marcus led the way. The sky was like granite and the steady drizzle of rain dripped through the overhead tangle of thorny vines. They walked hurriedly in silence. After a time they came in sight of another path branching off in the direction of the outer wall of the monastery, which faced the back road.

"It is here we must say good-bye, my friend," said Marcus. "Your father's servant waits by the fountain."

It seemed unthinkable that having arranged for his escape, Marcus would not join him. "Together we may accomplish something of lasting value for our generation," Justin urged.

"No, brother, I cannot go with you to London," said Marcus firmly. He avoided Justin's gaze, resisting the inward tug of friendship and something else, what was it? "I believe as you. Only, I will work here in Rome. The power of the archbishop can open doors that neither of us could open alone. And it offers a safe haven from which I can work toward reform. What good to die in a cell like John, or to be burned? Who remembers martyrs?"

Justin gravely considered, "It matters not if the world pauses to remember. It matters that Christ does."

Marcus stood shivering in his dripping robe.

Justin knew well the ambitions of Marcus and he knew what was possible if one had influence and wealth. His own escape and the fact that Marcus could remain in safety was proof of that. The abbot would not touch Marcus because he was thought to be the nephew of the archbishop who held the key to his advancement into the Vatican Palace. But what of future controversies? What would befall Marcus when he was older and the archbishop was no longer there to protect him? Would his convictions then lead him to death?

Justin warned quietly, "Think not that position alone will give you room to bring about reform. Good men have tried in the past to be rebuked to silence."

Marcus smiled thinly. "One could learn much from Erasmus when it comes to walking the cliff's edge. I will be leaving Rome and going to Florence where Savonarola served. I will now attend the Platonic Academy to pursue my studies and Greek."

Marcus grew thoughtful. "Remember the night in the chapel when you spoke of the path branching? It turns now and I choose another way. Nay, I have not recanted. My father did not ask me to, and I did not offer. The abuses in the Church must be stopped. But I will seek reform within the Church. I cannot, and will not, break with it."

"I respect your decision. Let us leave to the sovereignty of God His method to bring reform," said Justin. "It is enough we agree on the need. The bodies of such heretics may die, but their ideas, if born of the Spirit, will live. And if the light of truth burns brighter through the death of men like Savonarola, then it must be."

They paused together upon the place where their paths would divide, and for a moment said nothing. Behind them was the past. Marcus would go to Florence with the promise of a bright future, and he would return to London, and what?

"Then here we part," said Justin. He smiled into the face that usually bore a cynical expression. "I wish you true peace, my friend and once protagonist, Marcus."

"And for you, said heretic, true answers."

Then Marcus removed his silver cross and handed it to Justin. "The peace of Christ be with you."

Justin quickly embraced him. Marcus hurried away in order that his emotion might not be seen except by the silent friends of nature who told no tales. So the last of the nodding roses, whose petals drooped, moved gently in the silent rain, and a lone bird, who sat on the tree branch of his once secure summer home, took to flight as the leaves fell, leaving the limb stark against the oncoming blight of frost.

When Justin reached the end of the path he looked back, thinking he heard Marcus following.

There was no time for disappointment. And who knew the variance of God's ways when it came to his own? He was sure His hand would be upon Marcus. And John? His memory was everywhere in the garden, but his soul was with Christ.

The ancient Roman fountain was in ruins. Moss grew on the stones, and a few flowers, unwilling to say good-bye to the summer sun, bravely turned their faces into the rain. Justin paused and looked about for Felix. Then from the shrubs came the familiar voice he had not heard in years.

"Heaven be praised! You are still in one sizable piece, Master!"

Justin turned. Felix crawled out of the bushes. The two black eyes gleamed with relief. Justin laughed and embraced him, then held the lean figure disguised in a monk's robe at arm's length. "Felix! Your hair is turning gray."

"Yes, Master. The years pass as swiftly as the flight of a raven. You have not kept count."

"So you think! Where did you get the monk's cowl?"

"Anything can be bought in Rome, even a robe for Felix."

"I knew matters were bad, but things are worse than I thought when even Felix can buy a priest's robe," he jested. Then he grew serious. "Did my brother Stewert send you?"

Felix's eyes were troubled. "Nay, 'twas the fairest of women, Lady Regina."

Mention of her name took Justin by surprise.

"There is much to tell you, Master, but it must wait. We must leave at once. After I spoke to your friend Marcus, another monk saw me and knew I was a stranger."

Justin halted him. His head jerked back toward the path. The sound was unmistakable, the rush of feet, and more than two voices.

Felix motioned ahead. "That way! There is a wall!"

They ran through the tangled shrubs, Felix surged ahead, but tripped over his robe. "A robe is a curse, young Master. How have you borne it!"

"Not well, but better than you. Hoist it up under your belt. Watch those vines."

They came to the end of the wall. Felix had the rope in place and was up and over. Justin climbed swiftly, grabbed the top of the wall and dropped to the other side.

"They will never get over the wall," Felix said confidently. "They must turn back to the gate."

"Never underestimate hounds after a fox—two foxes now. Hurry."

Below was a steep slope. They slid and twisted their way to the bottom where a quiet dirt road waited. In the distance several riders on horses were approaching. From their dress they looked to be mercenary soldiers.

"Master Justin, quick! Cross the road!"

They darted into the welcoming shadows where trees grew close together, running as though the huntsmen were at their heels. At long last they emerged on the other side. Safe for the moment, they sank into the grass, gasping, and neither spoke until their bodies cooled and their hearts ceased to race. Justin stared up at the sky, enjoying the soft drizzle of rain on his face, and the clouds that seemed like sailing ships.

Lord, thank You.

5

Therefore, I love thy commandments above gold;
yea, above fine gold
(Ps. 119:27).

Inside the Roman inn, Felix sat cross-legged on the floor. The room was long with only one entrance and soon would fill with travelers. Justin leaned against the wall, tasting his new freedom. Only a few vagabond soldiers had come to the inn. They sat wearily in a corner talking among themselves and drinking from a shared jug.

Felix used his dagger to carve a chunk of meat from the leg of lamb. His eyes twinkled. "A woman with wit and courage," Felix said of Lady Regina Redford. "I would trust her with my life—and yours, Master."

Justin remembered back to younger days near Windsor Castle. Regina had always been adventurous, much to the dismay of her father Lord Simon, and her brother Marlon. Regina rarely, however, gave them cause for concern. She was, in truth, not only a girl of wit and courage, but owned the charms of a lady of nobility. He remembered how she had sent her servant to Saint Catherine's with the price of his indulgence for helping the Wycliffites to escape, and the time shared in the woods when they read the forbidden English version of the Gospel of Matthew.

"What news do you bring from her ladyship?"

Felix reached under his robe and handed Justin a letter. " 'Tis with sadness I bring you this news, Master, but we thought you should know."

Expecting the worst, Justin read Regina's letter dated in August from King Henry's palace in London. Her artistic handwriting leaped up at him as he read.

"Learning from Felix that one of your father's ships was soon to set sail for Rome under the command of your brother, Captain Stewert Brice, I have given this letter to Felix, thy faithful friend and mine, to deliver to you at Saint Athenians. Since my other letters and parcels have gone unanswered . . . ."

His jaw tightened and a feeling of frustration seized him. *So she had written to him and he had not been able to answer. What must she have thought of him? Did she believe he no longer cared? And yet, what hope was there?*

When Felix first came to me about your father's condition, I traveled at once to Antwerp to find him in the home of a merchant friend, Thomas Poynitz. I found your father just as poorly as Felix had described. Ewan Brice is a man tormented in soul, and I fear for his eternal state. I have tried in vain to console him with hope in Christ, for I have learned much recently under the lectures of Dean John Colet at Saint Paul's Cathedral. Yet it seems I am not the one to break through your father's spiritual barrier. The dear man is twisted by guilt and regret over your fate in the monastery at Saint Athenians. I regret to tell you that your sisters, Catherine and Mary died of the sweating sickness this winter. Captain Brice is sure that he is to blame. He is woefully convinced that he is doomed to abide with the heretics in hell. I shall let Felix explain his thoughts to you.

Justin paused. *So his little sisters were gone.* Stabilizing his emotions he read on.

I have written, hoping you might receive permission from the bishop in Rome to come to London to visit your father, for I do not know how much longer his mind will hold. Through the kindness of his friends, the English merchants in Antwerp, I have managed to bring him to my father's country estate in Devonshire. The countryside, I felt, would do him good.

I wish also to tell you of a wonderful happening here in London. Dean Colet is lecturing on the Pauline Epistles to overflow audiences. I have attended whenever possible, though my father Lord Simon is upset with my independence. I have talked Marlon into coming with me on several occasions and he is quite excited at hearing the Scriptures so plainly taught. I could wish for you to hear also.

At the lectures, Lord Marlon has met a most interesting young Oxford scholar at Cambridge by the name of William Tyndale. You must meet him. Yet I dare say no more on paper except that his scholarship is noteworthy. His zeal for Christ and the Scriptures is like a flame of fire.

As ever, Regina

Justin sat staring at the letter. His emotions were divided in several directions at once. Being in touch with Regina if only by letter awakened a strange desire within his heart. The thought of John Colet lecturing on the Pauline Epistles thrilled him. Of the Oxford scholar, William Tyndale, he knew nothing, and could only wonder why she would mention him along with a Master of Arts like Colet, who taught the Word of God as no one else was doing in the university. But his father—he tensed, his appetite gone. He must go to him at once. He must share what he had learned from the Epistle of Romans before it was eternally too late.

"And Stewert," he said of his brother, "where is he? I would see him at once. Where is his ship?"

Felix scowled. "I wish not to speak evil of your brother, Master, but," he spread his hands. "What shall I say to you?"

"The truth, Felix, as always. Spare nothing."

"The Brice ship is docked at Genoa and will be there for a few weeks. Captain Stewert is about his business in buying cargo to return to Antwerp. Most of the crew is on leave, and he thinks I too revel in the city. Your brother does not know I am here. He warned me not to come to you."

Justin was troubled. The years between him and his older brother Stewert were many, and they had never been close. Adding the years Justin had spent with his studies, he realized they hardly knew each other. Yet was this reason enough for Stewert to forbid Felix to bring him news of the death of his sisters and his father's condition?

"Captain Stewert is a jealous man," said Felix darkly. "He thinks ill of you."

A ghost of a smile touched Justin's lips. "Jealous? Of a brother in a monastery? While he sailed the open seas?"

"Stewert fears the love your father has for you. The bond your father feels between you and your mother, has always been deep. Stewert's mother, poor woman, was never loved. Wherever Captain Brice has sailed, it was you, Master, that troubled the mind of your father. Stewert fears that your return to London will mean the Brice galleons will be left to you, and not to himself."

"My father expects me to remain in the monastery. Why would he unexpectedly change his will?"

"That his own conscience might find a token of rest." He leaned closer to Justin, his voice lowered. "Your father is a tormented soul. After your journey here to Rome, we sailed to Cadiz, and on to the Golden Horn of the Turkish Empire. He knew no joy, Master. He would not eat, nor drink even his ale.

He took to badgering Stewert until there arose a great argument between them over you. Stewert accused your father of caring nothing for any of his children, except you. One night Sir Ewan called me to his cabin, greatly disturbed. 'Felix,' he said, 'I did well in sending my lad to Rome, did I not?'

" 'Aye,' I told him. 'Heaven is pleased, Captain Brice.' He looked at me squarely and said, 'Then why does the peace of God still elude me?' 'I know not, Captain,' I told him. 'Why does the blood on my hands gleam red in the dark!' 'I know not, Captain,' I told him. 'It is but a wicked dream sent by the spirits of those you slew fairly in battle. They rise from the sea in wrath to goad with pricks. Pay them no heed."

Justin groaned deeply within. *Father, your conscience is aware of sin and has no knowledge of the sufficient work of Christ* he thought.

Felix went on in a whisper, " 'I did the lad ill,' Captain Brice kept saying. 'I forced him. God is not pleased. Even the ghost of me wife comes to scowl upon me.' 'Tis but a dream, Captain Brice,' I kept assuring him, but he would not listen.

"It was then your little sisters took ill and the news reached him of their death, both in one night. He became like a ranting lunatic. I grew fearful for the health of his mind, and pleaded with the honorable Thomas Poynitz to send word to Lady Regina about his state, thinking she might influence the Bishop to seek your release from Saint Athenians."

Justin was deeply troubled. "I wrote my father that God had mercifully turned my journey to Rome into a discovery of light. There is no reason for guilt."

"No letters came, Master. Nor does it seem that you received those from her ladyship."

The morning sun broke from behind the clouds to send a glimmer of gold upon the dark blue water of the Tiber River. Slaves stroked the oars slowly as a guard galley passed the water gate, and their voices chanted in time with the oars.

Justin and Felix walked the flagstone road to catch the small ship bringing them to Genoa. "What city is like Rome?" Felix breathed with awe.

Justin stopped before a great cathedral and read aloud the inscription. "Christ our God, guard Your city from all disturbances and wars. Break victoriously the force of the enemy."

"A noble prayer," said Felix piously.

"Yes, it was taken, if I am correct in my history, from one of the gates of old Constantinople. But one must remember Jerusalem, Felix. There, the glory of God once dwelt. When the priests departed from His word, He departed from them. Is this great city any less responsible?"

Felix thought about that and made no comment. For his eyes beheld the buildings of many fine cathedrals. *With so many great and awesome buildings dedicated to the honor of God,* he thought, *how could the city be said to have departed from Him?* Felix wondered about this, but was reluctant to ask Justin for fear of showing his ignorance. *My mother was a Moor,* he thought. *How easily I can be judged to be an infidel. And I, Felix, am not a follower of Mohammed, no indeed. It is Christ who is the light of the East and West.* He felt pleased with his pious thought and glanced at Justin's robe and cross. His satisfaction increased. *Why, I, Felix, walk beside a very priest of God!*

Justin made his way through the throng of merchants and buyers, the jostling, bargaining, and arguing fell upon his ears as irksome babble. He came to a particular stall with a lean, bearded man in charge. Justin caught sight of the weapons. He paused. The keen eyes of the dignified Arab merchant fixed upon him. He raked the clerical tunic with the controlled insolence of a race who had conquered the East.

Idolater, the Arab thought. *A worshiper of women.*

Belonging to a race who looked upon women as little more than personal property, he considered Christianity to be the worship of the virgin Mary.

Justin pointed. "A Damascus dagger?"

"What else, my friend?"

Justin ignored the hint of pride. "I will take it." He nodded toward Felix. "My friend will pay," he told the merchant.

The merchant smiled for the first time as the exchange passed hands. "May Allah twice bless you," he said, too piously.

Justin ignored him and walked on, but Felix felt obliged to reveal his zeal. He leaned across the booth and pointed a finger toward the man's well-kept beard. "Beware, you infidel," he whispered. His bravery sent a little chill down his spine.

The merchant drew back insulted, but Felix grabbed a basket of oranges and tossed him another coin. He ran after Justin, peeling one with vigor. "Eat, Master," he said.

Justin had never seen so many churches, yet beyond the chanting of voices, the glimmer of candles, and the rising of sweet gray incense, there was no distinction between truth and error. Did anyone know? Did people or priest? Growing traditions mingled with Eastern mysticism, while the culture of Plato and the philosophy of the humanists were incorporated with the words of the apostles. Clarity was needed.

"And what could unveil historic Christianity more completely than the renewed teaching of all the Scriptures?" Justin asked him.

Felix was cautious. Yet he had traveled enough with Captain Ewan Brice to understand the thoughts of the common man toward Rome. He mingled with them and he knew their growing resentment over the apparent wealth of Rome, and the drainage of their tax dollars into the papal treasury. The papal attempt to get more money out of Saxony by selling indulgences would anger the Augustinian monk Martin Luther into nailing his ninety-five theses to the door at Wittenberg.

The rulers of Western Europe had also begun to resent the loss of money, and with the nobles and middle class, were casting eyes toward lands owned by the Church. Moreover, political independence from the decisions of Rome was growing. King Henry would one day battle the pope for the right to marry Anne Boleyn by getting a divorce from Catherine who bore him no sons to inherit his throne. By doing so he would eventually break his ties with Rome, and declaring himself head of the Church in England.

Beside the drainage of wealth, complicated by inflation and rising prices, the middle class saw the corruption in the Church and the abuse of clerical power. It angered them that self-seeking clerics could buy and sell offices, called sinecures, where they were paid a salary yet did none of the work. Justice, too, was bought and sold in the clerical courts, and for the right amount of money, rulings could be obtained that permitted acts which the Scriptures clearly condemned.

"Your friend Marcus said that you are in trouble with the abbot," whispered Felix for the first time. His black eyes rolled.

"It is good you have come, Felix. I must escape Rome. If caught, I will be tried as a heretic."

Felix's mouth dropped. The dark eyes widened. Words failed him. "A heretic?" he hissed at last. "I cannot believe it, Master!"

Justin paused on the wharf with the cool wind from the water blowing his cowl. "Can you read Latin?" Justin asked innocently.

"Master, you mock me."

"It is not I who mock you, Felix. What value would you place upon the words of Christ if you possessed them in your own tongue?"

"You mean, . . ." and he hesitated to voice the suggestion. " 'English'?"

"Yes. The tongue of merchants, sailors, yeomen, peasants, and slaves."

Felix hesitated. He glanced about and watched the dock workers loading and unloading cargo, and a peasant child running past carrying his breakfast and lunch in one hunk of bread. His eyes searched Justin's face for mockery. He was relieved to see that it was not there.

In response to his question, Felix impulsively emptied his pocket of the remaining coins and sent them rolling into the cobbled street likes flecks of golden light.

"To possess such words in my own tongue would deem gold cheap, Master."

Beggars and waifs converged on the spot and fought for the coins.

Justin raised a brow at the dramatic act, but Felix lifted his dark head with dignity. "A profound question, demands a dramatic answer, Master," he explained.

"It is for my desire to put the words of Christ into our tongue that I am branded a heretic," said Justin.

"What will you do, Master? Become another Wycliffe?"

Justin smiled and repeated his words. "Such honor would deem gold cheap."

A beggar tugged at Justin's worn sleeve. "Alms, my father, alms? For the love of the saints?"

Justin held palms forward to signify he had nothing, and grabbing Felix's arm, hurried him through the gathering crowd. They were being followed by the shouting waifs.

"Now you've done it," said Justin.

They darted through the street ducking here and there among the shops and buildings until they found themselves nearing the harbor. They paused now to walk, awed by the morning's magnificent view extending southwest toward the Mediterranean Sea. They looked at each other and smiled. Justin anxiously pulled Felix down the steps to the wharf, which groaned with the movement of the water's swells beneath their sandaled feet.

The private boat slipped quietly from the waterway and moved west on the landward side of Italy toward Genoa where the Brice ship waited to take on cargo. Moving astern Justin watched Rome slip from view. A thousand memories played with his emotions. The sea was picking up, still tumultuous from the storm of a few days before. The cold spray blowing against his face tasted salty on his lips.

Felix came forward and fixed his gaze not toward Genoa, but south and to the open waters of the Mediterranean. Justin thought he knew his concern. "Stewert is late in bringing the ship to harbor in England."

"A mistake if you ask me, Master. We have delayed too long. The year is late to be risking the voyage."

"Is he a good man with the sea?"

"Already as good as your father, but proud and arrogant, he is. Ye cannot tell him a thing. Yes, the sea will be no friend to the ship of Captain Stewert Brice. The weather will be sore enough."

"How long will the ship remain in Genoa?"

"Another four to five days."

"That will give me time to get aboard. Stewert must not know until we are far at sea. I wish no argument with him now."

6

Faith cometh by hearing,
and hearing by the word of God
(Rom. 10:17).

In Genoa the Brice ship was loaded with the fine, rich materials that had swept the English palace of King Henry VIII, especially the brightly colored velvets and cloth of gold. Genoa was known for its merchants and ships which aggressively competed in trade with the world's markets.

It was night when he and Felix neared the Brice ship that huddled among the numerous masts docked quietly in the waters. The night was still, the sky was clear after the storm, and the moon was a silver crescent in the black canopy over the water.

One of the crew members on watch recognized Felix. The crewman cast a glance over his shoulder to see if the few men left on board were watching him. They had their faces to the sea, anxious to put out again and return home to Antwerp. The cargo had been loaded and they only waited for Stewert and the crew to return. The ladder was tossed over the tall ship and Justin latched hold and climbed up. A few brief strides across the deck brought Justin to the cargo hold. Taking the ladder down, he was about to close the door over his head when above in the ship's masts, he saw a young lad with flaxen hair.

The lad swung from a rope like a monkey, watching him with wide eyes transfixed on his monk's cowl, and on the cross which caught the light and glinted.

Justin felt an uncomfortable twinge. The lad stared at him as if he believed Justin possessed special powers. As their eyes briefly locked, Justin sensed that it could mean trouble. Because of the lack the knowledge of the Scriptures, the Christianity of even the most devout often mingled with medieval superstitions.

Felix followed him down into the hold. "You will be safe here."

"The boy, who is he?"

"Only a lad. 'Tis his first voyage. He will say nothing. He fears Captain Stewert."

In the cargo hold Justin lost himself among the barrels and caskets of goods to be brought home to London. *How easy to smuggle things aboard the belly of a ship,* he thought.

They had been at sea for several days when Justin awoke to find the ship tossed and battered by the Mediterranean Sea. The hold was in total blackness. In the bowels of the ship his bed of cushions pitched up and down, and for a confused moment he could not remember where he was. His head buzzed strangely. Felix had given him some strange exotic tea from an Eastern port. The last thing he remembered was the meal he enjoyed the night before, smuggled to him by Felix. "Eat, Master. Drink. You will need much rest."

Much rest—how long had he slept? He sat up. What was in that tea? He studied the movement of the ship struggling through high wind and heavy seas. The ship lurched, the timbers groaned and shuddered as if ready to split apart. A gale. As Felix had warned, the sea was not easy to master this time of year.

He struggled to his knees, his head still buzzed, as he tried to keep his balance. Years away from the sea made his stomach churn. His robe—where was it in this blackness? And his dagger was gone! He felt blindly about the floor, bumping into a wooden barrel. At the sound, he heard someone startle, then freeze.

"Felix!" he whispered fiercely. "Come here, you scheming practitioner."

It didn't take Justin long to realize that it was not Felix. Whoever it was, he had taken his cloak, his cross, and the dagger. And in his hurry to get away, he was bumping into barrels and sending them crashing and rolling.

It had to be the boy! What he wanted with his belongings, Justin did not know. The boy's stumbling feet reached the steps and Justin staggered in the direction of the sound.

"Wait," Justin called. "I promise not to harm you."

The boy scampered upward. Justin felt his way, grabbing one of his ankles just as he pushed open the cargo door.

The sudden blast of wind and spray against his face shocked Justin out of his grogginess. There were voices shouting above the wind, and running feet. The strong booted legs of a crewmen now halted above the hold. He thrust a swaying lamp into the opening. "All hands on deck! Who dare cower down there with the rats?"

Another crewman came beside him. "It's the lad," he called above the din of wind and sea. "Trying to escape yer duty, are ye? Ye scurvy bloke!"

"No Sir, no Sir, the gods of the sea are angry and I was seeking relics to bless us!"

"Now look here, Boy. Did not the captain warn ye to keep out of the cargo? Ye have got the fingers of a thief! This is yer last sea voyage on a Brice ship—what ye got in yer hand?"

The seaman grabbed the robe as the boy cowered against the steps. He held up the lantern while the other man shook out the tunic. They looked at each other surprised. "A priest's robe."

"Where'd ye get this?" he called at the boy. The boy shrank back.

"On yer feet, ye bloody cur! Eh, what's that yer clutching to yer heart!" He pried open the boy's hand. "A cross!"

They grabbed his arms and hauled him through the opening while he shouted for mercy. The boy landed hard on deck. "Ye'll tell us where ye stole these or. . . ."

"I did not steal them! I only meant to borrow them. They are blessed."

"Whose are they? Speak, Boy!"

"I found them below in an old trunk."

"Yer lying. Yer a thief and the son of a thief."

The boy began to shout and struggle as they strung him out. "A lash is too civil fer the likes of ye. Tie him to the mast."

"Let him go," said Justin.

They whirled, hands to their sword hilts.

"I am unarmed," Justin stated. "The tunic and cross are mine."

They stared at him, astounded. "A stowaway. Call the cap'n."

Captain Stewert Brice was already angry at being called away from the rudder in such a storm. The rugged Scot left a good man as pilot, but none handled a ship as well as himself.

"What goes here?" Stewert demanded.

"A stowaway, Captain. He is a priest."

Every eye fixed upon Justin. For a moment no one spoke. The night was inky black. Not a star guided their way, and the ship had been off course for over a day. The wind lashed against them sending Stewert Brice's cloak flapping. They struggled to hold their positions.

"I was going to return them, Captain," the boy whined. "I only wanted them because they are blessed. The wind screams danger. We are doomed!"

"Hold your tongue," Captain Brice demanded.

Justin turned to the boy. "Nothing of mine can ward off the storm. I shall take back my clothes, and the dagger," he told the crewman.

Stewert stepped back as if struck. The voice had ended any doubt as to who the stowaway was, but even so, he could not believe it. "You," he breathed.

"It has been a long time. Greetings, my brother."

Stewert stepped forward and peered at him. "Hand me the lantern," he told the crewman. He held the lamp before Justin.

The light shone in Justin's eyes and he could see nothing, but Stewert was satisfied. He sucked in his breath and muttered. His face hardened.

Some of the crewmen now recognized Justin and shock turned to relief. They looked at each other and began to laugh. It was Justin Brice! The fair son of their true captain, Ewan Brice.

"Silence," Stewert demanded. He found little to bring him pleasure in the unwanted presence of his younger brother.

"Captain," one man cried as if Stewert did not understand, "this is Justin Brice. Yer brother!"

"I can see who it is," Stewert growled.

"Are ye not going to, . . ." the seaman stopped as the icy blue gaze above the lantern confronted him. He knew the look all too well. The men sobered and stepped back.

The wind increased. The great swells, black and threatening, sent the ship rising and falling.

The boy appealed to Justin like a frightened animal. "The wrath of God is upon the ship! Bless us, My Father, and we will live!"

Stewert squinted toward the sky. He could see nothing but blackness. The rain splashed against his face. He turned in cold rage to Justin. "Blessing?" he shouted. "His presence brings a curse." He thrust his arm toward Justin. "You run from Christ. You bring your sin with you on my ship!"

The crewmen stared at the clerical robe and cross as if they were now the omens of a sinking ship. Their countenance changed from smiles to wary glances. One man touched his lips with his tongue and swallowed. "The wrath of God," he whispered.

"No! A storm," corrected Justin. "It is the season for storms on the Mediterranean. Any good English seaman knows that. And you are all good seamen. God is not angry. There is nothing supernatural about our danger."

A murmur of decided agreement broke out. Yes, he was right. Justin looked at his brother. "You should have finished your voyage and docked at London two weeks ago."

"Your mouth, My Brother, has always opened the way for your trouble. Hold your tongue unless it is in prayer." He grabbed the tunic from the crewman, shouting, "Get to your posts. Can you not see the storm is upon us?"

The men scattered, leaving Stewert with Justin. Large drops of rain heralded worsening winds. In the distance sounded the faint rumble of thunder. Stewert hurled the tunic against Justin's chest. As the cross landed near the boy's feet, he gave a fearful gasp expecting a terrible judgment to strike them.

"Have you fled your duty to God to meddle in matters best left alone? Leave our father in peace!"

"Peace? Is his soul at rest? Is yours! Far be it from me to trouble either of you, but to bring the true message of Christ."

"You flee from God!"

"If I flee, it is not from God."

"No, you stow away till we be far at sea then bring curses upon my ship. Your presence is the work of Felix. I warned him to stay away from you."

"Had Felix not shown mercy and brought news of my father, I would still return to London. If not on this ship, then another. I will not return to Rome, nor any monastery. You must accept that, and Father as well."

"So, you have run from the monastery like a wicked son. Your broken vow dishonors the name of Ewan Brice."

"If a vow be broken, it is not your concern. It is between my God and me. But come, my brother! Your self-righteous indignation shows you a pious fraud. Is it a broken vow that you are concerned with or my return from a grave you hoped I would stay in?"

Stewert's eyes narrowed. "If I wished you dead, I could do it now. The sea could be your grave."

The ship lurched, and they were sent sprawling. The boy, still tied, cried for mercy.

Stewert Brice was first on his feet, and leaving Justin, he staggered back to the helm of the ship where the pilot was clinging to the rudder.

Stewert saw one of the men propped against the side with a cut on his head from the tossing of the ship. Felix attended the wound.

"Captain, there is land ahead, perhaps the Balearic Islands, off the coast of Spain. The wind demands her own way, Captain Brice, I cannot hold her."

"We are cursed," breathed the crewman propped against the side.

The thought of losing the Brice ship to the sea was more than Stewert could stand. It was easy to blame Felix for an ill omen by smuggling his brother aboard ship. He jerked Felix to his feet. "You conniving Saracen! Infidel! You went to your Master Justin. Do not deny it. Confess!"

Felix did so, bravely, and bowed his head. "As a servant to Justin Brice these many years, Captain Stewert, I could not forgive myself if I had not brought him word. It is your father I think of, not only your brother. Ewan Brice would wish to see him before he dies."

"You have disobeyed your captain's orders. I think I know

why. With Justin Brice as your captain you would seek to rule the ship yourself!"

He hurled him to the deck. Felix took it without flinching. His bravery provoked Stewert. It made him feel suddenly small and dishonorable. He lashed out with angry words of defense. "You have cursed me by bringing him aboard my ship. He has come between me and everything I strove to attain. My father would leave him sole heir for love of his dead mother. And now you jinx my ship, you infidel!"

"No, Captain Stewert, no, I am a Christian. Master Justin will give me the words of Christ in my own tongue."

Stewert drew his sword and grabbed him by the throat. He dragged him to the side of the ship and pressed him to the railing. The point of the blade pricked his flesh. The wind raged against them and the black swells curled upward toward Felix's head like anxious fingers ready to pull him into the deep.

"Your life for his, Saracen," Stewert shouted above the wind.

"Captain Stewert, please! I am no infidel! Lord save me!"

Stewert released him. The water cascaded over the sides sending them both to the deck. Stewert held onto the wooden railing, then staggered to the rudder, shoving the pilot out of the way.

Justin desperately struggled to loose the boy from the mast before another surge of water splashed over the side. The foam swirled about his feet. "Get below," he shouted. But now the boy went on his knees before him, his eyes wild, clutching at him as though he were a saint.

"Bless me, lest I die," he shouted above the wind.

For a moment Justin froze. "Get off your knees!" He grabbed him, but the boy fell on his stomach and clung to him all the more. The look of despair on the still-childish face pierced him like a sword. The ship was heaving up and down, and the sea swirling about them. Together they slid as the ship tilted, the boy still clinging to him.

"Bless me," he kept shouting until Justin thought the words would drive him mad. The hunger and fear in the voice would forever burn within his soul. "Bless me."

The sea water splashed over Justin's face bringing him up choking. He tried to speak. The boy clung to his ankle with only one hand.

"Have you no hope? Seek Christ! Seek His sacrifice alone! You will find it sufficient."

"Bless me!"

"I cannot bless you! I can only give you His Word."

His Word!

A streak of lightning blinded him. The sea momentarily lit up. As it did, a shout of alarm from aloft mingled with the gale. "Ship ahead! Ship ahead!"

A second flash of lightning burst across the sky. The thunder echoed. And now the rain was drenching them. The Brice ship attempted to turn to avoid collision.

From the second vessel a desperate alarm sounded followed by shouts so near that Justin recognized voices. The Brice ship took the full force of the impact and Justin was flung against the side. With a shudder the vessel groaned. Justin felt the impact throughout the ship, it throbbed through his very skull. Then there came an abrupt cracking of timbers. The vessel reeled out of control and the dark waters rushed in. Justin caught sight of the wave nearing the side and shouted to the boy to grab hold. Before his eyes he watched the sucking wave lift the boy over the side and sweep him away with the debris.

Dazed, Justin clung to a post. Gone, the boy was gone. One moment he was there, alive, asking a blessing in fear of death. And now he was gone, forever gone.

I lost him, he kept thinking. *He was my responsibility. I lost him.*

The alarm was still sounding. His mind remained fixed on the boy.

As if hurled back with the raging wind and sea, the boy's face appeared, but now it became many faces, many boys. "Bless me, . . ." and his voice merged as into the shout of a multitude.

Above the sound of running feet came the cry to lower the boats, but the swells were too high. Other crewmen hung from ropes and ladders and were being slammed against the side of the hull until they fell.

Justin was still holding to the post when Felix struggled toward him, clinging to the rail. "Quick, Master. A boat. This way."

"Where is my brother?"

"On one of the boats!"

At the side of the ship the rope ladder swung precariously. A boat rode the swells and the sailors strained to hold it. Felix was hauled aboard but the waves worked against Justin. He swung over the side and slipped badly. Relentlessly, the wind and waves beat him into the hull as he hung on the ladder, scraping his knuckles until they were raw. The sailors fought to bring the boat nearer. Felix shouted desperately for them to hold the boat.

The swells beneath Justin were first mountains, then valleys. Again there came the hammer-like impact against the hull, and this time his grip weakened with pain. His right hand slipped and he hung swaying hopelessly from side to side. In a moment his life passed before him like a small cloud racing across the sky.

"Lord," he prayed, his eyes not above, but on the raging black swells beneath, "if I brought them Your Word would I not bless them? Was it not Your Word that the boy cried for, though he knew it not? Lord! For the many—like the boy—and like Felix. I do not know how, but. . . ."

The rope slipped from his numb hand. Down he rushed, hitting with a splash, and was immediately pulled under. The cold shock, like needles, stunned him. He sank deeper into the black pit. Then up, gasping, choking, only to find a towering swell that drove him still further away from the bobbing boat. The voices of his comrades shouted in alarm, then ebbed into the fading distance. The mammoth sea claimed him. All was lost as again he went under, the monk's robe wrapping about his legs like seaweed, dragging him down. But to Justin it seemed that stronger hands, unseen, were lifting him upward claiming him for their own, and the sea had no will to contest. Without explanation, when he bobbed up choking, he found himself close enough to the boat to be tossed a rope. The sailors were startled to see him. They turned to each other, their voices stilled. An act of God!

Felix was in the boat and hauled him over the side. Justin lay on his stomach, gasping.

"Master, I saw the giant swell bear you away, and I thought I would never see you again." Felix wept now, unashamed. "Christ is good to us, very good. We will live to serve Him."

7

Near the Balearic Islands Off the Coast of Spain

I will speak of thy testimonies
also before kings, and will not be ashamed
(Ps. 119:46).

Justin awoke, alert to the threat of danger. He was alone. Ahead of him lay the stormy beach, and behind him, carved into the windswept cliff, stood the dread slave castle of the island of Baron Soleiman. It would not take long for his corsairs to gain sight of the disabled Brice ship, and be searching for them.

Justin listened without moving. Nothing stirred but the wind in the branches. The steady drip of rain monotonously ran down the back of his neck.

Where was Felix? He had lost sight of him just before the swells had capsized their small boat. Justin had been hurled along, choking, swallowed by the flood until he found himself upon the sand, lapsing into unconsciousness. When he awoke the rain was beating upon him, but in the darkness he saw none of the crew, only pieces of wood making their way to shore with the heavy pounding of the surf. Had they gone on without him? He had clawed his way up the beach to the shelter of the trees, and lay gasping.

Hours had passed since then. The first light of dawn was

breaking through the clouds and the great storm was passing, but still the wind blew.

The crack of a twig made him tense. Someone was in the trees near him. He waited, listening. His dagger lifted a little, expecting attack. One of the crewmen stumbled forward clutching his wounded arm. Justin grabbed hold of him and pulled him into the thick shrubs.

"Where are the others?" Justin whispered.

The crewman shook his head. His eyes were bloodshot, and dilated with fear. *He is out of his head,* thought Justin.

"Do you know where we are, Priest?"

"Yes."

The crewman was not satisfied with Justin's toneless response. He wanted the black words to be mouthed with as much dread as he felt surging through his heart. He rasped, "Baron Soleiman masters this islet."

"I know."

"He serves the enemies of your father. We are trapped, Priest." He clutched the front of his tunic. "Trapped! Where is your God?"

"Watch your tongue. Speak His name with awe, or speak it not at all."

"No man on this islet has ever escaped the baron's slave castle, or his evil galleys!"

"Where is Captain Brice?" Justin demanded.

"On the Spanish galleon.

"It is afloat? When did he board it!"

"Last night. Your brother intended to leave you."

So Stewert was willing to sail without him.

"There is still a chance to catch the ship. We must hurry." Justin grabbed him to his feet.

"The baron's men are searching the island. They will catch us before we get there."

"We must try."

They stumbled through the wet overhang, often tripping over fallen limbs. The seaman was bleeding heavily, so Justin was forced to stop. He ripped a piece of cloth from his shirt and pressed it tightly into the wound. The man did not look good and was paling.

"Leave me not, I beg of you!"

"Neither priest nor warrior abandons a friend."

With the man's arm about his neck, they plodded on. Several minutes later they found themselves out of the trees and facing the beach.

The gray waters were still thundering onto the shore, overtaking the sand, and scattering debris. Several dead seamen were sprawled there with the waves washing over their bodies. There had been a fight for the remaining boats and the strongest had prevailed.

Automatically, Justin's eyes sought Felix among the dead. With relief he saw that he was not there. *Stewert must have forced Felix to go on without searching for me,* he decided. *He would never do it of his own will.*

The crewman caught his arm, pointing. "There she is! There is still time, Priest!"

Justin caught sight of the Spanish treasure ship.

The two stumbled to the water's edge where the oncoming waves tore the sand from under their feet. It was all Justin could do to keep them standing. Could those on the ship see them? Would they send a boat? Was the Spanish captain still in command, or had Stewert taken over the ship?

Justin could swim, but the swells were rough and he could not manage both of them. He made a quick search for a piece of wood large enough to lay the crewman on, although the act seemed hopeless. Anything to keep the man's arm from strangling his neck. The sand was barren.

He must try. They entered the water but it was too late. The baron's men came suddenly from the trees behind them, hundreds of corsair warriors brandishing improved Toledo swords, lances, and crossbows.

Another large group carried boats and shoved off to scale the Spanish treasure ship, bending their oars with a will as they fought the shining dark swells.

An arrow whizzed, striking the water beside Justin. Another struck his companion and, with a cry, he went under the rolling waves. Justin grabbed for him, but a blow to the back of his own neck sent him face down into the cold water. A great hand took hold of the collar of his tunic and dragged him back to the beach.

The corsair stood big and strong with a shock of golden hair and a square jaw. His conical helmet was absent, but he wore a mesh shirt of iron chainwork reaching to his elbows to ward off glancing arrows or sword cuts.

"I am unarmed, Corsair!"

The sharp blue eyes fell on the cross glinting against his dark tunic. The corsair hesitated.

"Or does that matter?" challenged Justin.

The granite blue eyes glinted and a smirk crossed his lips. "Well, what have we fished from the sea! A warrior-priest without a sword? You must be a Greek," he mocked.

"I am a Scot!"

"If you insist that so great a blood is yours where are your knightly weapons, Lad?" The eyes continued to mock him. He suggested distinctly, "Is it not an ancient law that a warrior-priest possess helmet, mail-shirt, sword, lance, and a horse?"

Justin was well acquainted with the militant state of mind among certain sects of the Church. The Church and its lands were ruled mainly by Spanish bishops and abbots who were often the brothers of those fierce barons who ruled the rest of the land.

He was also aware that this grinning corsair was enjoying his ability to sport with him.

"I am willing to do without the Great Horse," mocked Justin in return. "I would be content with a ship, however. Surely there are a few about that you have pirated. What of the Spanish ship?"

"Fear not, Priest. You will travel by ship again, but not until we have taken its treasure. Content yourself with a sword," and glimpsing a dead man still clasping his sword, he seized it, and tossed it toward Justin's feet. A malicious smile was on his face. "Now. what is your excuse? Get up and fight, Lad. You are among warriors."

"And if my conscience forbids me to take off your arrogant head?"

The corsair grinned. He unsheathed his sword from his scabbard that hung by leather straps on his left side. "Then I will lop off yours."

Was he serious? There was something affable about him, but he reeked with violence. Still, Justin hesitated to clasp the sword. The corsair saw his internal struggle and it aroused his interest. Nevertheless he took the toe of his boot and flipped the handle of the sword closer within Justin's reach.

"Get up, Lad. Learn to fight, or you will die. If not by my hand, then by Baron Soleiman's. He will wish you to go to sea with him on future ventures."

"No, Corsair. I go nowhere but to England."

"We shall see, Lad."

He swung his sword and Justin ducked, as he felt the breeze of the blade. He clasped the sword and jumped to his feet.

"That is better." He lunged and Justin parried his blow, but the man swiftly countered with such force that Justin lost his footing. The corsair unexpectedly laughed, then began to torment Justin for his poor use of the blade. He toyed with him, backing him further toward the rolling sand hill.

"Come, Lad, where's your stuff?"

Painfully Justin began to recall some of what he had once

known well, but not until he had retreated halfway up the beach. He found himself growing angry, and the corsair knew it, and was enjoying it. This only made Justin feel more ashamed. His conscience struck him. *Am I a servant of God or a half-wild barbarian?*

Justin's sword smashed against his opponent's; he thrust, and parried again. The blades rang.

"Ah! Better!" But then the corsair lunged at him, and the force again sent Justin sprawling back against the sand. A hearty laugh followed.

"Forget your boast! Get it over with," Justin challenged.

"Surrender, do you? Look at him, will you! And his sword still in his hand! Get up and fight!"

Justin's left hand was across the sand. He threw the grit into the corsair's face and in defense he covered his eyes. On his feet, Justin's sword could have rammed through his heart.

The corsair rubbed his eyes blinking, he shook his head. "You have a good wit about you in the heat of a fight. A strong body as well. Who are you, Priest?"

"I should ask you that question. But from your murderous attack, I can easily see you are one of Baron Soleiman's thieving corsairs. You have killed my friend," he said in reference to the wounded crewman.

"You are in no position to hurl insults, Lad. I did not kill your friend, but I could have killed you. Your garb stayed my arm. Be thankful. What is your name?"

"Brice! Justin Brice! That should tell you a lot."

It did. At once the corsair was silent. His pale blue eyes swept the handsome young man from head to toe. He knew that name well. His own liege, Soleiman, served an enemy of Justin's father.

"A Brice! Soleiman will be pleased I have spared your innards from being washed upon his beach."

"No doubt. Gold from my father is worth more than my

head," Justin said dryly. "But my father is in no position to pay ransom."

"The cross about your neck, Lad, will be worth more than all the gold your father could pay."

"The cross must be worth little to a pirate like Soleiman."

"Ah, yes Soleiman has his castle looking like the finest in Cordoba, but the worth of the cross is not in its gold, but in your office as priest."

At once Justin was uneasy. The corsair then nodded in the direction of the foreboding castle. Justin followed his gaze to the windswept cliff where the castle stared down upon him.

"Soleiman is a religious man." The glint in the corsair's eye told of his intended irony. "He wishes to have his own priest. Where did you come from?"

"Rome."

"Ah. . . ."

"I joined my brother's ship at Genoa. We were on our way to London when we collided with the Spanish ship. My father is ill and I must reach him. I beg you, let me go."

"If Soleiman has his way, you will not be going to London, Lad, but serving our entire company as a priest."

"I will not serve as a hired priest to any man, least of all a clan of pirates. Do you think I can evoke God's blessing on thievery and murder?"

"What, Lad? Not partake of gold?" he mocked. "Duty calls!"

"And Greed calls with her, does she not?"

"I shall give you a serious word of advice," said the corsair. "If you value your life, you will do nothing to provoke Soleiman. He is not a man given to wisdom, though he prides himself as a scholar. You may find his religious beliefs to be mere superstition, but for the present, like it or not, your one hope of survival rests in your position as a priest."

"For the present I shall consider your advice."

"Now about that sword, Lad. One day I may teach you how

to use it. They call me Andrew. I am first in command of Soleiman's affairs."

The Spanish ship was being taken by Soleiman's corsairs. The distant sounds of battle were heard on the wind, or was it the thunder of the waves? Justin could make out men fighting on the deck, and many falling over the sides. His concern was for his brother Stewert. He was an egotistical warrior. His pride would not permit him to surrender easily. Andrew's sun-bronzed face was unreadable.

"Even without the storm we would have taken her. Word was sent to Soleiman weeks ago. She bears wealth untold from the New World. Let us go. Soleiman comes. He will also be delighted to find the son of Ewan Brice as an unexpected prisoner!"

It was raining again and the wind had picked up. They stood on the beach guarded by rugged corsairs. Baron Soleiman was so delighted with his catch, that for a time he could not control his sometimes silent, sometimes wheezy laughter. His bulging eyes restlessly swept his prisoners.

"Ah," he said long and deeply, "ah yes, ah yes."

The Spanish captain bore the unconquered elegance of an ostentatious monarch. He was handsome, dark-haired, and boasted a fine-clipped mustache. His hat, while damaged by the sea, bore a cocky plume, and his cape was decorated with gold brocade and gemstones. "You will pay for this foolish act of piracy, Senor Soleiman! You will have his Excellency Ferdinand after your head."

"The king has his old enemy of France to worry about," said Soleiman. "A Spanish ship to decorate Soleiman's islet is too little to concern him now."

He turned then to Captain Stewert Brice who was sprawled

111

against the back of a tree. His wound, taken in the battle for the Spanish ship, was a bad one.

"So, the son of Ewan Brice!" A wolfish smile of delight spread across Soleiman's jowls.

"The one," growled Stewert with a challenge.

"A double blessing from the sea!"

"I will live to double your woe," breathed Stewert. "You will pay for taking my men prisoners. My father has loyal men in many ports, including Cadiz. They will take this islet."

"And they will find you swinging from a tree on the beach. Let that be their welcoming flag!"

Andrew, the corsair Justin had met on the beach, moved quickly, hoping to avert their deaths. He pointed to Justin.

"Ah! But there are two sons of Ewan Brice. Are they are not worth a great ransom, my liege, Soleiman? Think what the old retired pirate will pay to receive them whole? And," he bowed toward Justin, "this goodly lad is Justin Brice." He clasped Justin's shoulders. "A priest!"

Soleiman's eyes riveted upon Justin, forgetting all else. For the first time he took in his attire, then smiled broadly, his temper receding as waves washing out to sea.

"A priest? Is this so, my Son?"

"Yes."

"Where?"

"Rome."

"Excellent, excellent," he kept repeating.

Every eye fixed upon Justin, taking in the black woolen tunic, the soiled maroon cloak, and the cross. His hair was brown, just tinged with reddish-golds, his features strong and handsome, his eyes a blue-gray.

"He is no priest," came a cold voice from behind Soleiman.

Justin turned toward the voice. For the first time he saw a tall, lean man wearing some sort of religious garb that reminded Justin of a soothsayer. A deep scar ran across his left eyelid and down his cheek. He carried a whip. Justin judged him to be Soleiman's personal servant. The man had taken an immediate dislike to him.

"I suggest that he is no more then a common mercenary soldier in disguise," continued the man. Give him and his brother to me. I shall put them in the dungeon."

The corsair, Andrew, stepped into the circle and bowed to Soleiman. He was obviously trying to make matters go as well for Justin as he could.

"O Soleiman, man of wisdom. Surely he is a priest, and also a lad with wit. Look at him." His hand smacked hard against Justin's stomach. "Fine looking, lad! He has good Scottish blood and the arrogance of a Frenchman! Strong, too. Look at those shoulders! Look at that height! What baron will own a more awesome warrior-priest? When I have finished his training, he will be fit for battle on any ship we take to sea, as well as for prayer. Who could ask for more? Ah Soleiman, my liege, you have yourself a prize."

Soleiman smiled broadly. He grunted. Then laughed, slapping his muscled thigh.

"Rome, you say? Are you also a scholar? Can you read Latin?"

When Justin paused, the warning glint in Andrew's gaze prompted him to relent.

"Indeed, O Great One."

"Ah, and write letters?"

"With prolific hand."

"He will know what secrets are written in the parchment taken from the churchman from North Africa," suggested Andrew. "Unlike your soothsayer over here," he bowed mockingly to the man with the scarred eyelid, "Justin Brice can read Latin."

"A parchment from a churchman?" Justin asked, his interest instantly aroused.

"It was 'accidentally' taken during the capture of an enemy ship," suggested Andrew, tongue in cheek. "I thought the leather envelope contained jewels. Alas."

"I would be anxious to translate it."

Soleiman beamed at Justin and rubbed his big hands together. He had waited over a year to learn its secrets.

"He lies," said the man with the scar. "No one can read the magic writing of the gods."

"If the soothsayer cannot read the writing of the 'gods,'" Andrew mocked lightly, "then may I suggest, My Liege Soleiman, that the priest be permitted to try?"

The soothsayer glared at his protagonist, Andrew, for the two men vied relentlessly for the highest position beside Baron Soleiman. Andrew, in order to gain his own ship and escape his slavery; the soothsayer to gain prestige and subservience from the superstitious corsairs. His good eye burned hot with jealousy as it fixed on Justin. "I say it is secret writing, Profane Priest!"

"If it is written in Latin, it will be no secret to me," said Justin. He turned toward Soleiman. "I should very much like to see this parchment, Baron Soleiman."

"Indeed," Soleiman told him. "I have long waited for someone who could translate it for me. "See?" he said glowering at the soothsayer. "You told me no one could read the writing. My patience is coming to an end. Are the spirits of the gods in you, or no? Ah, this has been a great day, Andrew! You shall be thrice rewarded for saving the holy man. What will you have?"

Andrew said smoothly, "I shall think long and hard, Soleiman. Perhaps to captain my own ship, and to forage with the ships of Portugal and Spain to the New World. To bring you back treasure and slaves, of course."

"We shall see, we shall see." Soleiman was again appraising Justin with delight.

"Priest, you will serve me in the castle. Then travel at my side upon the sea. The catch of fine ships laden with treasure will need your blessing. Do you not know how generous Soleiman is to the Church? Yes! How often have I given great treasures from my booty to the bishops of Spain."

"No doubt, Baron Soleiman, the bishops are in thy humble gratitude," quipped Justin.

Soleiman took the remark at face value. "I will treat you well. You will perform your religious duties, and entertain me with tales of wisdom, but! I shall be the judge of whether you tell the truth! Even a priest can lose his head. Remember that, Justin Brice."

Here was a man whose vanity urged him to become wise, but Justin felt certain that he had no real heart for wisdom. Soleiman must be humored. Realizing that he would be given training with the sword, and have some freedom in the castle, and therefore gain opportunity to escape, Justin bowed with humble pretense.

"As it is written by the wisest man who has ever lived: 'Receive my instruction, and not silver; and knowledge rather than choice gold. For wisdom is better than rubies; and all the things that may be desired are not to be compared to it.' "

Soleiman beamed. "The wisest man who ever lived? Who! Who wrote that?"

"Solomon."

"Ah! Soleiman!"

"No, Solomon, king of Israel. He reigned in Jerusalem."

Soleiman was instantly disappointed, and a little irked. "Then if he is so wise, why did he not rid the Holy Sepulchre of the Saracen infidels? Why are the pilgrimages to Jerusalem halted by Moslems?"

Justin could see that he was in for a difficult time. He said nothing.

"Fools," muttered Stewert Brice, lounging against the tree.

"Ye stand there in the rain speaking of wisdom, and I am bleeding to death."

Soleiman gestured toward Stewert. "Look to the Scot! Wisdom cries that his old fox of a father will pay very much gold to free him from my galleys. Put him in the dungeon. Let the famed Captain Stewert Brice contemplate with the rats the folly of contesting my corsairs on the sea! Send what remains of his crew to the fields to tend my pigs," Soleiman mocked. "I was told that pigs are wiser than sheep. Perhaps Captain Brice's crewmen shall learn a thing or two. You, also," Soleiman said, gesturing with disdain to the indignant Spanish captain. "And give me his plumed hat."

Soleiman placed the dashing hat upon his own broad head and smiled widely at his men.

8

Whoso despiseth the word shall be destroyed,
but he that feareth the commandment shall be rewarded
(Prov. 13:13).

Neither shall ye use enchantments,
nor observe times
(Lev. 19:26).

The knifelike figure in the elegant robe of brocaded blue and
gold stopped before the door to Soleiman's private chamber.

"He sleeps," warned the guard, but squarely fixed by the
Soothsayer's gaze, pressed the Soothsayer no further. *The Soothsayer can bring curses or blessings,* the guard thought. The guard was
a big man and courageous with his sword, but, like many of
the other corsairs, he feared the Soothsayer.

To the guard, the one good eye of the Soothsayer was a
curious novelty because it never appeared to blink. It was the
blind eye, however, that was chilling, for its cloudy color reminded the guard of darkness and thunder. In fear of the
Soothsayer's curses, he mumbled something and stepped aside.

The Soothsayer crooked a jeweled finger and rapped three
times on the door.

The door swung open and a great Nubian servant stood to
bar his entrance, an ivory dagger at his waist. He stepped aside

when he saw who it was, and the Soothsayer passed into the room as silently as a shadow.

The chamber boasted rugs from Baghdad and wall hangings of scarlet and deep blue. Soleiman sat on cushions. Around him was a rich assortment of pillaged loot taken from the Spanish ship. He chuckled as he produced vessels of gold, honey-colored agate, and containers of little brown beans that the Spanish captain assured him should be ground and boiled, then drunk hot. *Coffee,* he called it. Soleiman handed those treasures he wished to display, to the Nubian, and consigned the others to a chest to be stored in the castle treasury.

Soleiman was a heavy man, but solid, and an expert wrestler. He enjoyed nothing better than to hold matches with his tallest corsairs, whom he delighted to pin helplessly to the floor.

Fool! The Soothsayer thought watching Soleiman. *I should sit in your seat!* Outwardly he stood with a frozen smile and waited for Soleiman to beckon him to come forward. When it came to the Soothsayer's desire for power and gold, it was fortunate that his liege reverenced fortune-tellers, as well as priests.

The Soothsayer had served him for three years, having beguiled Soleiman with his mysterious "peepstone," a device that he claimed had been passed down to him from Moses on Mount Nebo in the Holy Land.

Soleiman looked up from his treasures and grinned, for he was in a celebrative mood. He hadn't been this happy since the day he proclaimed himself a baron.

"Ah, Soothsayer, come, come! You are just the one I wish to see."

"My Liege, I must speak to you alone. It concerns the danger that Brice brings to your castle."

"Captain Brice is below with the rats," Soleiman cut him off. "He poses no danger to anyone but himself."

"It was not Stewert Brice I had in mind, My Liege, but the

younger one. Yes! The heretic who masquerades in a monk's robe!"

"Heretic!"

"I have not been idle, My Liege. From a crew member aboard the Brice ship I have learned that Justin Brice fled the monastery in Rome to avoid being burned at the stake for heresy."

"A heretic! Surely these are the lies of jealous men. He boasts a robe and a cross, and he reads and writes Latin. What else is needed? It is enough."

The Soothsayer stiffened. "He must be destroyed at once, My Liege."

"Destroyed! What is this you say?" Soleiman's voice grew loud. "Destroy him?" He stood. "My priest? My very own personal priest? Are you mad, Soothsayer?"

At Soleiman's display of indignation, the Nubian servant stepped forward, and the Soothsayer shrank away.

"The priest sails my ships!" Soleiman stated. "Is that clear? And if we sail to the New World, he shall bless our voyage with fair weather and good health. I will hear no more lies to upset my plans."

The Soothsayer hastened a low bow. "I meant no offense, only," he hesitated, "he must be watched." He looked up, his good eye cautious. "For your sake," he whispered.

Soleiman grew silent. His eyes narrowed. "What do you mean?"

"My Liege must keep in mind, that although the man claims to be a priest, he is still a Brice. Are you not a known enemy to his father? Have you not fought Captain Ewan Brice with sword and ship?"

Soleiman scowled at the reminder. "Andrew believes the priest can be trusted."

The Soothsayer leaned toward him. "Andrew schemes, My Liege."

Soleiman pondered the words. He had heard them before

from the Soothsayer. There were a few times when Soleiman also suspected that Andrew might be thinking of stealing a ship and going to sea as captain of his own corsairs. The Nubian servant, however, assured him it was not so.

The Nubian's deep voice was silky. He bowed at the waist. "Baron Soleiman, you know Andrew is a brilliant captain. One who is passionately devoted to your service, as am I. If we sail to the New World as the ships of Portugal and Spain do, we will need him. He once sailed on a Spanish ship and knows the way."

The Soothsayer stared coldly at the Nubian bodyguard. "Andrew only claims to have sailed on a Spanish ship to Peru. He comes from the Netherlands, from Antwerp. He was the son of an English merchant until taken a slave by Baron Soleiman."

"Hold your tongue, Soothsayer. Is it not envy which drives you to these charges?" Soleiman suggested.

"I wish only your honor, My Liege. I am your truthful servant. I have gazed into the peepstone and the gods warn of deceit in the impostor."

Soleiman was troubled. The secret peepstone of the Soothsayer was a thing to ponder.

Seeing his troubled scowl, the Soothsayer pressed, "Shall I seek his true nature with the whip, My Liege?"

"If one ugly mark tarnishes his handsome flesh, I will have you thrown in with the rats."

The Soothsayer went down on one knee, head bowed. "The peepstone does not lie."

Soleiman hesitated, irritated that his delight in owning a priest was marred by the Soothsayer's suspicion. "I am beginning to wonder. Walk softly, Old Crow. If Priest Justin proves himself false, it is I who will be his executioner."

The Soothsayer bowed in stiff silence.

Soleiman was appeased now and sighed deeply. He motioned across the chamber toward his private sanctuary, pleased with what he was about to do.

"Look not as if you were weaned on sour fruit, Soothsayer. I have not forgotten how you served me these three years. Do not I have an honor for you, Soothayer? Come!"

At the word *honor,* the Soothsayer lifted his head and followed his liege into the sanctuary.

Soleiman smiled and swept his arm to the prayer bench. The Soothsayer's eye fell on the prized scarlet robe embroidered with stars and crescent moons.

"My Liege! Surely you do not mean, . . ." overwhelmed he lapsed into silence and stared.

How he coveted the robe, how he had plotted ways to convince Soleiman to honor him with it. Who among the other wise men in Soleiman's castle dare claim the robe?

The Soothsayer stood riveted, the fever of excitement raced through him.

The robe!

Taken from a pirated vessel, it had become a religious status symbol. Soleiman was so taken with the texture, color, and design, that he had dedicated it. Almost at once, the unclaimed robe became a mark of supremacy among all the counselors of Soleiman. None dare ask for it, but all coveted it, and none more than the Soothsayer. For Soleiman had sworn that it would be worn by the man he delighted to honor—the chief counselor of his religious wise men. To this day Soleiman had not been impressed enough with any of his counselors to bestow it. So it remained in the sanctuary. Here the robe was kept to greet the Soothsayer each time he entered. And the longer the robe stood unclaimed, the more he desired it for its renown.

"Me? Me, My Liege? I am not worthy," he murmured.

Soleiman didn't hear him. "The coronation will take place tonight in the sanctuary. O Soleiman, how the gods have looked down upon you. How you have been rewarded for your piety. And they said I was but a corsair! That God was displeased with my sin. Hah! How could He be displeased? Has He not brought me a priest to wear the holy robe? To teach me wisdom? To interpret the secret words?

"See to it, Soothsayer. I want everyone of importance here tonight." The broad face widened into an indulgent smile. "And you, Soothsayer, will have the honor of escorting the priest into the sanctuary."

With fanfare Soleiman handed him the robe. "Have Justin Brice brought to the bath and prepared. He will look splendid in the robe! Are you well, Soothsayer? You have turned a strange color. And posthaste bring me the religious parchment. I will present it to him tonight. The priest will translate the secret words. Who knows what majestic mysteries lay within my reach?"

Soleiman turned and knelt, saying a prayer. He arose, then glowered.

"Do you still stand there? Go! And send Andrew to me. He has an important function in the ritual."

The Nubian giant wore a faint smile and his eyes gleamed with amusement. He watched the Soothsayer depart wearing the expression of a man about to be hanged.

The Soothsayer disappeared into the castle library. Here, he took the bunch of keys in his possession and unlocked a small drawer. Slowly, he removed the church parchment.

"The secret words of the gods," he muttered. Could Justin Brice interpret them? If he did, his own position before Soleiman would be undermined. Soleiman was a fool, and the Soothsayer had worked for three years to trick him into believing in his magical powers to know the future. Justin and the parchment could easily destroy all this with one stroke.

He set the robe on the desk and picked up the candle, his hand shaking as he brought the parchment close to the flame.

Could he not claim that the rats gnawed it to rubbish? His heart pounded, echoing in his ears.

What of Andrew? He would remember that the parchment was safely locked in the drawer. Andrew did not reverence his position as Soothsayer. He was not superstitious; Andrew mocked him.

He must destroy Justin Brice before they sailed toward the New World.

The Soothsayer whirled at the tread of boots. Andrew stood behind him.

"Do you spy on me?"

Andrew smirked. Then his eye caught sight of the parchment, and the candle, and the way the Soothsayer's hand shook. His smirk vanished and his eyes hardened.

"Beware, Croaking Toad. The parchment will be given to the priest tonight. Be sure of it."

"Do not I always honor Soleiman's wishes?"

"To his face, you are always his humble servant," Andrew mocked.

"And you, O Great Military Lord?" the Soothsayer challenged. "Is your loyalty only with your tongue? Do you think I don't know that you intend to break away from your master?"

Andrew knocked the candle from his hand and stomped it out. The chamber dimmed.

"Babblers have died for saying less. How much more a servant of darkness?"

The Soothsayer turned pale. For a moment they stood eye to eye. The Soothsayer whispered hoarsely, "Only a frog babbles. My lips are silent, O great Lord."

"Good. The 'great lord' does not like frogs who croak in the night. I dislike soothsayers even more. Now then, see to the prisoner I have brought you. His name is Felix. Put him with the cook. When you do, tell the baker you have a message from

Andrew. If one more varmint ends up in my bread, I shall pay him a visit."

At the end of the passage, the giant Nubian waited. "The time is near. Tonight the small boat will be unguarded."

Their strategy to escape the islet in a small boat for Valencia, a port on the coast of Spain, had long been in preparation. Andrew felt confident the plan would work. Soleiman expected his slaves to try to escape by confiscating one of the galleons.

"We must bide our time and wait. The sea is too rough for a small boat."

"The longer we wait the more risk we take," said the Nubian. "The Soothsayer is suspicious. Who knows who else?"

"It is a chance we are forced to take. If we take to the sea now, we will never make Valencia."

"What of the priest?"

Andrew shrugged. "We shall take him, and Felix."

"What of Captain Brice?"

"Can he travel?"

"He has the strength of a bull."

"Can you get him from the dungeon?"

The Nubian held up the keys.

"Then let us also take the Spanish captain. For our generosity in helping him to escape, he can repay us with supplies to reach Bayonne. Breathe nothing yet to the others. A secret is best kept by two."

Unexpectedly, the door to Justin's chamber was unbolted. The Nubian's strong body rippled with muscle, and his skin looked as though it had been polished. He wore ebony trousers edged in gold.

Justin thought he saw a ghost of a smile on his lips, but the voice was toneless. "Tonight a special honor is to be yours from Baron Soleiman." The dark eyes scanned his shabby tunic.

"An honor?" Justin asked cautiously. "Will I be given the parchment to interpret?"

"Among other notable things. But come."

The chamber to which he was shown was larger than his own quarters and lavishly decorated with pirated goods. There was a marble bath and bench, fine rugs, and carved vessels to fill the tub. He watched the Nubian pour scented oil from a gold urn. Justin smirked.

When he emerged from the tub, putting on the clean robe, his reflection appeared that of a stranger. Nothing remained of his clothes but the cross lying on the bench.

He followed the Nubian. The door to another room was thrown open and three guards stood there. Justin gazed upon an assortment of rich gifts.

"Baron Soleiman bids you accept these gifts from his hand," said the Nubian, spreading his arm wide.

There were black woolen trousers, silk shirts, brocaded vests, mantles trimmed with marten fur, and boots.

The door opened and the Soothsayer stepped in, somewhat hidden in the shadow.

"So, Impostor! You managed to beguile Baron Soleiman."

The Soothsayer stepped into the light. On his arm was an elaborate scarlet robe, embroidered with gold stars and crescent moons.

"Do you wish the honor of putting the robe on him, Soothsayer?" asked the Nubian innocently.

The Soothsayer scanned the Nubian as if he were an insect. Face taut, he placed the robe on the table and, sweeping his cloak about him, walked out.

With the robe across his arm, the Nubian came to Justin with a deep bow, murmuring, "Tonight Soleiman will proclaim you chief of his wise men—a position most coveted. This robe, too, is coveted."

"Coveted? The Soothsayer may have it. It fits him well." Justin walked over to the other pile of clothes. It was satisfying to put on the black trousers and white shirt. Over it he wore a long-sleeved doublet, full at the sleeves but gathered at the wrist. But the masculine boots of fine cordovan leather were the best. Three years had passed since he had worn boots! He dressed, ignoring the guards until he noticed the silence. Looking up, he saw the Nubian still standing patiently with the robe. Justin sensed his determination.

"There is no choice, Priest Justin. You must wear the robe."

Justin's determination was a match, but he smiled. "I think not, Friend."

The guards smiled slightly and waited anxiously for their sport. The Nubian sighed and gestured to the guards. "Force him."

Before Justin realized it, the weight of several bodies impacted with his own. Jarred, his breath knocked from him, he was slammed to the floor. "Do not mar his flesh," the Nubian calmly commanded. He circled the struggling bodies.

"Watch his face! Hold him!"

Justin could not move. With determination the Nubian knelt, robe in hand. The robe was soft and smelled of some sweet perfume that Justin found repulsive. The face of the Nubian was blank. He avoided looking at Justin as if afraid he would smile. The three guards were now scowling, angry because it took all of them to keep him down.

"I will not entertain your liege like some troubadour," Justin warned. "Rats are preferable to this."

An amused voice sounded from the doorway. "Rats make for unpleasant company. Especially when the night holds pleasant surprises. There will be feasting and singing, and tomorrow night? Who knows?"

Justin recognized the voice of Andrew. The corsair walked up and stood looking down upon him. Unlike the others he did not hold back the wolfish smile as he took in the robe.

Andrew was dressed in the substantial clothing of a warrior, but the clothing was of quality, and his manner had taken on some surprising elegance.

Still pinned to the floor, Justin gazed up at him. "Well, Corsair," Justin said dryly, "so you *can* look civilized."

"Ah, Lad, my one hand bears the golden manners of English nobility." he bowed. "Do you not know I am a respectable merchant-adventurer from Antwerp? Ah! but my other hand," he held it up, "is the fist of a warrior! Be glad of your privilege of serving such a future captain."

At the term "future captain," Justin eyed him. A promised hint of escape glinted in the amused eyes staring down at him.

"I will yet teach you how to use a sword," suggested Andrew lightly. "Let him up."

They released him and stepped back. Justin was on his feet. At once his eyes locked with Andrew's and he removed the robe with emphasis.

"If he does not wear it," said the Nubian, "Soleiman will be in a rage."

"There is only one way to handle this. The lad will not submit to force," said Andrew. He took the robe and flecked off an imaginary speck of dust. Deliberately he made no attempt to put it on Justin.

The others watched wondering what he had on his mind. Andrew sat down on the table and folded his arms. His blue eyes glinted.

"Do you remember the parchment taken from the North African ship?"

Justin remembered in a flash.

Andrew paused waiting for the words to sink in, baiting

Justin before going on. "It is a portion of the Writings," explained Andrew.

Justin was alert. "How do you know?"

"The good churchman told me. He was quite upset. And alas, he died, good man though he was. I made him a vow at his last breath. If ever the Lord sent the right man, I would see to it that it was put to proper use."

"And you haven't told your liege what it is? The Soothsayer beguiles him into thinking it is secret writing."

Andrew shrugged. "Even if I had, he would need a man to read Latin. None of us can. How much is it worth to have the Scripture portion in your hand, Justin? To read it, to translate it, to know its words as one knows a familiar path?"

Justin wondered that Andrew had the sensitivity to understand his feelings. He wanted the Writing as much as he wanted freedom. Andrew knew it. And it told Justin more about the character of the man than any of his actions.

Andrew smiled his victory. Calmly, he handed Justin the robe. "If you behave wisely before Soleiman, the parchment will be given to you tonight."

Justin hesitated, then grudgingly took the robe. "Where did you get this monstrosity? Did you pirate it from a ship as well?"

"What! You insult the Baron's taste in fashion?"

"I will wear it. I make no other promises. I will decide from minute to minute if I can proceed with what he has in mind."

"Opportunities may be yours," Andrew hinted, "if you cooperate."

Justin scanned him. What was he hinting at?

They turned at the sound of the Soothsayer's footsteps. Andrew rose from the table and bowed pretentiously.

"See who arrives to lead the pompous ceremony! Soothsayer, do I notice a livid complexion? Does your 'peepstone' forecast some gloomy image to disturb your peace this night?" he mocked.

The Soothsayer stood clutching two lamps burning with fragrant oil. He was dressed in his own religious garb, representing what, Justin had no idea. Perhaps it was of his own imagination, like the peepstone.

"The only image I foresee is your head rolling from the block, Andrew. And it affords me no gloom." Seeing Justin in the robe, his one eye hardened.

"Come, Impostor. Entertain the baron with your masquerade. But when you gaze upon the Writing you shall be blinded by the gods. Soleiman waits in the sanctuary."

Justin found him as annoying as a buzzing fly.

"Remember my advice, Justin," Andrew told him quietly as he walked past. "Soleiman is a man to be humored. If you anger him, you will be cast below with your brother."

9

The wise men are ashamed;
they are dismayed and taken: lo, they have
rejected the word of the Lord; and what
wisdom is in them?
(Jer. 8:9).

The entrance of thy words giveth light;
it giveth understanding unto the simple
(Ps. 119:130).

With sullen face, the Soothsayer led the processional down the passage. Candles flickered. Justin's eyes were busy as he entered the sanctuary. Soleiman was seated on a dais with a number of men standing behind him, and Justin guessed them to be his counselors. The Nubian, his chief bodyguard, stood to his right. Torches blazed along the walls, and beneath them the corsair warriors stood lined up still wearing their weapons. Each, however, had a fine mantle trimmed with fur thrown about his shoulders.

The Soothsayer bowed stiffly before Soleiman and placed a lamp at each side of the dais. Spiraling gray incense, too fragrant to be pleasant, drifted upward.

"Come forward, Justin," Soleiman cried jubilantly. "You look splendid!" He gestured to Andrew. "What do you think?" Soleiman asked. "Is he worthy of the robe?"

Andrew seldom missed the irony in such situations. He spoke exuberantly. "Soleiman my liege, alas what can I say at this awesome moment?" He turned toward Justin and deliberately hesitated.

Justin wondered what Andrew could say, and met his gaze squarely, affecting sobriety.

"Magnificent! Auspicious! Sanctimonious!" Andrew declared. "Surely such a robe makes a man of God."

Soleiman was unsure of the intent of his words. With Andrew he was never quite sure. "Are you asking me or telling me? Never mind, let us proceed." He stood from his dais. "All bow in reverence to God. Any remaining on his feet will be deemed an infidel. Posthaste he shall be hung from Soleiman's gallows."

There was a shuffling of feet and clink of metal as the great warriors went down on their knees.

Soleiman, however, remained on his feet. He smiled, pleased at the sight. "Very well."

He begin to pace back and forth, carrying his halberd.

"Let it be known from this day and forward that I, Soleiman the Great, a devotee of Christianity," he paused and cleared his throat with a wary glance toward the Soothsayer, "and all other gods of the deep, doth hereby choose Priest Justin Brice to be the chief head of all my religious counselors. All in agreement with my wise decision, give praise."

They were now on their feet, giving a great cry and stretching out their arms. Above the din of voices steel clanged as the corsairs jerked swords from their sheaths in a salute first to Soleiman, then to Justin.

Soleiman smiled, then beckoned for Andrew to proceed.

Followed by two warriors bearing the gift of weapons, Andrew stopped before Justin. A slight smile was on his face.

Soleiman's oratorical voice rang out, "Soon we embark upon the greatest of expeditions, joining our forces with those of

Portugal in a journey to the New World. Notorious though we be, piety hovers over us like the wings of an angel!" He paused, thinking his language rather inspiring, then spread his arm in Justin's direction. "A warrior-priest will sail with us. He shall lead us forward with sword and cross! Bestow him, Andrew!"

"On one knee," Andrew commanded.

Justin hesitated. Instantly, he felt the heavy hands of the guards shoving him down. Andrew gave an extra shove against the back of his head, forcing his face toward the floor. Justin unwillingly stared at Andrew's polished black boots sporting silver buckles.

Andrew's flat sword struck the base of his neck, and his clear voice rang out. "In the name of God, I make you also a knight.

"Now arise, Justin Brice, a warrior-priest fit for battle and for the duties of God."

Andrew lifted him to his feet. "Be proud," he said. He took the belt from the guard and thrust another sword into its sheath. He smiled as he handed it to Justin. "Use it well."

There followed the other pieces of armor: the mesh shirt of iron chainwork, the hood of similar mesh, the sleeves, gloves, hose of mail, and the conical helmet. Justin's mind went back to his youth. He had been in training to be a belted knight when his father sent him to the monastery. Then, he would have given anything to become a knight; now, he found himself sobered by the truth.

"The warrior-priest!" exclaimed Soleiman. "Together we shall claim territory for England, and Soleiman. What say you, O great seamen?"

"For the splendor of God!" came the great male chorus, echoing the cry of William the Conqueror.

The splendor of God, thought Justin. *What do any of them know about the splendor of God?*

Only the Soothsayer, standing near by, held tight lips, his

one eye burning with envy. He thought only of his lost position as Soleiman's chief wise man.

Amid the noise, Andrew spoke in a low tone. "Soleiman will call you before him. Do as he demands. Humor him. You will be commanded to dedicate the men and ships for sailing."

"Is it a light thing to engage in pretense in matters concerning God?" Justin whispered.

Andrew ignored his determination. "Your honor impresses me. It will not impress Soleiman. If you want to live to return to England, you must do something. Listen—I may be able to get you to London."

Not until Soleiman raised his arm did silence cover the room.

Justin stood before Soleiman as the elaborate ceremony continued. Andrew was at his right and the Nubian at his left, a brocaded cloak about his shoulders. A servant drew near bearing a silken pillow on which the parchment lay. Justin's eyes were riveted to it. Andrew had said the parchment was a portion of the Scriptures. Was he right? It must be. Why would the cleric on the pirated vessel lie?

"You will now speak good words of courage to us, and dedicate us for our upcoming journey."

Unexpectedly, Justin grasped the parchment, aware that he was risking Soleiman's anger. Could he turn events to the Word? He lifted it in the fashion of those lifting their swords.

"Baron Soleiman, though I offer a hundred prayers to evoke His blessing, I cannot evoke His favor. Therefore, you are wise when you say 'speak good words of courage.' I hold some of those words in my hand. True words. His Words. I would give them to you now, from Christ Himself. Surely a man of your religious zeal will not waste this noted gathering on ceremony alone, or on my prayers. Now is the opportunity to hear a true word from the One you claim to serve."

Confusion made Soleiman's bushy brows rush together. What was this? He wanted the ceremony to move as simply and sanctimoniously as the incense pouring up around him. Yet, having been pronounced wise, he was led to accept Justin's suggestion.

"Then, the secret words are from God?"

Andrew had better be right. "Locked within this parchment is the Word of truth, knowledge, and wisdom."

Soleiman's eyes gleamed. "Ah?"

"It is so, Baron Soleiman."

"I will possess this wisdom. Read the secret words of truth, Priest Justin."

Justin released a silent breath of relief and begin to open the parchment; but Soleiman halted him like a child whose attention was fixed on a brightly wrapped gift.

"But first bless my sword and our upcoming voyage," he said with petulance.

Silence fell. The Soothsayer sensed that the moment for him to move was now. Also risking the displeasure of the baron, he seized the opportunity.

"He speaks of written words few can read," mocked the Soothsayer. "How then, may we judge? And yet he claims the ability to tell us the meaning of the secret words of the gods. We have no proof he tells the truth. Pardon my presumption, Baron Soleiman, but have you not been hasty in making this man your Chief Counselor? But I! I have seen with my eye visions in this stone, visions that transcend mere words."

The Soothsayer held forth his famed "peepstone," a clear stone that sparkled in the light of the torches.

"I have seen such stones before," said Justin. "My father brought several back to England on his ship. I believe it is mined from the earth and called a quartz. One thing I do know, Baron Soleiman—God does not speak to this Soothsayer through that stone."

"Not so. On my pilgrimage to Jerusalem I came upon Mount

Nebo where the great priest and king, Moses, ascended to paradise on the wings of a Great Horse."

Justin interrupted. "Baron Soleiman, far better that you make the Soothsayer your minstrel than your counselor. Beside his exaggerated humor, his biblical facts are in gross error. Why will you hear folly, when you may hear the Words of God? Do not let him deceive you. He seeks not your welfare, but his own greedy ambitions. I challenge the tales he has told you these past years. How many have come to pass?"

Soleiman's shaggy brows lowered as he fixed his eyes on the Soothsayer.

Silence.

"Not even one?" said Justin in mock surprise.

The Soothsayer hastened to extol his wisdom, growing exuberant in his agitation to convince Soleiman of his powers. His arms flailed, his voice rose to heights of passion, yet as he proceeded, faint laughter begin to be released by the rugged corsairs until even Soleiman begin to laugh. The Soothsayer felt his spiritual captives slipping through his clutches, so he tried harder.

"A little spirit took my hand as I bowed in prayer, and led me to a hole in a rock. Behold! The peepstone of King Moses gleamed as fire. Take it, said the little spirit. Thou, Olin, son of the great Norman Viking Odo, have been chosen to bear this awesome revelation. A revelation handed down by King Moses himself. It is the very stone he used to speak with God. This stone gave the twelve commandments.' "

Justin interrupted firmly, his eyes riveted on the Soothsayer who now refused to look at him. "The Soothsayer would convince Baron Soleiman that truth is progressive. God has already spoken once through His Son, and the apostles. Their words alone, are final authority."

"I have beheld great mysteries!"

"Neither man nor angel dare add to that revelation, or else he will be found a liar," said Justin.

Soleiman leaned toward the Soothsayer with narrowed eyes. "I think you have been beguiling me with your stone," he said through clenched teeth. "I am a wise man, but you seek to make me into a fool."

"My Liege, you are too wise to be deceived these three years."

Soleiman had but to lift his sword from his scabbard. "Toad, I grow weary of your croaking. Away! Let the man of God read the writing."

The Soothsayer shot Justin a look of daggers, then slunk away into the darkest corner of the chamber.

The servants drew near with torches. Justin cautiously unrolled the parchment and his heart hammered. His eyes strained to pick up the feel for the words staring up at him. *Andrew was right, Scripture.* He felt a vigorous surge of excitement. The parchment was a portion of the Book of Acts handwritten in Latin. The light was poor and he strained to read the sometimes faded lettering searching for a clue as to what section from the Book of Acts he held. He was unfamiliar with it, but the moment that he grasped the content, a strange joy came over him. Had he doubted the providence of God to this moment, he could doubt no longer. The Scripture portion in his hand seemed the perfect document to read to the manner of men assembled. Silently he thanked God for His guidance. The assurance of the nearness of the Lord persisted. God was not only aware of him, He "knew" him. And he knew all those assembled. With a confident look toward Soleiman, Andrew, and the Nubian, he nodded, and then glanced about the chamber to the soldiers to show they were included. He begin to read clearly, first in Latin, then in English:

Then Paul stood up, and beckoning with his hand said, Men of Israel, and ye that fear God, give audience.

. . . God according to his promise, raised unto Israel a Savior, Jesus:

And as John fulfilled his course, he said, Whom think ye that I am? I am not he. But, behold, there cometh one after me, whose shoes of his feet I am not worthy to loose.

Men and brethren, children of the stock of Abraham, and whosoever among you feareth God, to you is the word of this salvation sent.

For they that dwell at Jerusalem, and their rulers, because they knew him not, nor yet the voices of the prophets which are read every sabbath day, they have fulfilled them in condemning him.

And though they found no cause of death in him, yet desired they Pilate that he should be slain.

And when they had fulfilled all that was written of him, they took him down from the tree, and laid him in a sepulcher.

But God raised him from the dead.

And he was seen many days of them who came up with him from Galilee to Jerusalem, who are his witnesses unto the people.

And we declare unto you glad tidings, how the promise which was made unto the fathers,

God hath fulfilled the same unto us their children, in that he hath raised up Jesus again; as it is also written in the second psalm, Thou art my Son, this day have I begotten thee.

And as concerning that he raised him up from the dead, now no more to return to corruption, he said on this wise, I will give you the sure mercies of David.

Wherefore, he saith also in another psalm, Thou shalt not suffer thine Holy One to see corruption.

For David, after he had served his own generation by the will of God, fell on sleep, and was laid unto his fathers, and saw corruption.

But he, whom God raised again, saw no corruption.

Be it known unto you therefore, men and brethren, that through this man is preached unto you the forgiveness of sins:

And by him all that believe are justified from all things, from which ye could not be justified by the law of Moses.

Beware, therefore, lest that come upon you, which is spoken of in the prophets;

Behold, ye despisers, and wonder, and perish; for I work a work in your days, a work which ye shall in no wise believe, though a man declare it unto you.

Justin stopped. A great silence permeated the hall. He sensed the reading of the Word had gone forth in God's power and for that, he knew joy and satisfaction. It was the Word of God that was needed in the English tongue! This Word was the sword needed to cut through man's spiritual density and religious error. The Sword of God must be recovered from the darkened cloister and used to set his generation free.

The torch light flickering on the faces of those assembled revealed men moved by the presence of the Lord. Justin rolled up the parchment and turned to face Soleiman.

"The apostle has written of justification by faith through the finished work of Christ. Baron Soleiman, and all those among us who have listened with sincere heart, this declared righteous position before a holy God is given freely by grace, and is by no means attained by any merit of our own, no, nor by any religious work, however sincere or costly. Forgiveness of sin and acceptance by God rests alone in the merit of the death, burial, and bodily resurrection of his Son Jesus Christ. A work secured once and for all by His resurrection from the dead. A resurrection that has declared Jesus to be, as Saint Paul has written in the Epistle of Romans: 'the Son of God with power, according to the spirit of holiness, by the resurrection from the dead.'

"If salvation began with Christ, and is made complete by his work, and if it is kept operative by His resurrection life, our faith is to rest in that God-oriented work, and not in our own. As the Spirit of God has said through his apostle—"I work a work in your days, a work which ye shall in no wise believe, though a man declare it unto you.'

"I now declare that work unto thee, Baron Soleiman, and to all the men here gathered. Believe, and as he hath said, 'perish not.'"

The silence continued but Justin knew the words had penetrated their souls. Soleiman stirred and the moment was broken. He leaned forward, his great hand outstretched toward Justin, trembled.

"You have given us good and fair words, my Son. Words that will not be forgotten—no, nor go unheeded. May this great God be blessed for sending you to us to interpret the secret words. And now we know the truth, and now you have given us true wisdom."

The silence was interrupted only by the awkward clink of metal and boots as the men in the hall stirred. Soleiman stood. "You will read them to us again, Priest Justin. Tomorrow."

"I would do more then that, Baron Soleiman. Give me paper, ink and quill, and I will translate them this night into your spoken tongue. You may read and meditate upon them yourself wherever you go. And they will be yours to read to others also, for who knows where you may traverse?"

Soleiman gestured to the Nubian. "See that he has all he needs." He turned hard eyes upon the Soothsayer who remained standing in darkness. "I will have the words of Christ for myself. No longer will I trust others to speak for God to me. The words, and only those words, will I hear from henceforth."

Soleiman gave a gesture of dismissal, and the chamber begin to empty. Justin was staring at the parchment. *God's truth is revolutionary. Who would have expected a man like Soleiman to receive the words so humbly? Yet he had. An unlikely man had responded with humility to the grace of God in Christ.* What it would mean in the future to Soleiman's way of life, and to his corsairs, Justin could not guess. Instead, he found himself pondering the results of such a proclamation. *What would happen in the Church if this truth were taught from one end of Europe to the other? What would be the outcome? Peace, or wrath? Liberation, or imprisonment?*

More than ever Justin was convinced the Scriptures must be translated into English. Were there others who believed as he did? He must find men who would join with him in that endeavor, whatever the cost. If a man like Soleiman would listen and wanted the words before him, what about the common man in England and Scotland? They must not be denied access to the Scriptures.

Throughout the night by light of the candle Justin translated from Latin into English. When he had written until the darkness turned to dawn and the candle burned low, he went to the window where the cold wind awakened him anew.

Far over the sea came the golden streaks of dawn and strong winds from the sea. Below in the courtyard, soldiers moved about and would soon come for him. He was to meet Andrew for sword practice.

Under guard, he waited for Andrew on the beach. The smell of the sea after a storm, and the feel of the sharp wind was stimulating after the long night in his chamber. He had not realized how much he missed the out-of-doors, and he anticipated the training session with Andrew.

To his surprise Andrew appeared with Felix and the Nubian. The guards were dismissed and Andrew motioned for the Nubian and Felix to join them. The Nubian knelt, and with his finger drew on the white sand. "We leave tonight by small boat for the seaport of Valencia. From there, our journey will continue by land to the sea port of Bayonne."

Andrew gave Justin a measured look. "There is risk involved. Will you come, or not?"

"I shall be ready! But what of Stewert?"

Andrew questioned the Nubian with a raised brow. The Nubian's gaze was confident. "He and the Spanish captain will join us."

Night had fallen upon the Mediterranean. Justin waited in his dark chamber. The time was near.

The English translation had been delivered to Soleiman that day, and tonight Justin placed the Latin version in his bag with his other possessions and waited for the Nubian to appear at the door of his chamber.

A cautious step in the hall and a rattle of keys and the ebony giant appeared clad in armor and cloak. Grabbing his leather bag, Justin followed.

On the beach, the others waited. Stewert's arm was in a sling, his cloak flung carelessly over his shoulder, and his sword was replaced in its sheath. He was silent, but watched Justin skeptically, trying to judge the reason for his generosity in seeing to his release. When Stewert had sought to escape on the Spanish galleon after the shipwreck, he had left Justin behind. Yet he said nothing and took a position at one of the oars to use his good arm.

The Spanish captain was horrified when he saw the small size of the boat. He stroked his dashing mustache and raised his brows. "Senor Andrew! To Valencia in *this?*" But one glance back toward the castle silhouetted against the cliff above, and he boarded, manning his place at the oar.

The Nubian strode aft. He drew from his tunic a chart and handed it to Andrew. Felix whispered to Justin with an anxious glance toward the incoming clouds. "May the God of creation be with us, Master."

The boat slipped out to sea, the oars surged in powerful strokes, and the hull made headway through the glassy darkness. An offshore wind picked up and the small vessel took to the open sea; the wood creaked and the roll of the sea became deeper as the shoreline disappeared. Andrew, an experienced navigator, headed west to the Spanish port of Valencia. The dawn gave way as the rising sun shown on the full sails. An exuberant shout arose from the men on board.

A few drops of rain fell but the weather held stable. For days they edged along the coastline of Spain until the seaport of Valencia came to their view.

Once ashore the Spanish captain made grateful provision for their journey to Bayonne. Horses were procured and provisions given for the landward journey. They traveled the trade routes north toward the border between Spain and France to rendezvous with an English galleon. And reaching Bayonne in good weather, they caught a ship sailing north around the coast of Brittany and through the narrow English Channel, bringing them to port in London and the Thames River.

On the morning of their long journey's end, Andrew stood on deck with Justin. The ship nosed her way slowly into the fog-bound morning on the Thames estuary. All were on deck for the cautious berthing of the fine ship. A cry from the man at the masthead echoed through the misty salt breeze as the sailors in the shrouds barked their orders. The gray water slapped the hull and a group of crying sea gulls wheeled and swooped overhead.

The vessel was made secure and the planks were laid to join the cobbled quay. Justin picked up his leather bag and faced Andrew.

"Where now, Corsair? Are not the laws of London too civilized for you?" he jested.

Andrew's answer took him by surprise. "To Antwerp to visit a merchant friend at the English House. And you? Once your father is on his feet, will you not join him, and your brother, and take to privateering? You are good with the sword and at the pilot's helm. Be careful, or Stewert Brice will be jealous of his younger brother."

Andrew didn't realize his jest was true. He imagined Stewert being proud of his younger brother. Instead, Stewert resented his competition. Justin said nothing and cast a lingering gaze to the sea. It was still in his blood, there was no doubt of that. "My future is yet unknown. If I am to translate the Scriptures into English, I must master Greek. I am thinking of attending Cambridge."

Andrew's golden brow crested into a frown. "You are no longer among corsairs or merchants. Your speech must be bridled. This is the England of King Henry and Cardinal Wolsey. Heretics are burned."

"I know that only too well. I have recently escaped Rome from where I could have been burned at the stake."

Andrew's surprise at hearing this faded into a stalwart expression. "Then you know what you are about, and are determined to see it through."

"Yes, though I do not know the means."

"Should you come to Antwerp, you may find us at the English House on the harbor."

"I owe you both a great deal. I will seek a journey to Antwerp to repay you if my fortunes prosper."

"You owe us nothing. But come to Antwerp. We would hear again of your endeavors at Cambridge. Speaking no Latin myself, I am in sympathy for your concern for us English. Even I would muse deeply over such a Book, if I had it in the tongue I know."

To hear the rugged corsair admit this, pleased Justin more than he was willing to show. "Then I will come. And I shall see to it you have the Book."

"Caution, Lad, caution. This is one battle where Toledo swords are rendered useless. Since it is the only sword I know, I could be of no aid to you in danger."

Justin remembered the fleeing Wycliffites. In spite of danger they had risked meeting together in the woods to hear the Word of God. "Some things are worth risking one's head over. But let's not think of it now. The sun breaks through the mist and it looks to be a fair winter's day. I shall see you in Antwerp."

Stewert Brice had gone on alone, and Felix waited for Justin on the wharf. They walked the crowded cobbled streets among rotting two-storied wooden houses crammed together, and around them sailors carried loads on their backs. The street vendors were busy, and the pieman and fish peddler had their carts loaded for the day's work.

They paused at the pieman's cart to buy meat pies, still holding some of the heat of the old man's morning oven, then hurried on.

A hubbub of voices filled the mist shrouded morning. Sea birds bickered over discarded fish bones and decaying debris, and cats stalked. From above a wooden structure, a woman leaned out and emptied a bucket of water onto the street below.

When at last they reached the landing stage by the Tower of London, the morning sun had burned through the mist. Here they caught a small hired boat filled with street vendors on their way into the better part of the city to sell their wares. London Bridge came into view and Justin recognized the leaning wooden buildings on top, which had been so curious to him as a child. As the foundations rotted, the structures leaned precariously toward the water.

But beyond the Bridge the scene changed as he and Felix entered another world. Here were the magnificent palaces of the Strand, where gardens ran down to the water's edge, alleyways offered climbing roses with sweet fragrance, and a maze of varied greens from the intricately clipped bushes and low trees. A large fountain shot a glistening waterfall of blue into the air, and white-winged doves flew through the mist. There were small private boats docked between the landing stages belonging to lords, bishops, and abbots, which carried their masters and mistresses over the water under gaudy awnings of scarlet and gold.

It was here that he would meet Lady Regina Redford after nearly four long years.

Part II

10

The Strand, London, A.D. 1518

> Thy testimonies have I taken as an
> heritage for ever; for they are the
> rejoicing of my heart
> (Ps. 119:111).

Lady Regina dressed quickly in the ribbon-trimmed gown of green velvet, with its long skirt and belled, elbow length sleeves. Her dark hair was swept gracefully up from her shoulders and secured with combs of jade. She turned quickly as the door of her chamber opened and Lisbeth stood there, flushed with excitement.

"Sir Justin Brice is here, M'lady, and waiting in the garden. And" she breathed in wonder, "he wears no monk's robe."

Regina tried to calm the thumping of her heart. "Have Trigg bring the coach to the gate." She snatched up her fur-lined cloak and started toward the door.

"Trigg's already waiting, M'lady."

Regina was in such a rush she almost forgot the prized gift she intended to give Justin. She couldn't wait to see his expression, or show him how knowledgeable she was. Where her fluency with Greek and Latin offended Lord Robert, the Earl's son, surely it would please Justin. And the extensive notes she had taken on the lectures of Dean John Colet on the Pauline

Epistles, were scholarly enough to have belonged to a Master of Arts. She smiled to herself. Justin was the one man who would appreciate her labors. Carefully she slid the portfolio into the leather bag.

Lisbeth watched with puckered lips. "One day, M'lady, I fear you'll fall into dire trouble over your interest in such forbidden things," she whispered. "King Henry holds no sympathy for. . . ."

Regina cut her off with a good-humored pat to her cheek. "Tsk, tsk, Lisbeth. You fret like a stewing hen. Mind your tongue and let us go. Is everything packed?"

"Yes, M'lady."

In a manner her father would frown upon, Regina picked up her skirts and ran out into the hall. Then she sedately followed Lisbeth down several ornate corridors to the southwestern section of the palace and to the flight of stairs. Wide-eyed, Lisbeth now hung back and watched over the banister as her lady descended in a swirl of shimmering green.

Regina paused. From where she stood on the stairs, the view onto the private terrace showed an absence of guards. Past the gallery, a flight of steps stretched down to the scenic garden sitting silently in the noon sun.

Heart thumping, she forced herself to breathe, slowly trying to gain a measure of control before she faced him. One, two, three.

Her heart slammed in spite of the effort. Beyond the sloping garden, the water was a gray blue, dotted with small boats traversing to and fro.

Lisbeth, dressed in hat and cloak for the ride to Redford House, ushered the servants bearing Regina's trunk to the waiting coach.

"Shall I send for Sir Brice, M'lady?"

"No, wait for us in the coach."

Regina walked down the grassy slope toward the Thames

River. Justin waited by the landing stage near the barge. He turned as he heard her coming.

She stopped when her eyes fell on him. Still expecting a cleric, she stared. His costume was equal in brilliance to his appearance. The suit was black velvet, the shirt made of fine white linen, and a riding cloak was draped about his broad shoulders. His boots were polished, sporting silver buckles, and on his head was a dashing hat of the French fashion.

He came toward her sweeping off his hat with a deep bow. "Your servant, Madam."

Regina rallied her floundering courage and became at once Lady Redford. She clutched the leather folder behind her back, wondering. This could not be the young man who had spent years in Rome at Saint Athenians? She had expected a monk's cowl, a subdued, if not altogether "religious," demeanor. Instead he looked a lord, at least a cavalier, and she was both wary and pleased all at once.

His propriety and formal tone was quickly matched. She lifted her chin with studied nobility. "Sir Brice, how pleasant to see you again. Have you received my letters?"

Regina had no idea that Justin had dreaded this formal moment. Felix had accumulated the fashionable clothes, declaring he could not possibly visit Lady Regina Redford in anything less dashing. The plumed hat Justin had considered twice; yet Felix had won. "And when you greet her, Master, be sure you bow very deep and sweep it wide. Offer your servanthood with profound dedication."

"I remember the customs, Felix," he had said dryly. He could have added that he had also once raced with her on horseback through the woods around Windsor Castle. But, the years had considerably changed matters. They had grown up.

He looked at her now, his poised manner showing nothing of his inward dilemma. He dare not contemplate the feelings raging in his heart.

"Your kindness to my father is graciously accepted, My Lady. How can I ever repay you?"

"Perhaps I shall think of some way," she murmured, and dragged her eyes from his. "Shall we go? The coach waits."

Two fine coaches were parked in the cobbled driveway and the attendants waited in their bright uniforms of red and black. One coach was for her and Justin, the other for her servants. Felix waited beside Lisbeth, and seeing Lady Regina, he made an elegant bow.

Regina went to him at once and planted a kiss on his cheek. "I shall reward you for your faithful service, Felix. I shall not forget your voyage to Rome on my behalf."

Felix grinned and hastened a bow over her extended hand. " 'Twas an honor, My Lady. And no easy task. Wait until Master Justin tells you of our shipwreck."

"Shipwreck!" she looked over at Justin. He bowed.

"And made slaves by pirates, My Lady!" Felix added.

"A harrowing tale, My lady," said Justin, too gravely. He opened the coach door and handed her in.

"I will hear everything, Jus . . . I mean, Sir Brice. I must know every detail," said Regina.

Justin cast Felix a slight smile, who grinned back.

Ah! thought Justin. *By the time I explain my life in the monastery, the wondrous discovery in Rome, and the adventure bringing us back to London, the formality between us will once again melt into a comfortable relationship, I hope. If she is still the Regina I remember, she will relish every moment.*

It was 1518. The coach bearing them to Redford House left the crowded streets of London and took Whitechapel Road past the many little villages that, despite their close proximity to London, differed little from the countless other villages throughout England. The church of Saint Anne stood beneath a cluster of trees, and the half-timbered cottages with over-hanging upper stories, were thatched. There was a village green used on festive celebrations such as May Day, the cottage of the blacksmith, an apothecary, a few other tradesmen, and a small tavern-inn with its aged sign hanging on a wrought-iron arm over the one street.

When he at last finished sharing his discovery of the truth found in the Epistle of Romans and concluded with his escape from Saint Athenians, they were well on the road taking them into the English countryside where Redford House was located.

"You must be cautious, Justin. Returning to London will in no wise give you the liberty to criticize the teachings of the Church. Emotions run high since the Augustinan monk, Martin Luther, found public support for his teachings in Wittenberg. The word *heresy* is bantered about on the wagging tongues of everyone from Cardinal Wolsey to King Henry. If they find out that you were to be tried in Rome, I wonder if you will be able to enter Cambridge. I, myself have recently been rebuked in a letter from Cardinal Wolsey for having 'erring feet.' "

Justin had remained calm and unflinching until she mentioned the danger to herself. He searched her face at once. "The Cardinal took time to question you? Why? What have you been doing?"

His concern caused her lips to curve into a demure smile. *So he was interested!* But she swiftly masked her pleasure and grew serious. Her brown eyes became remote.

"You will risk all to stand for truth before the Roman abbot. But I must stay to the safety of my chamber and to my embroidery."

He lifted a brow. "I know you too well to believe anything so comforting. Tell me," he winced, "You did not 'publicly' criticize the Cardinal?"

She smiled wryly. "Even I know better than that. It was not criticism of Cardinal Wolsey but support for Colet. It seems I have been too vocal in my praise of Colet's teaching. But once you have seen what he has written, you will understand my enthusiasm, if few others do."

She then produced the leather folder that he had been eyeing with curiosity since leaving London. She handed it to him with eyes shining.

"I have something for you. I was going to wait until we reached the manor but I cannot hide my excitement. Here!"

Justin raised a questioning brow and opened it. He stared with shock at the contents—the Greek New Testament of Erasmus!

She smiled, her dark eyes gleaming. "My tutor of many years, Master of Arts Whitfield, knows Erasmus," she explained. "I have one of the first printed copies of his Greek scholarship."

Justin opened the precious Book, bound in leather, and turned the pages slowly. The thought of holding in his hand the Word of Truth from Matthew to Revelation was as awesome as it was disheartening. He tried his meager knowledge of Greek and found himself woefully lacking. He *must* learn the original language from the Masters at Cambridge. Erasmus was no longer there, but his work was, and those whom he had taught.

Regina knew Greek well. Cautiously, she probed his ego. "I might begin to teach you some Greek, if you would not find it offensive to have a feminine teacher." She proceeded with her carefully laid plans. "I was hoping you would stay at Redford House through the winter and spring. It may take that long before your father is well enough to return to Antwerp. I thought we might study the New Testament together."

He met her eyes squarely and she couldn't read behind the slight smile, or the glint in his eyes.

"When do we begin?"

His readiness took her off guard. She hesitated. "Anytime you wish—tomorrow?"

153

"Tomorrow I shall be waiting for you, Master of Arts Redford."

She smiled, embarrassed, and then quickly diverted his attention to what else was in the folder.

"Erasmus's New Testament is not all. This is my own portfolio on the lectures of Colet. I wrote it in Latin. Since you could not hear him at Saint Paul's, at least my notes would be of benefit to you. They are quite extensive," she apologized, glancing sideways to see his reaction. Was he pleased with her education or did he feel threatened?

Justin quickly leafed through the pages. *The lectures of Dean John Colet on the Pauline Epistles!* he could hardly contain his joy.

"There was so much to write down," she hastened, thinking his silence meant disapproval of the portfolio's size.

She couldn't contain her zeal. "Oh that you could have had heard him. Instead of quoting the teaching of the Church on the Writings, he taught the Writings themselves. He straightforwardly quoted what the Scriptures themselves say. He expounded the very words from their original meaning in the Greek. And this he did with all of the Pauline Epistles." She leafed through her ponderous notes, "Romans, and the letters of Corinthians, Ephesians."

His blue-gray eyes focused upon her now with such pleasure that she halted, feeling her face grow warm. No one, least of all Lord Robert, shared her enthusiasm for the Scriptures. The unity between their spirits, around Christ and His Word, gave her a sense of warm delight, hitherto unknown.

She averted her eyes to the papers and ruffled them. "I . . . I wrote in Latin . . ." her voice trailed. There was a moment of silence in which the clip of the horse's hooves was loud.

"Your work is excellent," Justin stated. "This means more to me than you can know. How I envied your opportunity to hear him. And to think you have actually captured so much exposition on paper for me."

"I must confess that Marlon also took notes for you."

"Marlon?" he smiled ruefully. "Now I am overwhelmed. He who hated the sight of pen and ink."

"He has changed, Justin. He met Colet and talked with him for hours. He has a great hunger for the Scriptures."

"Marlon?" He was delighted.

"Yes, and he also met a young man by the name of William Tyndale who. . . . "

"Your gift is priceless, Regina." He begin to leaf through her work again.

"I wanted to send it to you at Saint Athenians, but thought better of doing so. It would surely be greeted as a heretical work."

"You were wise to do that. What is the reaction of Colet's own colleagues?"

"As expected, his work has created a stir among other scholars at Oxford. Even the New Thinkers are cautious."

"As well they might be. To develop the literal meaning of the Pauline Epistles, when most theologians are more interested in allegory, must be a shock. So this is what you have been endorsing in King Henry's palace! No wonder Cardinal Wolsey took time to write you an admonition."

He grew sober. "My Lady, you must do nothing that will call you before the king. The Tower is no place for one of your beauty or learning. I would have to give up all plans of going to Cambridge in order to attempt your rescue."

Her expression now looked like anything but a young scholar. She dimpled. "I find your chivalry quite flattering. Would you indeed, Justin Brice, risk your head to save me?"

His gaze was unwavering. "I would, My Lady."

Even among the conservative scholars at Oxford and Cambridge the truth of the essence of biblical teaching was unknown. The lecture halls of the two universities, being the foundation of Christian learning in sixteenth-century England, were governed by the inflexible laws laid down centuries earlier. The opposing ideas of nominalism and realism were always at odds. The masters of scholasticism lectured not on the biblical text, but cited what the authorities said about the text. The theology of Thomas Aquinas permeated the doctrine of the Church, and as Erasmus had said to Colet, to speak against Aquinas now, was to speak against the Church itself. It was to John Colet's credit that he told his students to keep to the Scriptures and the Apostles' Creed.

"His lectures were so crowded one could hardly find room to sit or stand," Regina said. "They stood for hours. Not students only, but monks, and the other Masters of Arts."

"All men should teach as he does," said Justin. "The words should be given in literal context and explained clearly, not to those who understand Latin only, but in English. For too long the Church has taught dogma and neglected the foundation of Christianity, which is the Person of Christ and His Word."

"So I agree, and Marlon, too. We tried to get our father to attend the lectures and to speak of them to the King, but he would not," she said quietly. "Yet recently Marlon has spent time with him in hearty discussion. His interest is awakening. And now that King Henry will send him on business to Cambrai, we hope Father will take time to visit Wittenberg to also meet with Doctor Martin Luther."

Justin thought of the stalwart Lord Simon Redford. He was highly respected by the king. But today's favor could be tomorrow's trip to the Tower. Lord Simon Redford walked softly —a necessity for anyone in service to King Henry—as Cardinal Wolsey was to find out in future years. (Unable to get the pope to grant Henry the VIII a divorce from Catherine to marry Anne Bolelyn, Cardinal Wolsey would be sentenced by the king to die for "treason.")

"What does your father think of Colet?"

"He is thoughtful, but will say little. He warns us to be

cautious in offending Cardinal Wolsey. But I did get him to read Erasmus's *In Praise of Folly*. He thought this satirical work identifying the abuses within the Church very clever, but then, Erasmus is so gifted in his satire."

"Marlon and I mistakenly thought we might get our father to aid William Tyndale, but he will not."

"You have mentioned this William Tyndale before."

"He is a godly man, a true scholar with a destiny. I am sure of it. He has acquired a masterful knowledge of the biblical languages and abhors obscurantism. I want you to meet him. You share much in common."

Now was the moment to ask what had been on his mind so long. "When Felix told me you had not married, I could hardly believe it. How is it that you have escaped Robert's wish to marry you?"

"Like you, I, too, have been in a cloister."

She explained by touching the volume of her hand-written works. "When a young woman buries herself in her chamber, and is content to stain her fingers with ink, rather than jewels, a frivolous man like Lord Robert quickly grows bored. It is as I planned it, for I do not love him. And so he is content to busy himself elsewhere."

He was relieved, but rebuked himself. Her disinterest in Lord Robert did not mean that she loved him.

"I was offended when you refused to answer my letters," she said.

"I never saw your letters. The abbot destroyed them."

"I soon understood that."

He hesitated, wondering if he dare express his feelings. And if he did say he loved her, then what? Lord Simon Redford would never consent to their marriage. Was it not wrong then to test their love further? And what of his personal commitment to the Lord? How could he risk involving her more fully in what he knew would be a future wracked with danger and uncertainty?

"At least marriage to Lord Robert would mean your safety," he stated.

She turned on him at once. "Do you think I am frivolous? That I care for nothing but ease and baubles? That I have no commitment to things of value? That I fear the harshness of reality?"

"You are a rare young woman of valiant spirit. I would be a fool to question either your courage or your devotion to matters of serious import."

Her eyes shone. "Remember Wycliffe's translation of Matthew?"

"How could I forget?" he whispered emphatically.

Her emotion matched his. "Neither can I forget. When we shared the Word together in English for the first time, I knew I had found something important, something worth risking not only the comforts of my position but my life."

"I would not see you risking your life!"

"Yet will you risk yours? If I find myself involved in heretical views, they began before your return to London. I told you about William Tyndale, but I have not explained his ambitions. He intends to translate the Bible into English. And I vowed to do all I could to make it possible."

He stared at her, struggling with torn emotions. Hearing of another who heralded his greatest desire caused the blood to pound in his temples. But the risk was great. It was one thing to risk himself, but Regina?

"Regina, you are sure of this? This William Tyndale spoke to you of his desire?"

"And especially to Marlon. You will think highly of him, Justin, as we do. He is dedicated."

"He has impressed me already. I must meet him."

"You shall meet him. Marlon and I have mentioned William

and his ambition to our father, hoping he might speak to Cardinal Wolsey, or to Bishop Tunstall about receiving authorization from the Church to work under their supervision. But Father turned red with rage."

"More than likely it was the ghastly color of fear," said Justin quietly. "Wolsey is the last man in England to ask. William Tyndale's name or whereabouts was not mentioned to the cardinal, I hope?"

"No! Now it seems Master Tyndale must one day go to Bishop Cuthbert Tunstall himself for permission to translate. But he will need a letter of introduction."

The Bishop of London seemed the best choice in seeking patronage for Tyndale's work. Tunstall was a scholar in language and embraced some of Erasmus's ideas of Church reform. Justin, however was skeptical.

"Even if William Tyndale seeks the patronage of Bishop Tunstall, it is not likely he will get it."

Lady Regina scowled. She still hoped to talk her father into writing Tyndale a letter of introduction to the London bishop. "Why not?"

"For the same reasons the abbot in Rome failed to risk his position to religious and political criticism when I mentioned the Scripture in the vulgar tongue—ambition and fear."

"You are too cynical. Not every bishop in the Church is so concerned with his position."

"There are good and dedicated men in the Church. I meant not to claim otherwise. But there are few in authority who will risk being called a heretic, any more than Erasmus. They may satirize or denounce the evil, and by doing so, they sow the seeds of reform. It is needed, and every man has his own gift. The teacher exhorts his student to put his knowledge into action. And Erasmus has been a great teacher, as others have been. But more is now needed. Now the time of harvest must come. Something positive must be done. Some action must be taken. If William Tyndale is a scholar of the original languages and is zealous to put the Scriptures into English—if he is willing to risk his life to do it—then I will do anything I can to help him. And I will consider it the greatest privilege the Lord has given me."

"And you do not think the work can be done with the Church's approval?"

"No. Therefore, your father is right to turn red when his son and daughter come to him and ask him to speak to Cardinal Wolsey. I only wonder what Master Tyndale will do if he is refused permission from the Church?"

Regina hesitated to speak for Tyndale, for he had made no comment on what he might do. But she believed he would go ahead with the work anyway and told Justin so.

"Undoubtedly he knows the consequences," said Justin. "I, too, am willing to do what is necessary. But you. . . ."

She interrupted tonelessly. "But I am to remain safely cloistered in the palace and watch the smoke rise from Smithfield?"

"Neither I nor this Master Tyndale have plans of visiting Smithfield," he hastened soberly, speaking of the place where heretics were burnt.

Regina was not at peace. Her will was committed. "If risking your future to help a man like Tyndale is deemed a worthy sacrifice to serve our Lord, am I to be denied my loyalty? Did I ask to be born at this hour in history? And if I possess the authority and goods to help so noble a cause, am I not held responsible to use these things in good stewardship? Or, because I am a woman, does that mean I should shackle my wits to my bedpost?"

A smile crossed his face, for he could not resist. "Your wits, my lady, should be shackled only to a man who appreciates them."

Her energy spent, she now was at loss. She stared at him, but he looked away. He could not involve himself. He must go to Cambridge and learn the languages.

The words burned in her heart. "Are you that man?" She wanted to ask, but she wisely held them back.

11

Redford House

> He hath sent me to bind up the brokenhearted,
> to proclaim liberty to the captives, and the
> opening of the prison to them that are bound
> (Isa. 61:1).

The sixteenth century was a time of sweeping change in Western Europe, shaking the foundations of both Church and monarchy. More than eight years had passed since, in 1508, a young teenager named William Tyndale from Gloucester, England, entered Magdalen College at Oxford.

As Tyndale entered Oxford, it was a crucial time in Western civilization, overlapping the end of the Dark Ages with the beginnings of the Renaissance, the discovery of the New World, the Spanish Inquisition, and the Protestant Reformation. But Tyndale, involved deeply in his learning at both Oxford and Cambridge, and later as a fugitive from the Church and the king, was unaware of his crucial part in the whole picture of the movement of God.

In 1515 he received his M.A. from Oxford, and in 1519 moved to Cambridge to master Greek. In 1516 Erasmus edited the first published Greek New Testament, and also wrote his negative work called *In Praise of Folly* which satirized the abuses of the Church. And Dean John Colet had already lectured on the Pauline Epistles, giving the literal exegesis. And on October 31, 1517, in a town in Saxony called Wittenberg, Martin Luther had nailed his ninety-five theses to the door of the Castle Church.

During his stay at Redford House, Justin was lost in his own studies and unaware of what was taking place in Wittenberg. With Regina's help his command of Greek improved, but he was ever aware of his need to attend Cambridge and get his degree. As for his father, his dark mood worsened. Justin visited him in the small cottage at the end of the garden.

Captain Ewan Brice lay brooding, his mood as dark as pitch, his brows hunched low over his stormy eyes. No matter how Justin tried to reason with him, his father would not hear.

Felix shook his head. "What will you do, Master? You have spent months with your father, and yet he remains iron in his resolve to do himself harm."

"I do not know, Felix," he said wearily. "Lady Regina returns to London for the Christmas holidays. We dare not impose on the Redfords much longer."

Yet Justin was reluctant to leave his father in his despondent condition. The time was fast slipping away, and he knew he must help him. Even Felix had come to faith in Christ, but his father remained imprisoned in the darkness of his own doom, in spite of Justin's greatest efforts to free him. And Stewert? Somehow Justin felt he would never be given the opportunity to share the peace he himself had gained. As long as Stewert was jealous and bitter, Justin's words would fall on stony ground.

And his father. . . .

In the darkening sky lightning flashed above the trees, followed by the sullen rumble of thunder. "My Catherine and little Mary are dead . . . dead like their mother, lying cold in the ground. And, like your mother, I am to blame for the little ones sleeping cold . . . soon now the rain will come again and drench their beds."

Justin had heard the tale of gloom a hundred times. And when it rained his father's mood worsened. That was the reason Justin had joined him in the cottage.

"Catherine and Mary died of the plague, like Balin York, and a thousand others. God has not taken their souls to punish you, Father. Know that your sin, and mine, is covered by the blood of Christ. Rest with quiet confidence in that scriptural fact."

Captain Brice lay on his bed staring darkly ahead, his mind tormented. At the sound of Justin's voice, his remote gaze turned to fix upon him.

He blinked, then scowled. And, again for the hundredth time, he murmured, "You are not in your robe, nor does the cross grace your neck," he said.

"I have told you, I am no longer a monk. My service to the Lord will be invested in what I believe is a far greater endeavor."

"Do you not hear the thunder of God against heretics? Be quick to seek your forgiveness. 'Twas no light matter to flee the very city of Rome."

"The righteousness of Christ is my armor, and yours. Be at peace."

"No, Lad, you have wrongly returned from Rome to ease my torture. I will return to Antwerp and to my ship. I have a destiny to keep with a storm at sea. The Almighty awaits to send me to a just death."

"Father! Have you not heard a word I have said to you these past months?"

"Neither your presence nor your fair words will convince me otherwise. I have committed an unpardonable sin. The death of my innocent damsels was a judgment against Ewan Brice." He groaned. "I gave my son to Rome, what else more was there to do? Yet there is no peace. My hands are still stained. I have lost you, for I sent you against your wish—and now both of my daughters are dead; only Stewert lives, and he to curse me."

"I bear no grudge against your decision to send me to the monastery. In Rome I found truth, for I found the Scriptures. I have returned to London the better for going. And Stewert is loyal to you, though he bears a root of bitterness against us both. He can be won back to you by letting him know your feelings toward him."

"No. In my dreams a thousand screaming demons come to gnash upon my soul."

A flash of lightning and a rumble of thunder brought him upright. "Yes, the God of wrath thunders against Ewan Brice. Behold my way is dark, my soul cast from before Him like rotting leaves before the devil wind."

Justin stared at him, distraught by his inability to perceive the truth.

For the first time Justin saw him as tired and old. There was nothing left of the virility he knew so well. The strong personality was shattered into fits of gloom and depression that worsened as the days past.

"Obviously he is too guilt ridden to listen to your logic. He needs something else to free his mind," said Regina.

The Christmas holidays were over. They were in the library studying the Greek version of the New Testament with Colet's notes. Her comments, though simply put, arrested his attention. Slowly the profound truth in her suggestion gripped him. Was this the answer to his tireless prayers for his father's release from the bondage of guilt? Had he been depending upon his own arguments of logic to dispel the shackles, instead of using the Sword of Truth to cut through the unbelief?

Each morning thereafter, Justin met with his father to read the Scriptures. He refused to debate the reason behind the deaths of little Catherine and Mary, and when his father interrupted to trod again the worn paths of guilt and judgment,

Justin did not argue. He would wait in silence until his father's tongue grew weary and said no more. Justin would again read the Scriptures which heralded the liberty bought by the blood of Christ. He would conclude with prayer, thanking God for His guidance in his life while at Rome, then quietly reassure his father that he loved him, and leave.

Ewan Brice seemed not to hear, but as the days turned into weeks, Justin saw that his father was no longer interrupting as much as he had done previously. Soon there were no interruptions at all, and Justin then begin to labor over the sense of the words, explaining the merit in Christ's atoning death, what the resurrection proved, and how Christ ever lived to make intercession for His own.

"God is satisfied with the price of the bruising of His own Son. He hath put Christ to grief and made His soul an offering for sin. His travail did satisfy the holy demands of judgment, and by that righteous servant, many are justified, for He poured out His soul unto death. And though a man's sins be as scarlet, they shall be as white as snow."

The weeks slipped by and then one day Felix opened the cottage door and thrust his head in. "Lord Marlon Redford is here, Master Justin."

Justin left the New Testament on the table and walked toward the Redford Manor. Lord Marlon emerged ahead on the path, a handsome figure in his doublet and hat. Justin hardly recognized the man before him, and from Marlon's expression he, too, wondered at the masculine figure who had once been the stable boy.

"So you escaped the monastery to capture the heart of my sister, did you?"

Justin wondered. But Marlon grinned and came toward him with a hearty grasp of his shoulders. "It is good to see you again, Justin. I could not be more pleased. My father is here now with some masters from Cambridge. They have come to hear our guest who is a scholar from Wittenberg. He knows Martin Luther."

"A friend of Martin Luther here in Lord Redford's home?"

"Yes. My father has interest in the work of Luther," he said quietly.

"I am very glad. But it will mean grave trouble if King Henry hears of it."

"Caution is the reason for meeting here instead of in London." Marlon looked grave.

"Of Luther, I know little. It is William Tyndale I wish to meet."

"Ah then, so Regina told you of William? Good! You shall meet him."

Justin pressed. "When?"

"When will you return to London?"

Justin thought of his father. "I have stayed here too long. I must leave by spring if I am to enroll at Cambridge."

"I will arrange a meeting soon. But as for Luther," and his voice lowered by habit, "it seems lightning has struck over Wittenberg. Think what this means, Justin! He has openly criticized the Church in Rome for the abuses of the indulgence system. Not only that, but he has challenged a debate on the subject."

The parlor of Redford House boasted a fireplace built across one wall, and as the wind flung the rain against the windowpanes, the logs blazed on a bed of red coals. Several doctors were present from one of the superior faculties of Cambridge, wearing their scholarly birettas and violet robes, and the Masters of Arts wore miniver-lined hoods with wide sleeves.

Whitfield, a friend of Erasmus and tutor in the palace to Lady Regina was there. She stood beside her father Lord Simon. As Justin met her gaze, her lips curved slightly into a smile, but she now wore the face of Lady Redford, and she made no move to cross the room to him.

The discussion was already going on. At once his attention was drawn to the scholar from Wittenberg who addressed those assembled in Latin.

The visiting scholar was a graduate of the University of Wittenberg, where Martin Luther held the position of lecturer in biblical theology and taught in the vernacular on Psalms, Romans, Galatians, and Hebrews.

"Herr Doktor was gravely upset when Archbishop Albert received a papal bull to raise money by selling indulgences."

"Such exploitation of the people is not altogether new," said a Cambridge doctor cautiously.

"Yet the Archbishop was given authority to sell indulgences throughout Saxony for the next eight years," said the scholar from Wittenberg indignantly. "Doktor Luther has rightly asked, although dryly, whether the poor churches of Germany must go roofless so that Rome may have a roof of gold. But that is not the half of it. The Dominican monk Johann Tetzel is the Archbishop's 'peddler.' He goes about stirring up the people to buy. He even claims repentance is not necessary."

"Not necessary!"

"No! He has promised remission of the gravest sins if the sinner would only buy an indulgence. At his table he has a cash box, like so," and he sketched an airy gesture with his fingers, his lips pursed, "and beside it, hear this! a written price list of standard fees for indulgences. Herr Doktor has in these last years come to assured faith through the Scripture alone. Do you wonder why then he has been outraged in the name of true righteousness?" The German scholar jumped to his feet, his cheeks flushed, and with great drama enacted his scene before his engrossed onlookers.

"Herr Doktor walked like this," he walked with shoulders back across the room to the fireplace mantel. "And boldly nailed," he hammered, "to the door of the church his protestation!"

A rumble of thunder followed and the German scholar lifted his eyes toward the ceiling.

"What will come of this challenge to Rome?"

"Does Pope Leo know of the action?"

"If not, he will. Then what?"

"Luther will be burned."

"Let us hear these famed ninety-five theses," interrupted Lord Simon Redford. "Our friend from Wittenberg has a copy with him. Proceed, Learned Sir."

"I indeed have a prodigious copy," said he, retaking his seat. "It is so, my brothers, that the original in Latin has been translated into German and is spreading rapidly among the people."

"The trumpet has sounded," said an old doctor. "The call will echo throughout Europe."

The scholar from Wittenberg removed the parchment from his sleeve and began to read: "A disputation of Master Martin Luther, Theologian, for the elucidation of the virtue of indulgences. From a zealous desire to bring to light the truth, the following theses will be maintained at Wittenberg. . . . He therefore asks that all who are unable to be present and dispute with him verbally will do so in writing. In the name of our Lord Jesus Christ. Amen."

As he proceeded to enumerate each proclamation of the ninety-five theses, Justin felt a surge of passion. Oh that he could have been there!

Rain pelted the window with such sudden fury that the German scholar had to raise his voice, the Latin denting the walls of the chamber in staccato tone.

Lady Regina slipped from the side of her father and came up beside Justin, but no one noticed, so engrossed were they.

Justin was spellbound, for Luther's theses were not a long,

wandering apologetic, but rapid-fire declarations on the unscriptural use of indulgences. Luther declared,

—Those who assert that a soul straightway flies out (of purgatory) as a coin tinkles in the collection box, are preaching an invention of man (*hominem praedicant*).

—Those who think themselves sure of salvation through their letters of pardon will be damned forever with their teachers.

—We must especially beware of those who say that those pardons of Rome are that inestimable gift of God by which man is reconciled to God.

—Confidence in salvation through letters of indulgence is vain.

—A wrong is done to the Word of God when in the same sermon an equal or longer time is devoted to indulgences than to God's Word.

When the tense reading had ended, silence fell. Then glances were exchanged among the doctors and masters. The debate broke in urgency.

"He hath said no more than what men like Erasmus and Colet have said for years. I commend the learned doktor."

Another said gravely, "It is but the beginning. What next? And where will it lead? Have these theses been sent to the Archbishop of Mainz?"

The German scholar wiped his perspiring brow. "Indeed. And the Archbishop has sent them to the pope in Rome."

There was a groan. "Ah, so there we have it," said a grave doctor. "Know now that Martin Luther will surely be called on charges of heresy."

"The Dominicans," said the German, "even now boast that Herr Doktor will burn. But he has appealed to Prince Frederick of Saxony. Since a German must only be tried in Saxony, he will not be sent by Frederick to Rome. He will be required to appear before the Diet of Augsburg."

"Will it be an open debate?" asked Justin

"Yes. He shall be permitted to speak."

"Then the man will have the words to contend for the faith," said Justin.

The German's eyes looked kindly upon him, and he smiled. "You are right, Scholar. Martin Luther will never recant. It is, *sola fide* or justification by faith, and *sola scriptura*—the Scriptures are the authority."

Reginia took Justin's arm and led him into the hall. Her eyes shone and her cheeks were flushed. The voices dimmed behind them. "When we left London, you said the seed for Church reform was sown by men like Erasmus, but now bold action was needed. Has Luther drawn the sword of action?"

"Only God knows what the end will be. But I think Martin Luther has sounded the trumpet, and men all over Europe who have needed a leader will rally to his summons."

Her eyes clouded. "And you? Will you also go to Wittenberg?"

"I shall remain in England and seek your friend Master Tyndale."

12

He sent his word, and healed them,
and delivered them from their destructions
(Ps. 107:20).

Justin entered the cottage, bringing a gust of wind and rain
with him. Felix was bent over the cook pot steaming on the
hearth, stirring his concoction with vigor. He looked up surprised. "Master Justin, are you back so soon? I had thought you
would dine with the great doctors and masters at Redford
House this night."

Captain Ewan Brice was in the next room supposedly asleep.

Justin hung his wet cloak on the post to dry. One look at his
face and Felix stopped stirring. "Are you sick?"

"No. I am leaving with Marlon in the morning for Cambridge. You must take my father to Antwerp."

The sudden news came as a surprise to Felix. "Indeed,
Master, yet I thought we would stay at Redford House till
spring."

"I thought so myself, until I heard the scholar from Wittenberg. I can no longer delay my future, Felix. If ever I am to
master Greek, I would do it now."

He explained about Martin Luther. "It is time I was about
my own affairs in London. The news from Wittenberg has
stirred me to pursue what I know to be true."

A sound from the doorway leading into the bedroom caused them both to turn.

Captain Ewan Brice stood there alert, and with a curious arch of his brow. "How now, Justin! So you will go to Cambridge, will you?"

Justin stared at him. Ewan Brice looked as robust as the day he had taken to ship in good spirits. Felix, too, stared.

Then Justin caught sight of the New Testament in his father's rough hand. He had been trying to read it!

Captain Brice saw his eyes fix on the Book and he held it up with a scowl. "Are you sure the fine words you read me came from this gibberish?"

Justin's relief brought a smile. "It is written in Greek."

"Greek, Latin—'tis all gibberish to the likes of me. Have you none of the good words in me own maternal tongue?"

"My Father, you have touched upon the essence of why I go to Cambridge. One day you may read the fair words for yourself."

" 'Tis a good thing," he said with exaggerated irritation, "I cannot always have me son sitting near the bed reading for me now, can I!" His eyes gleamed, and a slight smile showed under his beard. "Especially since thy father will take to sea with Stewert, and ye shall go to your Masters of Arts."

Justin searched his rugged face and he saw what he was looking for.

"You have His peace, my Father?" he asked quietly.

Ewan Brice walked slowly toward him and paused, a look of emotion coming to his face all at once. Captain Brice flung wide his strong arms with unashamed affection. "I have His peace, My Son."

Justin embraced him and for a moment they wept together.

Then Captain Brice gripped Justin's arms Roman style. "What is this I have heard you say, that you have no worldly goods to keep a woman like her ladyship in silks and furs?"

173

"When did I say that!"

"You have always said so, has he not, Felix?"

"Indeed, Master Ewan, since he was a boy," Felix agreed with a broad smile.

"Do you not own half of everything I possess?" asked Ewan, throwing his arm about him. "And what of the Brice Castle and lands in Scotland? You are young and strong Lad. Venture forth and take it."

"I have a vow to keep, my Father. A vow that will bring God's word to the people in their own tongue. I made it when I left Rome the night our ship was lost in the storm. It is a vow that will mean great risk. I would not involve Lady Regina anymore than I have to."

"If you have made a vow, keep it," said his father firmly. He handed the New Testament to Justin and the corners of his mouth turned. "I will expect your vow to accomplish much."

"There is something I ask you to do in Antwerp. I have a friend named Andrew. You will meet him when you arrive at the English House. Reward him. It was he who made our escape possible from Baron Soleiman."

"I shall do as you ask. And now," he said with a gesture toward Felix, "let us eat and be merry for this one night, at least. You, my son, give thanks to our gracious Saviour. He hath removed the burden of guilt from my wicked old heart."

13

Cambridge University, A.D. 1519

My zeal hath consumed me,
because mine enemies have forgotten thy words
(Ps. 119:139).

The lesser parlor of the Inn of the White Horse of Cambridge became suddenly quiet with the news. The lively discussion among the learned men and students who often frequented the Inn—bringing books and notes with them to share about the fire—ended abruptly. In the silence that permeated the room, both masters and students exchanged somber looks, then one by one arose slowly from their seats and walked out into the night.

Justin grabbed up his books and papers and sought the quiet darkness of the evening. A melancholy sense of loss descended upon his spirits, and it seemed the light of a precious torch had been snuffed out. He hurried down the hall and up the staircase which led to the chamber he shared with William Tyndale.

William was busy at his desk by the window, his candle burning, his worn scholar's cloak pulled tightly about his lean body to block the chill. His quill ceased its scratching and he looked up above the flame, squinting to see what drove Justin to banging the door. One look at his face and Tyndale stood to his feet, ready for important news.

Had they burned Luther? He gripped the quill tightly but his face was outwardly composed.

"Have they burned the good and brave man, then?"

"No," Justin hastened, "it is Dean John Colet. He is dead."

The news of the death of Colet brought a quiet moment of reflection on his work of teaching the Pauline Epistles, and on what the loss of such an able scholar would mean.

"The Lord has seen fit to take a needed man," said William soberly, and he sat down again. "Yet, He makes no mistakes." Chin in hand he stared at the paper before him.

Justin laid his books on his own desk. "He will be hard to replace. With the storm of controversy over Martin Luther, we needed his voice more than ever. Master Colet had hoped for an English version from Erasmus."

William nodded. "Yes, I know it. But Erasmus *is* Erasmus. He has no wish to ignite a quarrel with the pope. He dedicated his new Latin version to him, thus stilling his own personal controversy."

Erasmus's action had brought criticism from certain men at Oxford and Cambridge, and they had retaliated by banning his works and books.

Justin, long an admirer of Erasmus, rushed to his defense. "Yet Erasmus opposes those who are unwilling that the sacred Scriptures be translated into the vulgar tongue. Has he not said they should be rendered into the languages of all?"

William's eyes gleamed with passion as he swept up the Greek New Testament and turned to the foreword where Erasmus had declared: "Let the husbandman sing portions of them as he follows the plow, the weaver hum them to the tune of the shuttle, and the traveler beguile the tedium of his journey with Gospel tales . . . ."

Tyndale spoke slowly but firmly. "Then if Colet be gone,

and Erasmus will not—you and I, if God permits, will translate into the English vernacular."

Justin pressed. "When?"

William sighed deeply and ruffled the stacks of work on his desk. "I have not yet the degree from Cambridge. To study Greek is why I came here. It must not be rushed. And there is Hebrew to learn. And, I would first seek permission from Bishop Tunstall."

"You are already a scholar of languages. It is I who woefully lack." Justin went back to his desk and pulled out his books. "I shall never keep up with you. If you wait for me, the translation will never get done. I have doubts about the bishop. Will he risk his approval in a time of controversy over Luther?"

"Yet, it is best we try the approved route. When we aim our bow at the target, and when God says, 'Let fly,' we will hit the bull's-eye. Now! To your books," Tyndall jested. "You are right. If I wait for you, the years will turn my hair white."

Justin brought his candle to William's and lit the charred wick. A small flame shot up, and he carried it back to his desk. He sat down and turned to his Greek, studying until his eyes watered and his mind ached. Long hours later when Tyndale had fallen asleep at his desk, and his candle was low, Justin's thoughts for refreshing diversion turned as always to Lady Regina.

With determination he resumed his studies. He must master Greek! The original language must burn in his heart, his love for it must set fire to his bones, consume his mind until it flowed as a musical river! Only then did he dare set to interpret the Holy Scriptures into his own tongue.

Justin turned in his seat and looked across the chamber at William. A feeling of despair came over him. It was a fact: Tyndale was the scholar. Justin was and would undoubtedly remain for many years, at least, the underling. Could the translation wait so long? What was the will of God? Had he been called to work side by side with William as he so desired, or did God have some other purpose for him in aiding Tyndale?

Justin shut his books and wearily blew out the candle, too tired to even tumble into his bed. The next moment it seemed the dawn peeped through the window and the watchman's call sounded clearly. A new day of study was already upon them. The rigorous schedule began with a rush as all over Cambridge the scholars jumped from their beds, shivering in the icy morning as they hurried to the hall for breakfast.

The new ideas sweeping Europe in 1521 shook the very foundations of the old beliefs. It was being said, "Luther has hatched the egg that Erasmus laid." Much in the theses of Martin Luther went straight to the root of the religious tree of tradition which the biblical reformers had been aiming their hatchet at for years. Traditional views based on a growing Church theology of centuries of reasoning were giving way to a new interest in what the Scriptures alone had to say on matters of salvation, sacraments, priestly positions, and the abuses of the hierarchy.

Martin Luther refused to recant at the Diet of Augsburg, insisted that the Scriptures were the foundation of Christian truth, and questioned papal infallibility in a debate. Had it not been for the intervention of God through Frederick, the Elector of Saxony, Luther would have met his death before the sect of the Dominicans, yet he found support among his own Augustinian order.

Luther's treatise *The Babylonian Captivity of the Church* was circulated and read in private at Cambridge, where it was received with caution. For "Lutheranism," as the movement in Saxony was now called, was frowned upon by King Henry, Cardinal Wolsey, and Sir Thomas More.

But it was Luther's biblical challenge in the pamphlet that went straight to the heart of the Roman system—salvation and grace dispensed through the Sacraments—that moved King

Henry VIII to write his own thesis attacking Luther and defending the sacramental system.

"King Henry has won from the pope a new title," said Tyndale to Justin, and his expression was wry. " 'Defender of the Faith.' "

"One wonders how long he will defend Rome if his own political advantage were at risk," said Justin dryly. "I have spoken to Lady Regina. Queen Catherine fears the king is looking askance at her since no male heir has been born. The king grows restless. The queen believes he may wish a divorce."

"It is unlikely Cardinal Wolsey will be able to get the pope to issue such a proclamation," said Tyndale.

"And so we shall see how his religious ardor may soon turn sour," said Justin. "The 'Defender of the Faith' may become the defender of his own political posterity. To those in his court who know Henry," explained Justin, thinking of the Redfords, "they believe the man is capable of breaking with papal authority and proclaiming himself head over the Church in England. He will do what is to his advantage to secure his throne."

"God may yet use even King Henry," said Tyndale. "Does not the Lord have His way in the whirlwind and in the storm? The wrath of man He can make to praise Him."

As the trying months of 1520 and 1521 lengthened across Europe, the brush fire begun in Wittenberg was sucked up by the winds of religious and political discontent and burned as hotly elsewhere. The work of the Reformation within the Church was moving forward.

In Scotland, John Knox, the leader of the Scottish Reformation would soon be heard from. In Zurich the Swiss Reformer Zwingli was taking a stand. Later in Geneva, John Calvin would stress the sovereignty of God in a development of a formal system of theology. And in England, yet unheard of except among his own peers, young William Tyndale was convinced the Church was in serious decline and stressed the need for the New Testament in the vernacular.

By summer the Inn of the White Horse, a meeting ground for much debate among distinguished scholars, received a number of masters from other universities, including Wittenberg. William Tyndale stood by himself and listened while the others questioned, applauded, or rejected what they heard.

"Did you expect the outcome to be otherwise? Luther's three papers from Wittenberg have struck in force. One, at the errors in the hierarchy; two, at the Sacraments; and three, at the theology of the Roman Church. The pope had no choice but to issue the bull of excommunication, and arrest."

"Luther meant not to attack the foundation. . . ."

"Of course he did. Are you naive?"

"An appeal for reform is not an attack on the foundation of the Church, but it is like lighting fire to hay, wood, and stubble," ventured old Doctor Royce. He then blew his nose with his handkerchief, as if adding emphasis to what he had said.

"Be not so bold, Doctor Royce. You, too, will find yourself defending your speech before the cardinal," warned another.

Doctor Royce tugged at his silver hair. "I can hardly burn for defending the Scriptures and the Apostles Creed," he retorted and looked about at his colleagues with sharp gray eyes. "Unless babblers who mistake truth for heresy are anxious to run to Cardinal Wolsey."

There was a silent moment, as the assembled close colleagues glanced at each other with caution. Cambridge was now looked upon as the seed ground for the Lutheran heresy. It had been threatened that Parliament was going to meet to debate the spread of Lutheran ideas at the university.

The scholars from Wittenberg shifted uneasily in their seats. It was William Tyndale who broke the silence. "Pray go on, Sir.

Have you said the excommunication bull was sent to Wittenberg?"

Grateful for the interest shown by the silent young man, the German scholar turned his attention to William. "It has. *Exsurge Domine,*" he said. "It was sent under the seal of the Fisherman's ring to the elector Frederick."

"Did not Frederick found the University at Wittenberg? Surely he will not proceed with Martin Luther's arrest?"

"He did not. Now Herr Doktor has instead been summoned by the new Emperor Charles V of Spain to appear for an imperial diet at Worms. He will go with the promise of Frederick's protection."

"Has he made mention of what he intends to say?" Tyndale pressed.

"He has utterly refused to recant and burned the papal bull. He goes with one plea, to be shown his error by the testimony of Scripture alone. If so, he will recant. If not, he has vowed to take his stand, and to appeal to God for help."

Tyndale considered for only a moment. "The man not only has courage but he is fundamentally correct. He should be judged for error by the use of the Word of God alone."

One doctor looked at him coolly, taking in his scholar's robe in meaningful rebuke. "Are you a newcomer to Cambridge?"

"I have been here since 1519. I received my Master of Arts at Oxford, Doctor."

"If Luther were less inclined to thunder in wrath," suggested the doctor, "he might spare the Church the agony of being torn asunder as a lion tears helpless prey. Think so?"

"Which do you liken to a lion—Luther, or the Scriptures?" Tyndale smiled. "Or perhaps both. I prefer to accept what the Scripture says of itself in the Book of Hebrews. That it is 'sharper than any two-edged sword, piercing even to the dividing asunder of soul and spirit, and of the joints and marrow, and is a discerner of the thoughts and intents of the heart.'

Therefore, if the Church system is being torn asunder as you suggest, Honorable Doctor, it is the result of the Word, and not of Luther. For he appeals to the Scriptures to be the lone judge of his error. Truth and error must needs be torn asunder from one another, as tares from wheat, as thistles and thorns from grapes."

The Doctor made no comment. "What did you say your name was?"

"William Tyndale."

The room tensed. Several distinguished men rose to their feet at the same time. "I fear the hour grows late."

The silver-haired Doctor Royce added: "If one is to get a wink of sleep before the tiresome watchman rings his miserable bells, you had best do as I. Turn in early and stuff your ears with bits of paper."

"I shall try it," said one wearily, groaning as he stood to his stiff knees. "Lately there has been much to keep me awake. I grow too old for all of this. Blessed be dear Colet, who is removed from our midst!"

William Tyndale stepped out into the refreshing night breeze, and paused below the inn's swaying sign. He was in trouble and he knew it. He turned to go back to his chamber.

He was joined by old Doctor Royce. "If I were you, Master Tyndale, I would remove my presence from Cambridge for a spell. Do you have a family anywhere about?"

"Yea, in Gloucester."

"A pleasant place in the summer, I would expect. I have not been there myself. I come from Canterbury."

"At times I forget how pleasant it was."

"Your family and friends would undoubtedly be quite glad to see you," Doctor Royce pressed easily. "And perhaps, you might find a teaching position somewhere until the fires over England cool somewhat," he urged with gentle but firm pressure.

William Tyndale sighed.

"Your study of the languages could be done in your leisure."

"Your wisdom is respected, Doctor Royce. I shall pay serious heed to your suggestion."

Justin stirred in his bed as William fumbled to light the candle. Preferring sleep to discussion at the White Horse, Justin had remained in the room and now raised himself on his elbow as William began to pack his books.

"What are you doing?" He threw off his blanket and grabbed his clothes, putting them on. "What is it, William?"

"I must leave Cambridge for Gloucester tonight. I have portrayed myself a supporter of Lutheran heresy."

"Openly at the White Horse?" Justin groaned. *What would Tyndale's departure from Cambridge mean to their plans?* "And why did you need to speak so loudly?"

"You're a fine one to scowl. You who said more to the authorities in Rome than I have among learned thinkers." He smiled ruefully. "You know I cannot but often speak my mind, especially when men who should know better are ignorant of the Scriptures."

"Yes, and rightly so. But we pledged to be cautious until commencement at Cambridge. You only had a year to go."

Tyndale sighed, then threw up his hands. "I said nothing more than what many there also believe. It was only that a man, whom I know not, in obvious league with the king's wishes, was there to call me on it. He wrote down my name, I am sure of it."

"Then we best leave at once."

" 'We'?" said Tyndale. "No. You were not involved. They will have nothing against you. Press on toward excellence, my friend. If we are to give a fair translation of a matchless work, we must needs be found disciplined in learning, and worthy in our mastery of the original languages. Else we will both go down in history as English clods! They may attack me, but my scholarship is something else. I, too, shall press on, no matter what else I may be forced to do for the present."

With Tyndale gone, his remaining years would not be the same.

"I may be reached through my brother Edward. He was recently appointed general receiver of lands, including Gloucestershire."

"I will ride with you for protection," said Justin scanning the slim figure.

Tyndale bore a ghost of a smile. "Will you also be Master of the Sword?"

After Tyndale left, Justin resumed his schedule with monotonous rigor. Only one purpose drove him on, to learn. Months passed and the summer gave way to the fall chill. He stayed clear of the Inn of the White Horse, and was careful in choosing his friends. It was with reluctance that he took on Tyndale's private Bible study. He wished to do nothing that might shut the door to his degree, planning for the long future rather than the need of the hour. But a young scholar rebuked him.

"Your Greek is better than ours, since we are but newly arrived. If you fear to resume William's place, we might as well agree to meet no more."

Thereafter he ventured to risk the meeting, believing it was one risk that the Lord intended him to take.

14

London, A.D. 1522

> A woman that feareth the Lord, she shall be praised
> (Prov. 32:30).
> And if I perish, I perish
> (Esther 4:16).

Regina's decision came with cool resolve. This was no time for her to be mastered by fear. She had much to fear in King Henry's court—intrigue flowed in the blood of the king's men; it was as much a part of their intellect as the hunts and tournaments. If caught trying to warn her father, Lord Simon, that his sympathies with the work of Luther had been discovered, Cardinal Wolsey would not hesitate to send her to the Tower.

Yet, she must try. What choice had she? Her father would be arrested when he came out of Parliament that afternoon.

The Redfords' enemies in the court bought and sold information that put an end to power. Dare she risk going to Lord Robert? Who in King Henry's court could she trust, beside Lisbeth her maid? With her brother Marlon in France on business for the king, she and her father were alone.

Robert would not fail her now. Hope in his declared love prompted the risk to somehow get past the royal guards and reach his private chamber. Little time remained to waste debating her actions.

The door to her chamber opened unexpectedly. Dressed as a bishop, Constantine entered. He stood in the handsome cloak of black and scarlet, trimmed with silver fur. The magnificent black eyes, alive with passion, and in contrast with his religious pretense, ran over her with abrupt appreciation.

Regina met his gaze with icy rebuke. "Do you come peaceably?"

Constantine arched a brow. "With blessings, my dear, if you do as I say."

"Your blessings?" she suggested coolly, "or Wolsey's?"

"The cardinal did not send me. I have come on my own."

"Do you dare enter my chamber without knocking?"

"You would do well to show more respect."

"Yes, there is the Tower, is there not?"

"You are too much like your mother, My Lady. We would have enjoyed an exciting relationship, if only she had controlled her tongue. Alas!"

"To wear the dress of a mercenary soldier would suit you better."

"What! And lose my seat at the king's sumptuous table?"

"No doubt Wolsey agrees."

"Wolsey has his problems, I have mine. I have come as a friend. Do hear what I have to say."

Her laughter mocked the term "friend." He ignored it and walked over to the gallery facing the Thames river. "For your sake," he warned softly, "cooperate with us."

"Neither you, nor the cardinal will dictate my beliefs."

"Go ahead and persist in your stubbornness, yet expect no aid from Lord Robert. He is too wise to involve himself in Church conflicts. He has unexpectedly decided to take an extended journey to Versailles, there to counsel your brother Marlon on the errors of returning to London. Set no hope in the Earl's ability to help you now."

Uneasiness began to erode her confidence. Robert had always backed away from conflict. With Marlon gone from London, she had been depending upon his influence with the king. Constantine now fixed her with a level gaze.

"Your father has already been arrested and sent to the Tower. The accusation is twofold—heresy and treason against the king. I see no hope of pardon by either court."

Regina felt her muscles turn to water. It was too late.

"Be thankful I have sent Lord Robert to advise Marlon not to return, else your brother, as well, would be arrested."

"On what charges!"

"The support of Lutheran heresy. The king views it as a political threat to his own security. There are peasant uprisings in Saxony due to Luther's condemnation of the Church hierarchy. King Henry fears the same teachings will bring uprisings in London, and rightly so. Your father is known to have entertained and supported a number of Wittenberg scholars in his house. Men are burned for less."

"My father has done no ill to the king! He is loyal to Henry and has served him faithfully since he took the throne. How can the king accuse him of treason! The scholars merely discussed ideas."

"Mere ideas, as you call them, breed revolt. Lord Simon was foolish to risk so much for so little. There is scant hope for him now. And if you would save yourself, My Lady, do cooperate with me now, before Wolsey moves against you. At the moment, he is content with Lord Simon. He wishes no grotesque display of burnings. But I cannot say as much for some other bishops in England."

Regina turned away, sickened. A thousand thoughts ran through her mind. *How can I save my father? If I cannot, what of Marlon? Can Lord Robert reach him in time to warn him? Will Marlon be wise enough to stay away from London, or will love and honor force his return in order to appeal the life of our father?*

"There is hope for you," he suggested tonelessly.

Regina refused to turn. Her palms went cold. *What does he have in mind?*

"I have knowledge of the heretical works here in your chamber. Your maid became terrified when I questioned her, and she told all."

Regina refused to speak.

"I could call guards now and, before witnesses, produce the works of Luther. And if that is not enough, the works of Colet and Erasmus, which you have foolishly been translating into English. Such works will call for your trial before the Church court. Must I say more of your fate?"

Still she said not a word, nor turned to face him.

Constantine crossed the room to the hearth where a log burned on a deep bed of red coals. "Think well, My Lady. We are alone. Hand them over to me and I will burn them."

Regina's heart slammed in her breast and a trickle of perspiration ran down her ribs. *Dear Lord . . . .*

"If you will not, I shall bring them to Cardinal Wolsey. How much better to burn books than heretics."

"And my father?" she asked quietly.

"I am afraid there is little I can do to thwart his destiny. It is in his own power to recant. If he is wise, he will. Both Wolsey and Henry would prefer to spare his life. But like you, he is stubborn."

"What you mistake for stubbornness is conviction."

"I, for one, prefer not to offer my head to Henry on a charger."

Regina shuddered inwardly. Her thoughts darted to Justin and took a measure of comfort in thinking of his stand before the abbot in Rome. *And what of Martin Luther at the Diet of Worms? He had refused to recant.*

Luther's books had been burned in great bonfires at Rome, Louvain, Liege, and Cologne. Some hostile demonstrations followed the burning of Luther's works, and in Wittenberg students had torn the papal bull from the doors of churches and slashed them with mud. Luther had met his enthusiastic students and faculty at the gates of Wittenberg University where the young scholars had kindled their own bonfire. Luther, who was patient in his own defense before the diets, was angry at the destruction of his life's works and flung the papal bull into the flames, tossing a volume of the canon law with it to be burned. Then the students paraded the street with the edict of Pope Leo on a pole. Another student carried a sword with an indulgence spiked to its tip.

"Cooperate, Regina. Become my mistress and you will be escorted safely to my villa. Your secret will die with the ashes in the hearth."

"No. Never."

His eyes grew remote. "Think again of your fate, My Lady. Are your heretical convictions worth the awful price you will certainly pay?" He walked across her chamber and stared at the floor. Regina's heart quickened. Beneath the plank was a small vault where she had recently hid her writings, and the three pamphlets of Luther. The first was *An Address to the Christian Nobility of the German Nation* where he stated that princes should reform the Church when necessary, that the pope should not interfere in civil affairs, and that all believers were spiritual priests of God and able to interpret Scripture. The second paper was called *The Babylonian Captivity of the Church,* and the third pamphlet, *The Liberty of a Christian Man,* asserted that the priesthood of all believers was a result of their personal faith in Christ.

Constantine tapped the floor with his toe. "Shall I call for witnesses, My Lady? Know that such evidence will be your end."

Regina stood rigid, her eyes fixed on the floor.

"Call for your witnesses, Constantine. I shall not, in order to spare my life, compromise both spirit and body to your demands."

For a moment he said nothing and she refused to look at him. She turned her back, hoping her fear was not obvious.

"You are a fool," he stated vehemently. He turned and walked to the door, flinging it open. "Guards, search this heretic's chamber." He pointed a finger at the plank. "There—you shall find a rat's nest."

Regina watched as the two Dominicans produced the forbidden works and her own English translation of the works of Colet and Erasmus. Her stomach turned queasy but she restrained herself. She would not fall before them in abject fear. Her mind was suddenly emblazoned with words from Scripture memorized from Erasmus's Greek New Testament.

Who shall separate us from the love of Christ? shall tribulation, or distress, or persecution, or famine, or nakedness, or sword? As it is written, For thy sake we are killed all the day long; we are accounted as sheep for the slaughter. Nay, in all these things we are more than conquerors through him that loved us. For I am persuaded that neither death nor life, nor angels, nor principalities, nor powers, nor things present, nor things to come, nor height, nor depth, nor any other creature shall be able to separate us from the love of God, which is in Christ Jesus, our Lord. (Rom. 8:35-39).

Constantine spoke to the Dominicans. "Bring the books to Cardinal Wolsey. Tell him I shall meet with him this afternoon."

Darkness enveloped Regina like a thick blanket, but gave no warmth. She sat huddled on the stone floor unable to control her shivering. The door to the dungeon opened, and Constantine stood in the yellow torchlight, guards behind him.

She shielded her eyes from the pain of the light. How many

days had elapsed? She struggled to stand, but her legs were weak. "And my father?" she whispered.

Constantine sighed. "I regret to say he would not recant."

The expected blow did little to ward off the grief. She slipped to the floor and wept.

"I am not altogether heartless, My Lady. I visited your father before the execution. He was not burned but went to the block. His last words were of hope and in praise of the coming 'awakening' across England. Out of mercy I granted him a last request. It was that you would be taken from the dungeon. I have arranged your incarceration elsewhere."

She lifted her head. "What of my brother?"

"He is safe in France with Lord Robert. Bring her to my house on the Strand," he said coldly to the guards.

He turned and left, the sound of his steps on the stone echoed with the empty thump of her heart. She sat there numb and cold. The guard took hold of her arm. "Do not struggle, My Lady," he said as she tried to jerk away. "We do not wish to hurt you."

"Help me get a message to one named Justin Brice at Cambridge."

"To help you would mean involving ourselves in heresy. It could bring our own execution."

As Regina was escorted across the courtyard, her eyes fell on Lisbeth. The maid watched from the distance and her hand came up against her mouth. Regina's hope was small, what could Lisbeth do? Yet she took her chances and cried, "Cambridge! Cambridge!"

Lisbeth winced as the one word struck her brain. She struggled to grasp the message. *Cambridge?* Then she looked up quickly to show her mistress she understood. Cambridge! But the guards were leading Reginia to a coach. Regina had enough time to glance over her shoulder toward Lisbeth. Lisbeth tried to wave her white handkerchief, but the coach bore Regina out of sight. As the horses clipped smartly over the cobbled way and down the street past Westminister, Regina caught a glimpse of the Tower standing against the gray and misty morning. *Father, Father.*

Simon Redford had gone the way of others before him. And who knew how many more would follow? Regina's heart swelled with pain, and she wanted to cry. But, as she twisted to see the Tower disappear behind her, a surge of peace and comfort that passed understanding came to bolster her soul. She was not alone however black the night, however hard and painful the future. She was not abandoned to the horrors of suffering and persecution. One stood beside her, yea whose Spirit was within, breathing the promise of strength and peace. The realization brought a surge of joy that was unnatural to her predicament. She had no doubt it was His joy and His peace. She took courage.

Lisbeth huddled with the young groom behind the stables at Windsor. Her cheeks were flushed and her voice shook, but her hand clutched his arm firmly. "Will you see my poor Lady burn?" she goaded.

"But must I see him in this 'ere Cambridge! I've not traveled outside London!"

"You owe her ladyship this much. Who bailed your own mother out of debt last year? Tell me, Hicks!"

Hicks, hardly seventeen, wiped his brow with his soiled sleeve. "And a good lady she is, I'll say that. 'Twas a crime, I say, for old Wolsey to take Lord Simon's head."

Lisbeth shuddered, ashamed at her own cowardice before Constantine and her betrayal of Regina's forbidden books. Her nails dug into the lad's arm until he winced. "Will you go, Hicks? Will you bring the message to Justin Brice?"

"Yes, Lisbeth," he murmured quietly and, with more determination, "I will see it through. Have you got the letter all written?"

She pressed it into his hand. "Milady taught me well. 'Tis all written. Here, take this bag of coins. But do not tarry along the way. Her Ladyship's future depends on our faithfulness."

"I will not fail you, Lisbeth, nor her ladyship, but if I'm missed here at the stable. . . ."

"I will see to that. Be on your way, Hicks."

He hesitated and his eyes dropped as a funny smile tugged at his mouth. She tiptoed, gave him a brief kiss, then pushed him. "Off with you, Hicks."

He turned and disappeared between the stalls of the horses, and Lisbeth mustered courage to face the new master of the stables. The man who had taken Balin York's position was a hard man to please. What would she tell him about Hicks' absence?

15

The law of his God is in
his heart; none of his steps shall slide
(Ps. 37:31).

The frost of mid-December struck Cambridge, and as Justin walked to the dining hall his breath was white on the air. At the high tables the masters ate alone while the scholars sat below envying their superior's fatter meals and warmer robes. A fire burned in the huge hearth, but where Justin sat it could not be felt. He was surprised when a fellow scholar came up behind him and whispered,

"There's a lad to see you. He says it's urgent."

Hicks stood awkwardly in the hall, unsure of where to put his feet. Justin had never seen him before, and scanned the rough clothing. "You have a message?"

"My name is Hicks, Master Brice. I work in King Henry's stables at Windsor."

Justin smiled. "I know the stable well—the message?"

Hicks fumbled in his tunic as his eyes roved around, taking in the halls of learning. Justin read the letter in Lisbeth's shaky writing:

Lord Simon Redford hath been sent to the Tower and died in the service to our God and Saviour Jesus Christ on Monday day five. Her ladyship Regina is being held by Bishop

Constantine until she is charged with heresy by Cardinal Wolsey's court. His lordship Marlon is in France, and has been warned to stay out of London by Lord Robert, son of the Earl of Roxbury. I am sending this message at her Ladyship's request by your servant, Hicks.

Signed, your servant Lisbeth, maid in waiting to Lady Regina Redford.

Outside the cold wind penetrated Justin's robe. Hicks was fast on his heels. "Will you return to London then?"

"At once. Wait for me in the street. I must get my things from my room."

The hall was silent and his steps echoed as Justin ran up the staircase, past the other cloisters, to the chamber he had shared with William Tyndale. The cold room greeted him with silent memories, but there was no time to dwell on them. He must move quickly. He grabbed his leather satchel and threw in his books, his writings, and his last small bag of coins. He started to run out the door, but it was as if the hand of Tyndale himself had reached out to stop him. What would the departure of Justin mean to his future? If he left, would he ever return to Cambridge? How could he? And what of his study of the language?

Justin glanced about for the last time. Tyndale's worn wooden desk sat empty. The charred candle was burned to its lowest ebb. He imagined William sitting there, his face intense as he struggled over some hard passage, his quill scratching. He saw other scholars gathered for their own study of the Greek Testament, and heard again Tyndale's exhortation to master the languages. He saw all his own work slipping through his fingers. Then Regina's image came before him, as pure and bright as any flame.

He must go.

Hicks left him in London and returned unobtrusively to the stables where the master eyed him above his thin nose, but said nothing. Lisbeth had taken the liberty of giving the stable master a pearl necklace belonging to Regina, and he was content to ask no further questions. But why a lad should be gone for so long and then return looking none the richer or wiser for it, he couldn't guess. He shrugged his heavy shoulders and turned his keen interest back to the royal horses.

Alone on the streets of London, Justin spent the last of his money on adequate clothing, getting rid of his scholar's gown, and dressing as any common mercenary soldier. There were swords and daggers for sale, fine weapons made of the best steel, and he found himself hesitating before the booth. He chose a sword from among those exposed. Tyndale's wry words came back. "Are you also a master of the sword?"

At once, the merchant behind the counter began his discourse on the qualities of the Toledo sword. "Look at it, M'lord! See how it balances in your hand? There's hardly a man who will stand before it, I tell you! It's worth its weight in the king's gold."

He pressed on. Justin was hardly listening. Everything he had ever learned in the art of warfare was embedded deep within his memory. "How much?" he said tonelessly.

The merchant uttered his price and Justin emptied his purse of the last coin, strapped on the scabbard, and left. He felt like a stranger walking in his own boots, his conscience tugging in two directions.

The waters of the Thames River were quiet tonight, misted over with the thickening wet air. The small boat rocked gently as it moved silently through the dark waters. London Bridge was ahead, with tiny lights gleaming in the ramshackled buildings.

The rhythm of his oars was smooth as the waters gleamed past. Between the arches Justin glimpsed the splendid houses and palaces of the Strand. Here King Henry would provide a house for Anne Boleyn as he plotted with Wolsey to divorce Catherine, and here a bishop or an abbot, a lord or lady, lived in comfort and finery.

Justin tied the boat and left it rocking in the wash of the private barge belonging to the bishop. He walked quietly through the hedges and the winter gardens.

Ahead, the gray stone wall of the villa stood above him, hardly visible in the darkness. The silence of the night was interrupted by the faint stir of the wind rustling the dried leaves, followed by the rush of running feet. Justin remained hidden near the branches of a tree. Lisbeth appeared, breathing heavily from her run, followed by Hicks. Justin stepped out.

"No one followed us, M'lord," she whispered. "We paused at intervals along the way to make sure."

"Wait for us at the boat, but stay hidden."

Hicks was perspiring, his face intense. "Once over the wall you can reach her chamber through the garden, but you must hurry. A change of guards comes soon."

"The present guard?"

Hicks grinned. "I clobbered the bloody bloke. He won't stir till daylight."

"How many more?"

"None in the garden, nor Milady's chamber. They're out in the passage."

Justin neared the high wall surrounding the garden of the bishop's villa. He listened. The garden was silent. He leaped— grabbing onto the outer wall, and pulled himself up. For a moment he lay flat on top. He peered below into the darkened trees and shrubs, seeing and hearing nothing. Above, in one of the chambers, a light shone golden. He dropped quietly to his feet and moved toward the side of the house. An inner wall covered with a rambling vine ran along the entire side of the house. Justin made his way through the trees and leaped, catching hold. He was about to drop to the inner court when he froze. Below, a guard looked up, startled. Seeing the glimmer of steel in Justin's hand, the guard made no move.

He found his voice. "Who are you, and what are you doing here?"

Justin considered his crouched position on the wall. Facetiously he whispered, "I am a guest of Bishop Constantine."

The guard's attention was momentarily arrested by the inconceivable suggestion. Then he said indignantly, "If so, why do you come like a thief over the wall?"

"I thought Bishop Constantine might be used to visitors taking the back door."

The guard muttered and reached for his sword but Justin leaped, bringing him down to the courtyard. At once he was on his feet, and as the stunned guard staggered to rise, Justin struck hard to the back of his neck, and he slumped to the stones. He pulled him into the trees then turned back to the dilemma at hand. Only the urgency of his position prompted him to undertake the precarious climb up the wall. Was it possible? He carefully noted the stone outcroppings he could use for footholds; if he maneuvered himself properly, he could just enter the gallery. But if he did reach her chamber, how could he descend with her?

Regina heard the soft rustling of the vine below the gallery and scraping on the stone. Whoever risked the climb was no friend to Constantine. He first had to get past the guard below.

Someone was on the gallery and moving cautiously toward the entrance. In a another moment Justin crouched in the shadows, sword in hand, scanning the chamber.

Regina was about to cry out with relief but caught herself. For a moment she stared at him, then rushed to his arms. They clung together as if they stood alone on a crumbling foundation.

"I was wrong to send for you," she whispered. "I was selfish to involve you like this."

"I would have grieved if you had not. You should know by now how much I care, Regina."

"My own feelings have been obvious, have they not? I have never loved Robert. I have done everything to delay marriage. There stands nothing between us now. My position is gone, my father, even Marlon. . . ."

"Think not of that now. It is enough I have found you safe. We must move quickly."

Turning swiftly, he crossed the room and put out the light. He was at the gallery peering below into the garden when she slipped into her cloak, and came up beside him.

"Do you see anyone?"

"It is quiet." He looked about for something to use as a rope. She crossed the room and pulled the braided sash from the scarlet drapes. "I was going to try it many times, but there was always a guard."

"The climb down is steep."

She shuddered at the long drop into darkness. "There is no choice. A number of guards are in the house and two in the passage."

Holding Regina with one arm and grasping the braided sash with the other, they started slowly down. A gust of wind caught their bodies as they clung to the face of the wall. His toe found a crevice and they slowly edged down. After a few feet, they reached an inches-wide ledge and paused there, shutting from their minds the thought of the braided sash fraying. They waited. "Ready?" he whispered again. She made no sound but let her feet go over the small ledge and they continued the descent. His feet groped for the vine-covered wall and found it. In another moment he swung her down, and, grasping her arm, they fled to the outer wall. He pulled himself to the top, then reached down to grasp her wrists. Flattening herself against the wall she used her feet to climb up.

Her dress was torn, she had lost a shoe, and there were cuts and bruises, but she was over the wall!

The boat was waiting where he had left it and Regina embraced Lisbeth. "I knew I could count on you, Lisbeth! Will you come with us to Antwerp?" she whispered.

"Nay, M'lady. I . . . I shall stay in London and marry Hicks," she stammered with a little smile.

Regina squeezed her. "I am happy for you, Lisbeth. Godspeed!"

"Thank you, M'lady, and good-bye. May God's peace keep you both from harm." Lisbeth kissed her cheek, wiping away her own tears. They smiled at each other.

Lisbeth and Hicks watched the boat carry Justin and Reginia into the low-hanging fog over the Thames.

They were free!

Part III

16

Little Sodbury, A.D. 1521-1523

> His word was in mine heart like a burning fire
> shut up in my bones, and I was weary with forbearing,
> and I could not stay
> (Jer 20:9).

To William Tyndale, the worn trail he rode on horseback was familiar enough. He was home, where he had been raised in the Vale of Berkeley in Gloucestershire. In his saddlebags were his precious books and his meager personal possessions. He was on his way to Little Sodbury to the manor of Sir John and Lady Anne Walsh, to take up his new position as chaplain to the family and tutor of their small children. The position was not exactly what he had in mind, but it seemed to be the leading of God, and William found himself content enough for the time.

It was early summer and the trees were in bloom, filling the morning air with the sweetness of apple blossoms. The Cotswold hills smiled down on the green grass as Tyndale dismounted and stood before the manor of honey-colored stone.

Sir John and Lady Anne were there to meet him, ushering him in with grace into the great hall of Little Sodbury Manor. Before a large fireplace, now empty, Sir John extended a chair.

The summer light filtered down through the high windows onto the long, wooden table.

"And these boys, Master Tyndale, will be your two pupils," said Sir John. Lady Walsh smiled as she produced the two youngsters from behind her skirt. The eyes, big and round, and somewhat frightened at this tall and angular Master Tyndale, stared up at him.

Tyndale smiled at them. "I am sure the three of us will become very good friends. We will begin our learning this afternoon with a pleasant hike through the apple orchard. There is much to see that God has made," he told the two boys. "And new ways to pronounce their names. We shall afterward play a game and see if we can match the English word with the Latin. And if we do, well," he hesitated with a look toward smiling Lady Walsh, who now raised her brows, "I am sure your mother will have something pleasant to eat."

She exchanged smiles with her husband and said—as the two boys showed sudden enthusiasm for the hike—"I am sure the cook shall have something worth your hearty appetites. But Maurice," she said to the oldest, "you must be sure to do everything Master Tyndale tells you."

Tyndale was well received at Little Sodbury, and soon found himself settling down to a quiet and comfortable life. His sermons at the little chapel of Saint Adeline in the manor grounds were given in English, however, and a few voices were raised in mild protest and brows arched. But Lady Anne approved of his teachings and silenced the objections.

"Why did you leave Cambridge?" Lady Walsh inquired one day after a well-delivered sermon following the Mass. They walked back together alone since Sir John was speaking with the locals on the green.

"Several reasons, Lady Walsh. In the universities they have ordained that no man shall look on the Scripture until he is saturated with eight or nine years of heathen learning."

"A sorry situation, indeed, Master Tyndale."

"So, armed with false principles, the scholar is shut out of the understanding of the Scripture."

"Yet you must be cautious with your criticism, Master Tyndale. The clergy here in the Vale are not as learned or liberal in their conclusions as you. They oft come to dinner on Sundays and you must be careful for your own protection."

"I shall take your warning to heart, Lady Walsh."

When guests were present at the Walsh table, William had expected to dine alone with the children or even in his room. But neither Sir John nor Lady Anne would hear of it.

The Walsh home was known for its hospitality to traveling merchants and to the clergy of other parishes. William sat silently at the table, hearing the comfortable but boring conversations. Country squires and merchants from Bristol discussed taxes, the cheap prices of their goods on the English market, and complaints against the economy of the king. Tyndale's mind stirred restlessly. After theological debates with doctors and masters and assimilation of the news of Luther's fiery stand in Wittenberg, the price of barley, wheat, and oats strayed undetached through his brain. As the meals ended and the guests lingered over the beakers of wine, Tyndale watched the seasons come and go through the window. The leaves greened, then became burnt golds and browns, and the bare limbs of winter moved in with the cold wind.

The delight of the Walsh children pleased him. They were especially delighted with the little box he created with a peephole in one end, and a wheel that, when turned, showed the letters of the alphabet. On long hikes through Little Sodbury, Tyndale watched the common farmers plowing their fields in contented peace, working hard from dawn to dusk, then returning to their humble cottages to gather about the hearths. He watched an older boy plowing his father's field, and as he did the words of Erasmus seemed to sing in his mind like the hand of a skilled weaver moving the shuttle. "I would to God that the plowman would sing a text of the Scripture at his plow and that the weaver would hum them to the tune of his shuttle."

"That, dear and wise Erasmus, shall not be . . . no, for these common folk shall die and their children and grandchildren with them, before ever a word of Latin or Greek is learned of them so thoroughly."

Life at the Walsh manor, however pleasant and however much he enjoyed the children, begin to disturb him. He found he had ample time for leisure, so to satisfy his spiritual desire he begin to preach in the surrounding villages, and traveled to Bristol to speak to the crowds assembling on College Green. But the minds of the Gloucestershire clergy were not inclined toward the thinking of Colet and Erasmus, and soon he found himself in arduous theological discussions. The clergy was startled by his opinions and offended that Sir John Walsh sought to protect him from their criticism. In the absence of the bishop, the clergy hotly accused him to the chancellor of the Holy See. So it I was that William found himself before the angry Chancellor Malvern.

"I have preached nothing but the Scriptures," Tyndale defended himself. "Do my accusers find this heretical in belief?"

"Silence! You are accused of daring to portray yourself superior in learning and divinity over your learned divines in Gloucester. You ridicule them before the common man and seek to show yourself the master."

Shocked, Tyndale stared at him. "But my lord Chancellor. . . ."

"Silence! If you wish to remain in this diocese, William Tyndale, you must govern your tongue and your haughty spirit with humility before your fellow clergyman. If not," he warned, "and I hear complaint again of your actions, you shall swiftly and without remedy be dismissed from Gloucester as an arrogant young rebel not to be tolerated here."

Chancellor Malvern stood to show the proceeding was over and he wanted no further words from Tyndale. William turned to leave, angry over the injustice when the chancellor added somewhat kindly, "Yet, I am satisfied with your orthodoxy. You may depart neither branded as a heretic, nor trammeled by any oath of abjuration."

William walked back to Little Sodbury in a disheartened mood. The sun was setting and it would be dark before he reached the manor. If his teaching of the Scriptures brought such intolerance from the clergy in Gloucester and false charges of ridiculing his fellows, what must the state of the Church be! He was strengthened in his convictions that the translation of the Word into the vernacular was the only hope for the common man. How else would they ever learn the truth of God? Certainly not from priests who rushed through the Mass, mumbled their prayers and hastened to a warm fire to eat their meal and drink their vintage wine! The Church was too comfortable. The ecclesiastics did not wish to be disturbed from their slumber nor to risk taking a stand for the truth. It was far easier to remain in their traditions and to reject the call of sacrifice.

One afternoon he found the old dream smoldering in his heart until the heat burst into a new flame. He returned from a walk in the country to find Sir John Walsh entertaining a group of clergy in the dining hall. He recognized some of the clerics as the same men who had privately accused him to Chancellor Malvern. At the dinner table one churchman in particular seemed determined to trap him into a confession that would mean his end in Gloucester.

"Surely, Master Tyndale, as a teacher of the Walsh babes, you would not teach theology where simple learning will suffice. The uneducated masses need milk, not meat, else they would choke like newborn infants."

Tyndale guessed where he was headed and refused to back down. Like wolves waiting for a goat to weaken with illness, they watched his every word, hoping to accuse him again before the the chancellor. But Tyndale's anger over their hardness solidified his position. What good was the truth if he could not speak it for fear of rebuke or incrimination? Was the word of Christ to be so guarded from utterance of human tongue that one did not breathe it for fear of angering clerics?

"Was it not Saint Peter himself who wrote, 'Desire the sincere milk of the Word that ye may grow thereby?' If that be so, the Word itself should be given to the babes to grow into strong and healthy men."

The man grew tense as he saw his bait being taken. Tyndale saw it too, but his mind was made up. He would not turn back. He pretended not to see the warning glances coming from Sir John Walsh, nor hear Lady Anne interrupting to ask the servant to bring in the dessert.

The churchman also pretended not to hear and pressed, leaning forward in his chair, "The unlettered multitude need protection from wolves in sheep's clothing. Think you not? The body of truth long since gathered as the theology of the Church under Rome is best fitted for those who need discipline and guidance by the superiors. Do you not think so?"

Tyndale stood calmly. "I think the wolves devour the sheep and prefer the Scriptures to remain in Latin that their own ignorance of the Word of God remain undetected by the flock. For if the flock could compare the truth of the New Testament church with the tradition built in Rome over these long centuries, they would too easily discover that we flounder in error and would demand change."

The churchman leaned back in his chair satisfied, and a thin smile crossed his lips as he exchanged glances with the man beside him who gasped, "Do you say we should not follow the laws of Church theology?"

"I say we should follow the laws of God contained in the Scriptures and judge all else accordingly."

"Even the words which issue forth from Rome?" he demanded.

"Whatever decree that keeps the flock of Christ in ignorance of His words must be defied by authority of God Himself!"

"You have heard him with your own ears," the cleric stated to all at the table. "The witnesses are many!"

The Walshes sat stunned in fear for Tyndale. Sir John's head lowered to his plate. *I should never have allowed this,* he thought, *I should have intervened.*

"Then hear this, Sir," said Tyndale, his steady gaze compelling those at the table to fix upon him with breath paused.

"If God spare my life, ere many years pass, I will cause a boy that drives the plow shall know more of Scripture than you."

Tyndale looked from one shocked face to the other, pausing at the churchman who had deliberately set out to entrap his speech. "Know, Sir, that my confession is uttered not in emotional haste, but wittingly. Good day." He turned with a light bow to Sir John, who sat gravely looking on, and to Lady Anne, who bit her lower lip. "I beg forgiveness if I have embarrassed or caused you moments of distress."

He turned and walked from the great hall. There was no turning back now. He would have to leave Little Sodbury Manor. His mind was made up. He would return to London and seek ecclesiastical approval for his projected translation. There was only one man he could even think of going to who might agree to work with him. Tyndale felt great relief as he packed his meager belongings into one simple bag. It seemed a great load had been removed from his soul. The decision was made. Whatever the cost, he would go through with it. The call, the desire, the assurance that he was in the will of his Lord burned like fire in his bones. If he kept silent the fire would consume him.

Tyndale decided to seek audience from the Bishop of London, Cuthbert Tunstall. Tunstall was a fine scholar, he told himself, and a friend of Erasmus. Surely the bishop would grant permission to translate into the vernacular. But how would he get into Westminister to the bishop's office to see him? He glanced down wryly at his worn rustic robe. He would look a beggar among princes.

It seemed his prayer was answered and the door opened wide by the hand of God when Sir John Walsh, learning of his journey to London to the bishop, offered a letter of introduction to Tunstall.

"Sir Henry Guildford, comptroller of King Henry's household is a friend of mine. I shall ask him to send word to the bishop of your desire to visit him at Westminister. I am sure he will do so."

"Surely the matter with the bishop will now go smoothly," said William. But Lady Anne looked troubled.

"Be not so sure, William. It may be that Bishop Tunstall is more anxious to stop the spread of Lutheranism than he is in risking his position to begin an English version of the Scriptures. Perhaps," she said quietly, "this is not the time for such an endeavor."

"When, My Lady, will the time ever strike with ease? He who observeth the wind shall not sow; and he that regardeth the clouds shall not reap, as it is written in Ecclesiastes."

She sighed. "I hate to lose you, William. The children love you so."

"For other children I will sow against wind, My Lady. And who knows? One day Maurice may have his own Bible to read and obey."

"Do be cautious," warned Sir John. "London is a powder

keg. The king will come down hard upon any conceived heretic who is deemed to peddle the wares of Luther"

"Permit me also to soothe my own motherly concern," said Lady Walsh. "I have a relative in London, a merchant by the name of Thomas Poynitz. His business often brings him to Antwerp. Perhaps he may prove of some assistance to you."

"And do go by sea to London," said Sir John in a fatherly tone. "From Bristol you can catch a ship. It will be safer than traveling by land where you may run into robbers."

Tyndale smiled. "With your advice I am sure to fare well."

It was a short week later when he found himself aboard a ship which made its way around the coast of England, from the Channel of Bristol to the Thames River estuary in London.

It was a September morning when William Tyndale climbed the steps of Westminster. The narrow street was crowded with barking vendors; he passed them lost in his rehearsed speech that he hoped to give to the bishop. He found the bishop's palace as it had been described by Sir John and took the side entrance. There he would be admitted by the guards into the antechamber, where others also waited for a precious and hard-earned audience to the bishop.

It was afternoon when Tyndale was ushered into Tunstall's office chamber. The man who sat with graven dignity behind a massive desk was a courtly gentleman who eyed Tyndale with immediate caution. At present, in London, Bishop Tunstall wanted to avoid the slightest hint of reform.

Tunstall shook his head. "Master Tyndale, you ask me for the impossible. The project must be put aside with due haste."

Tyndale felt his stomach jump.

"Such a worthy endeavor under your jurisdiction, My Lord Bishop, would surely find acceptance."

Tunstall stood. *Was this young unknown foolish enough to think he would even consider offering him his patronage at such a time as this?*

"In the name of reform, havoc spreads in Europe. There are

violent riots among the peasants, the overthrow of local authorities, and attacks on clergyman. And is it not Luther's common-language New Testament in German that is behind the movement of the common man? I am cautious of anything that hints of 'Lutheranism.' Do you think I am foolish enough to risk the incriminating charges that would be hurled against me to King Henry and the cardinal? An English version in the vernacular would light the faggots, Master Tyndale. I have far greater plans than to die a martyr's death at Smithfield."

Tunstall sat down again more calmly. He ruffled through a sheaf of papers. "I have no more to say. Except to warn you to forget this vision of yours. You will find no support in England, not now. Good day, Master Tyndale." He then pretended to lose himself in some important papers.

Tyndale stood there in rebuked silence. It was hopeless to debate. Tunstall, regardless of his own appreciation for scholarship, and his support of many of Erasmus's reform-oriented beliefs, bowed to the pressure of politics and state religion. He was unwilling to stand with those in support of an English New Testament.

Tyndale was aware that politics had won and, without another word, turned and walked to the door.

Bishop Tunstall glanced up over the paper, his eyes scanning the stranger in the worn scholar's robe with patched elbows.

The door shut behind William Tyndale, leaving Tunstall alone in his lofty chamber; the great red ruby on his finger caught the candlelight and glimmered red. Tunstall stared at the ring.

Rebuffed, the door to fulfilling his goal firmly shut, Tyndale returned to his lodging. There was little else to do for the present but survive. The way before him seemed dark, and the path was blocked by insurmountable obstacles. Were these obstacles meant to be taken as from God? Or had the voice of Church authority been like the authority of the religious establishment in Jerusalem when they forbade the apostles from preaching anymore about Jesus?

One thing was certain. There was no place in all England where he might translate the Scriptures and have them printed. With his purse nearly empty he did what was most practical— he sought temporary employment rather than return to his family in Gloucester.

That Sunday, Tyndale preached at Saint Dunstan's-in-the-West on the parable of the prodigal son. The congregation listened attentively, for he had first read the gospel message then translated into English. When the service was over and he removed himself into the side chapel to dress in his old tunic, a man was waiting for him when all others had gone home to their Sunday lunch.

He was a big man, and rugged, yet had an air of nobility in his manner.

"The name is Humphrey Monmouth," he told William. "I have listened attentively to your discourse this morning. I confess that your manner of preaching, though different from what I have been accustomed to, is of interest to me. Are you new here at Saint Dunstans?"

Tyndale did not want to appear rude, but moved cautiously. "Are you, too, a clergyman, Master Monmouth?"

He laughed. "No, I am a London cloth merchant. My business takes me hither and yon. Will you be preaching here from now on?"

"I shall seek to preach wherever I can throughout London until I have decided on the way God will lead me."

Tyndale briefly explained his meeting with Bishop Tunstall and why he had come to London. Seeing Tyndale's situation and that he was obviously hungry and without funds, Humphrey Monmouth insisted he return with him to his home.

"No, do not argue, I insist. My home is in the parish of All Hallows in Barking. Until you know how God shall lead you, my home is yours. No, do not protest. I shall expect some remuneration from you. Let us say I have hired you to pray for the souls of my father and mother and all Christian souls?"

Tyndale opened his mouth again to thank him, but Monmouth waved him to silence. "You will fare better among us merchants. One thing is for certain, you shall eat better. Come, let no more be said."

17

Antwerp, 1524 A.D.

> I will never forget thy precepts;
> for with them thou hast quickened me
> (Ps. 119:93).

Andrew and the giant Nubian faced Justin on board the Brice ship. "Will you not change your mind and captain your own ship?" Andrew pressed.

Justin had turned his galleon over to Andrew to make the voyage to Cadiz to take on cargo which would be sold in the London markets.

Justin smiled. "No. I must remain here in Antwerp."

Justin's mind was on William Tyndale. He had learned that he was no longer at Little Sodbury serving Sir John and Lady Walsh, but he did not know Tyndale had gone on to London. *Has he fallen into difficulty with the authorities?* Justin wondered. The weeks passed, and his concern increased. He must locate him.

"I have other work to do. I must find William Tyndale and see how it goes with him. The English version of the Scriptures must not be abandoned, even if I will not be his partner in translation."

"Careful, Lad. Aiding Master Tyndale will place you in more danger than being a slave to Baron Soleiman."

Justin was grave as he thought of Regina. Now that they

were married he had a serious obligation to see to her safety. And more so, because she was with child.

"Right well, I know that, and Regina does, too."

Justin walked the short distance from the harbor toward the English House, which was the headquarters for the English merchant-adventurers in the city of Antwerp. The solid building stood within easy access of the harbor and warehouses on the corner of the street between the Rue de la Vieille Bourse and the Rue Zrek.

Lord Marlon Redford saw his brother-in-law coming toward him and waited on the cobbled street. Marlon had been on his way to the Brice ship with important news when he saw Justin coming. Having arrived from France for Justin's marriage to Regina the year before, Marlon had since taken up residence in Antwerp to help Justin and Regina in their endeavor to aid William Tyndale. They had been looking unsuccessfully for Tyndale for months. Marlon now had important news.

"I received word today that William is in London."

"Why has he left Sir John Walsh in Sodbury?"

"It seems he came to a disagreement with the the Church in Gloucestershire."

"So I feared. He is not under arrest?"

"No. But he did dispute seriously with certain clerics over the translation of the Scriptures into English. He had to leave Gloucestershire."

Justin was pleased that Tyndale's convictions remained as fervent as his own. He must reach him in London, but for Marlon to travel with him was unwise. He would be arrested as a supporter of Martin Luther.

"That is not all," hastened Marlon. "He went to see Bishop Tunstall about receiving authorization to translate into English."

Justin expected the worst. "And what did the bishop say?"

"William failed to get the bishop's support. Tunstall believes the time is not wise to begin such an endeavor."

"Nor will it ever be, if left to the religious and political blessing of England. We cannot wait. Where in London is he?"

"He serves in the home of Humphrey Monmouth in Barking."

Justin stopped and turned to him with surprise. Marlon wondered at his reaction. "Do you know Humphrey Monmouth?"

"If he is the same man, my father has spoken of him. Is he a merchant, do you know?"

"He is. His house is in the parish of All Hallows."

"It is the same man."

They hurried on. Marlon guessed his intentions. "Returning to London is dangerous."

"More so for you and Regina. I must know what he intends to do and whether he will risk a translation of the Scriptures without permission of the Bishop."

"If you will venture forth, then so shall I. If I dress as a merchant, I will not be recognized."

"The risk is too great, Marlon. If I go at all, it is better that I go alone."

Marlon's dark eyes were determined. "If you will risk going to London, then I will join you. Our commitment to an English translation will bind us together. But why did you say 'if' you shall go? Is it because of Regina?"

"She is with child."

They entered the English House as dinner was being served. He smiled at Regina and wished to bend down and kiss her, but instead his eyes spoke his love, and he took his seat beside her. She leaned toward him and whispered, "Did Marlon tell you of William?"

"He did. We must meet alone after supper to make our plans."

Captain Ewan Brice was talking to Thomas Poynitz, who was related to Lady Anne Walsh of Little Sodbury Manor where Tyndale had previously worked before coming to London. It was from Thomas Poynitz that Justin had first learned of Tyndale's service at Sodbury.

His brother Stewert sat beside their father. Now that Captain Ewan Brice had taken interest in the work of Luther, and was more interested in theological battles than the risk of going to sea, the family rift had eased somewhat. But it still had taken some getting use to for Stewert to accept Justin as a partner in the shipping business. Knowing this, their father had wisely put an end to the reason for Stewert's suspicion. He divided all his worldly possessions between his two sons, making sure they inherited equally, from his ships, down to the last gold coin.

The prosperous merchants, some sporting richly ornate dress and expensive rings, ate heartily and discussed the work of Martin Luther. For the moment Justin's attention was diverted from Tyndale to Luther.

"Luther himself is no man of violence," said one. "I have met him and he deplores the use of anarchy, as some have propagated in Saxony."

" 'Tis no surprise to be plagued with troubles," said Ewan Brice. "With every movement there are fringe groups. Extremists who would turn the movement of God far right or far left."

They spoke of the peasant revolt in Saxony.

"I spoke with the peasant farmers. They are quite upset that Luther did not support their revolt."

"What do you expect?" said another merchant. "The peasants have heard him denounce the authority of the Church and assert the authority of the Scriptures and the right of individuals to come directly to God through Christ. They also applied these arguments to social and economic problems."

"It seems to me they had a right," argued another. "Feudal

abuses can be demonstrated as being in error by Scripture, can they not? Why should they not have expected his support? Instead he but urged them to patience."

"He feared a greater danger than the abuse of the peasants' economic conditions," said one gravely, "and in my opinion rightly so. An uprising by the peasants might endanger the movement. Does not Scripture also say to obey the magistrates? And so he feared the peasant uprising might endanger the orderly government in Protestant provinces and do more damage in the end."

"And so he urged the authorities to put the poor folk down, at any cost," said one in obvious disagreement.

"The authorities needed no urging," argued the other.

"Yea, and so one hundred thousand or more peasants were slaughtered!"

" 'Twas not Luther's doing," Ewan Brice spoke up. "I have met the man. He is compelled to do only the will of God."

"Yea," said the merchant who had just returned from Wittenberg. "Luther hath grieved deeply over this matter."

Everyone grew silent.

"It may not have been of his making, and it is true that he has deplored violence on both sides. But there is little doubt now that the German peasants will remain in the Roman Church. They feel betrayed."

There were other growing criticisms of Luther, for a man and a movement of such growing notoriety cannot help but have others in disagreement, even among those who supported his primary beliefs on justification by faith and the authority of Scriptures. Luther's repudiation of monastic vows and his marriage to the former nun Katharina von Bora was seen by some as improper.

"Luther feels he has done the right thing. And his home is a happy one."

Justin spoke for the first time. His own marriage to Regina

prompting him. "It is written that commanding to abstain from marriage and certain foods is doctrinally in error. I commend Martin Luther for recognizing his freedom in Christ and establishing a Christian home."

His father laughed heartily, as did the others. "With his lovely Regina, do you need to question my son's enthusiasm?"

"Putting aside such criticism of Luther," said another seriously to Justin, "hasn't your beloved Erasmus now turned against him?"

"Erasmus supported Luther's demands for Church reform," explained Justin. "But he stepped back from support when Luther broke with Rome. Like many, Erasmus wanted change within the Church alone. But it seems to me that Luther has tried, and the Church has no mind to hear just protest."

"Yes, and so they would rather issue bulls of arrest and have Reformers burned," said Marlon sharply.

The others followed his reasoning to the death of Lord Simon Redford and grew silent.

With events in Saxony as they were, Luther felt forced into the position of developing church organization and liturgy for the Protestants. He was convinced the common people had to be taught, and so he would develop a catechism for the parents and a shorter one for the children. A great lover of music, he wished praises to be sung by the congregations themselves, not monkish chants in Latin but hymns of faith and worship in the common language of the people.

After supper, as he usually did, Marlon joined Justin and Regina in their chamber in the English House.

"There is no one else in all England who feels the burning need to translate the Scriptures into English except William Tyndale," said Justin.

"As far as we know, there is no one," agreed Marlon, "that is, except yourself."

Justin shook his head. Having left Cambridge, there seemed

no possible way to resume his study of the original languages. Time was not on his side.

"I am no longer the man. I have not the needed command of Greek and Hebrew. It would take several years at least. We must rally to William Tyndale. Surely he is the man God has chosen for the task."

At times Regina felt guilt over being the one who had forced him to leave. Yet when she mentioned it to Justin, he rejected her theory. He had made his own choice to leave Cambridge. She had tried to get him to enroll in the University at Wittenberg, but he had been too involved with the shipping business. And now, a child was on the way. He seemed resigned to the fact that he would never translate the Scriptures.

"It is for us to stand with him," said Justin firmly.

"Without the bishop's authorization, Tyndale cannot work in London," said Regina. "What then can he do?"

"He must come to Antwerp."

"Indeed," said Marlon, leaning forward in his chair, "but will he come?"

"If he will not come to Antwerp, then he may go to Wittenberg to visit Martin Luther. At Cambridge, Tyndale had a high regard for the German's work."

"Then we will go to the house of Humphrey Monmouth," said Marlon.

Regina slowly rose to her feet. For Marlon to return to London was dangerous. But Justin, too, could easily be arrested. By now Bishop Constantine would have discovered who had rescued her from his legal custody.

Justin was silent. His mind was now on Regina. They shared a secret not yet known by the others, except Marlon. *Now that she was with child, is it be right to leave her and risk going into London? If something happened to me, what would become of her?*

His struggled heightened as he felt her intense gaze. Their eyes met. She seemed to know exactly what he was thinking and how difficult it was. She crossed the room to him and laid her hands on his arms. Her eyes looked directly into his.

"I shall be quite all right. It is important we find William and do all we can to assist him. Hold nothing back if you are sure God is leading you in this matter."

Marlon quietly got to his feet and left the chamber.

"Our lives were dedicated to serve Christ before we married," she whispered. "Should not our union also be dedicated to Him with the child as well? We must do what we know is right and leave all else to His care."

He held her close. "How is it that God has blessed me with a woman whose heart is devoted to Him? And yet, to leave you at a this time troubles me greatly."

"I know," she whispered, "but does it not help to know I wish you to go?"

"It does, but it makes leaving you no less easier."

"I shall be perfectly safe and well. Felix is here and so are your father and brother. And I have met some fine ladies."

"You are sure?" he pressed.

"Quite sure," she said with more confidence than she felt. She held him tightly. "I will be waiting for you."

He buried his face in her hair. "I am dedicated to you, Regina. My love for you is great. I need you desperately. If anything happens to you. . . ."

"Nothing will happen, My Love," she whispered. "You must go. And I must stay."

He raised her face to his. "But though we part, we are one in purpose and in love. We will do what we must and trust the Lord to bring us back together again."

"Yes," she whispered. "If He has brought us together, then surely there is a future. But what will it be, Justin?"

"It is not for us to know all that He has planned. He will guide us a step at a time."

18

London

> The words of the Lord are pure words:
> as silver tried in a furnace of earth, purified
> seven times. Thou shalt keep them, O LORD,
> thou shalt preserve them from this generation
> forever
> (Ps. 12:6-7).

With Lord Marlon, Justin sat in the pleasant surroundings of Humphrey Monmouth's ornately timbered house in Barking. Monmouth greeted Justin warmly, having known his father, Ewan Brice. To the home of the cloth merchant had come many other businessmen and adventurers who sailed the trade routes of the world. They listened while Justin urged Tyndale to come to Saxony.

"It is true," said Tyndale. "Not only is there no room in My Lord of London's palace to translate the New Testament, but there is no place to do it in all England."

Justin produced for Tyndale a copy of Luther's German New Testament. He watched Tyndale's eyes light up as his lean hand reached for it.

"Luther was not idle during his enforced residence at Wartburg Castle. Using Erasmus's edition of the Greek New Testament, he completed the German version in less than a year," said Justin. The intimation that Tyndale could also do his work in Germany was not lost on William. Their eyes met and locked. A slight smile passed between them.

"Can you read German?" Henry Monmouth asked William Tyndale.

"Not well yet. But I am learning." He turned back to Justin. "Neither have I been idle these years."

"Nor have others," said Marlon Redford. He turned to the respected handful of merchant-adventurers who were friends and associates of those at the English House in Antwerp. "Do you bring news of reform elsewhere?"

The merchant-adventurers had sailed the world's ports and knew firsthand of political and religious movements. "Yes, indeed, the fire spreads. Denmark, Norway, and Iceland have rejected the teachings of Rome. And Gustavus Vasa is the first in his line to rule a free Sweden."

"Not to mention Zwingli in Zurich," whispered another, "and there is a very young man by the name of John Calvin who may one day stir the Protestant movement anew."

"We need reform," Justin agreed. "But without the Scriptures being available to all in their own tongues, the Church can easily lapse back into tradition and abuse. The light of the Word must always test every Christian. The best of godly men will fail or lag in their zeal. Put no final hope in leaders, but in what is written."

Tyndale stood. "I am ready to translate into English," he stated quietly, "but I will need financial assistance."

Justin was on his feet. "You shall have it."

The other merchants were interested at once. Their travels had long ago enlightened them to the broader world. They not only had measured ideas, Church dogma, and the need for England's political freedom from Rome but found the adventure of supporting a translation of the Bible in their own tongue both valuable and necessary if England was to free herself from Rome.

Humphrey Monmouth was grave. "You are risking your life, William. And all those who assist you in any way, also risk theirs." He fixed a sympathetic gaze on Justin, and then on Marlon Redford.

"Yes, I know it," breathed Tyndale.

"None need associate with you unless he is burdened to do so," said Justin. "All sacrifice must be given willingly."

"The printing cannot be done in England. Do you know what happened to Luther's other works? They were burned," warned Humphrey Monmouth.

"Yes, and my father was executed," said Marlon firmly. "It is in his memory I seek to help light a spiritual fire in England that no burning of books or executions can ever silence."

Humphery Monmouth shook his head. "Your father was a brave man, Lord Redford. And I shall do everything I can to help financially."

"So shall we all," said the other merchants.

"Are there printers in Germany who would aid us?" Tyndale inquired.

"I have friends in Antwerp at the English House," said Justin. "They will know the right printer."

"I would first go to Wittenberg," said Tyndale. "I will enroll at the university and meet Luther."

"Then to Wittenberg we shall go," said Justin.

They were all on their feet now, their enthusiasm was like sparks, lighting each other on to bravery.

Marlon gripped Tyndale's shoulder. "We have waited long for this moment, William."

"Too long," said Justin. "The hour is now."

"Why do we tarry?" said Tyndale. "Let us go."

Wittenberg University

Situated on a sandy hill, Wittenberg overlooked the Elbe River. The university, founded by Frederick the Elector of Saxony, dominated the town. To Justin the atmosphere was as exuberant as its own Martin Luther, bursting with energy and changing moods. The Augustinian convent was now deserted, and here William Tyndale would be given a small chamber as he enrolled in the university.

But providing the diversity of God's gifted men, Philipp Melanchthon, professor of Greek in the University of Wittenberg and colleague of Luther in the reformation, was the scholar of gentle reasonableness to supplement Luther's lionlike boldness and energy.

Philipp graciously received them into his chamber. Not yet thirty, articulate, tall, and slim with deep black eyes, he had already mastered the classical languages and Hebrew. Like many others on the Wittenberg faculty, he was a friend to Luther and loyal to the truths he taught. His writing on the theology of the Wittenberg Reformers, *Loci Communes Rerum Theologicarum*, grew out of his studies of the Epistle of Romans and was published in 1521. The work, in Latin, had established him as the theologian of the Lutheran movement. Luther himself had called Philipp's work "immortal."

"It is an attempt to make clear the most common topics of theological science," Philipp told Tyndale, his voice quiet and calm.

Tyndale leafed through the book. "You have accomplished much in a methodical fashion for a purpose, no doubt."

Philipp smiled easily. "To incite people to the Scriptures."

"It is also my ambition. If God permits, I shall translate the New Testament into the English tongue."

Philipp approved at once. "Then you must meet and converse with Martin Luther while here at the university. He will see any visitor from England or elsewhere. Though his days are long and go well into the night, he shall be glad to see you."

Luther joined the group from England that night at supper. As scholars, they conversed in Latin so that they might understand each other. Only Marlon, whose Latin was weak, sat with a scowl, discouraged that he was missing out. Justin smiled at him, translating the more important parts of their discussion.

"Luther and Tyndale agree on important doctrines, but on some, Tyndale deliberately has distanced himself," Justin explained quietly.

Marlon arched a brow. "On what then do they disagree?"

Justin leaned over his cup. "Tyndale believes the Lord's Supper is a commemoration of Christ's death, and Luther holds to Christ's real presence in the wine and bread."

The voices between Luther and Tyndale raised slightly, and Justin turned back to the vigorous debate.

Marlon watched Luther's large fist come down on the table with a force that made the dishes rattle. Tyndale leaned toward him, his even gaze unwavering, and spoke firmly but quietly.

Philipp Melanchthon caught Justin's eye and his smile was disarming. Obviously used to Luther's stormy debates, he was trying to assure his friends from England that it meant nothing. Luther was enjoying himself and especially liked this William Tyndale.

Marlon leaned toward Justin. "What now do they argue about?"

"They do not argue; they discuss, with equal respect, their differences. Luther expresses his doubts about the authority of the Book of James."

Marlon scowled. "Why?"

"Luther believes it contradicts justification by faith, apart from works."

"And Tyndale?"

226

"Tyndale declares that it assuredly belongs in the scriptural canon. He likens the works that James speaks of as a good tree bringing forth appropriate fruit, not for salvation, but as evidence that it is a good tree with solid root in the foundation of salvation. Faith without works is dead."

"And what do you say?" Marlon whispered, although the voices of the two other men were so strong he would not have been heard anyway.

"I agree," said Justin thoughtfully, "that the Book of James is part of Scripture. And that the works spoken of are evidence of new life, not the cause of that life. They also differ about the use of music. Luther enjoys writing hymns and teaching protesting congregations to sing. Tyndale says that music tends to distract too much from the importance of preaching the Word."

"What do you say to that?"

"I think," said Justin with a ghost of a smile, "that I would heartily enjoy singing with Herr Docktor. It promises to be an experience of enthusiasm and joy. As for William Tyndale, I think he will not be a mere translator of Luther, but a servant of God with an independent mind. However, these two men have much in common. We have reason to thank God for raising such men up to light the path of reform."

Luther now jabbed a stubby forefinger against Tyndale's knapsack. In guttural Latin, he asked, "Friend Tyndale, what text will you use then, in your translation?"

"The latest edition of the Greek text by Erasmus, Friend Luther."

Luther was satisfied. He clapped his hands together. "Abide with us awhile. The university is at your disposal. Indeed, you and your friends will find Wittenberg a haven for your just and holy cause."

Tyndale settled at Wittenberg until around April, 1525. Here he found in the learned environment all that was needed for his formidable work. Undisturbed, with lexicons and dictionaries at his disposal and the support of like-minded scholars who heartily approved his zeal for translation, he set himself a goal of one year to complete the English version.

"The task before you is formidable. Won't you seek help?" Justin asked.

"I could ask for you to check and countercheck each reference," said Tyndale. "But I realize the request would neither be fair to you nor to your dear Regina. So then! Return in peace to Antwerp."

Justin's travel arrangements to Antwerp were already made. He and Marlon would leave that afternoon. "I feel a stranger to my own wife," said Justin. "Else I would be at your side from dawn to dusk."

"I know. And yet I surely understand your need to return to Antwerp. I have inquired for a clerk to aid me and there is one named Will Roye, an Englishman. He seems a skilled copyist, knows Latin well, and is comfortable with Greek. And the work must proceed while it is day and God grants opportunity."

Tyndale opened the Greek New Testament to Matthew. His lips moved in silent prayer, With quill in hand he bent over the work, sucking in his breath with burning anticipation. Laboring first over the Greek text, he began to translate into English. The quill hesitated, then with certainty moved across the paper.

"The book of the generation of Jesus Christ. . . ."

Justin stood there for a moment simply watching and hearing the scratch of the quill. No sound would fall as sweetly upon his ear as this one quill; and no other man, whether in a drab scholar's robe or expensive velvet, would ever mean as much to his soul as this one scholar from Gloucestershire.

Justin's heart pounded and seemed to echo with the rhythm of Tyndale's quill. At long last, the Greek New Testament began to find its way into the English language. A thousand prayers seemed to be uplifted in petition and thanksgiving to the throne of God. And there came to his memory a host of other men, small and great, who seemed to hover in that humble chamber—men like John Wycliffe, Dean John Colet, Martin Luther, Erasmus, and a host of others, some martyred for their faith.

The work seemed now to merge as one sublime task, coming together by the working of the Spirit until it hovered over a single man who sat diligently at work. One man, yet one completely yielded to the purpose of God. A humble man, a lone scholar, yet he was willing to give all and to face death by fire in order to complete the task. A fragment of Scripture from 1 Corinthians flashed through Justin's mind. "I have planted, Apollos watered; but God gave the increase."

God was at work in history. And whatever the cost to those involved, whether they were great or small, known or unknown by man, the result of Tyndale's work would be worth the price.

Justin stared at the candle on Tyndale's desk until his mind saw not the wavering, feeble flame, but a torch burning brightly, growing until the light of it hovered over England, touching not only the palace of the king, but vale and city, university and parish, and the light changed the direction of history, and would touch the world.

Slowly, he crossed to the door of the chamber and quietly put his hand to the latch. Tyndale was too engrossed in his work to notice. Justin smiled at the sight, and, moved with joy, he thought, *William Tyndale, servant of God, may the sustaining grace and power of Jesus Christ enable you for so wondrous a task.*

Hamburg, 1525

In the spring, with the translation completed, Tyndale and Roye, his clerk, made the trip down the Elbe River to Hamburg to receive the finances promised by the English merchants. Reaching Hamburg, Justin and Marlon met him, anxiously looking at the bundle containing the precious document.

"We must be cautious," said Justin and eyed the man Roye with an uneasiness he could not explain. He rebuked himself. *After all, hasn't this Englishman Roye been with Tyndale serving faithfully for an entire year?*

It was Tyndale's turn to be cautious as he fingered his precious bundle and listened to their news. "We know of a printer in Cologne."

Tyndale looked doubtful. "I have heard of the Archbishop of Cologne. He is antagonistic toward Luther and all things of the new doctrine."

"He is that," agreed Justin. "But the printers we recommend are known by the merchants of the English House. As businessmen, they are not inclined to ask questions about what they print. I have already paid them a visit and they have agreed to print all we can pay for."

"Not only that, they are craftsman," said Marlon. "The work of Quentel and Bryckmann is known throughout Germany."

"For the Lord's work, we should settle for nothing less than fine quality," said Justin. "We have arranged for our merchant ships to be docked in the harbor. From Cologne it will be easier to load the New Testaments among the exchange cargoes and ship them down the Rhine to London. A Brice ship waits now to bring us to Cologne," said Justin

Tyndale smiled. "You have convinced me. Why do we tarry? To Cologne we shall go."

"Only one thing," said Justin tonelessly. "As you have already intimated, in Cologne we shall be in enemy territory. We must watch our step at all times. Our business there must be kept in strictest confidence." He looked again at the man named Roye.

"His labors have proven dilligent thus far," said Tyndale.

Justin cared not for Will Roye. Then he rebuked himself. *If you had stayed with Tyndale as you promised to do at Cambridge, he would not need Roye.*

Marlon, too, gave Roye an abrupt once-over. "It seems to me I have seen you somewhere before."

"No, good Sir, you have seen me nowhere. Else I would have remembered you as well. I am lately come from England where I fled the Friars Observant at Greenwich. I came to Wittenberg in search of true freedom."

"Have you found this true freedom?" Justin inquired.

Roye quipped, with a bow to Tyndale, "And who might find freedom even for an hour when my master translates from dawn well past midnight? After so long an ordeal, it is a wonder my poor fingers have not been written down to the bone."

Justin said nothing more.

On board the Brice ship, Justin took Tyndale to the captain's cabin and together they went over the handwritten copy of the New Testament.

"Not since I was a boy and came across the English version of Matthew have I looked upon anything as marvelous as this!"

Tyndale was pleased. "And yet my work is only half done. "I will not be content until the Old Testament is also in English."

The dawn blazed with vermilion over the city of Cologne stretching for some miles along the left bank of the Rhine. Justin greeted the morning with anticipation. The spires of many churches poked up from steep roofs, and the timber houses greeted them with the morning light. Wharves and warehouses clustered by the waterfront were already awake with sailors and merchants. In the distance the bells of the monasteries chimed, reminding him of his years in Rome, and in the far distance his eyes fell on the majestic cathedral, still unfinished after three hundred years of building.

Tyndale was wide awake and at his side, the New Testament carefully wrapped in the baggage slung over his lean shoulder. Leaving Andrew in command of the ship, Justin and Marlon took Tyndale to the print shop in an alley behind the quarters of the leather workers. Peter Quentel recognizing them, came at once. "The manuscript, please," he said in low guttural German.

Tyndale produced the volume from his baggage and Quentel's deft fingers turned the pages. When he looked up his eyes pretended innocence. "I cannot read English," he said lightly. His eyes glinted. "Therefore, I know not what I print. The price, you have it with you?" Quentel asked.

Justin handed him a bag. "You will receive the rest when the manuscript is finished and it meets with Master Tyndale's approval."

Quentel nodded briskly and eyed Tyndale. "You may come as soon as the first sheets are printed to make changes."

"How soon until you have it finished?" Tyndale pressed.

Quentel stroked his chin thoughtfully and made low noises to himself. "Soon. I shall begin first thing in the morning."

Justin explored the hand-operated presses in the long, low building. The odor of ink, paper, and leather filled their nostrils. Quentel would use the Roman type. Three thousand copies of the volume were to be printed at first, with copious notes, including marginal glosses.

When they left Quentel's shop, they went to an inn. A sprightly old man met them wearing leather breeches and a gaily colored stocking cap, from under which a splotch of thick white hair hung down across his tanned forehead. Under thick silver brows, pale blue eyes probed each visitor alertly, as Tyndale spoke quietly to him in German.

"*Gut, gut,*" the old man nodded, and smiled suddenly. To show he understood perfectly he placed a long bony finger to his mouth, his eyes twinkling. "Shh, shh."

Around the white-tiled stove, wooden tankards were soon produced, also strong-tasting cheese, and black bread. The night drew on and the fellowship was warm and pleasant. They celebrated the success God had granted and dreamed together of the results in England.

Daily, Tyndale left the inn by the back door, walked alone to Quentel's printing shop, and again entered by the back door. At night he corrected the sheets that came from the printer and returned them the next day. By summer's end, as September dawned with the promise of harvest, the work was nearing completion and hopes ran high with the excitement they felt.

It was a warm fall day with the leaves turning red and gold. Regina sat on the steps of the house in Antwerp with her infant son Seth wiggling in her lap as she tried to read Justin's letter.

Above Seth's head she read aloud. "The work fast comes to an end. But I have a strange foreboding I cannot explain. Know that I love you very much and think of you and Seth with each hour. I wish you were beside me . . ."

Regina frowned. "What foreboding does he speak of?" she said to the small child, for she oft took to talking to him in the absence of others. "I wonder who this clerk Roye is? Surely he is trustworthy or William would not be working with him."

Seth's plump little fingers snatched at the letter in her hand, and the large blue eyes stared up at her, wide and clear. He gurgled happily and broke into a delightful smile. She kissed his forehead. "If it were not for you, Little Man, I should not be missing out on this greatest of adventures."

Almost as if the baby understood, suddenly his features contorted into a cry. Regina laughed softly and hugged him against her breast. "No, I would not trade you for all the printer's ink in Quentel's shop. Beside, you will soon be big enough to travel."

Seth smiled, contented again, and begin to jump up and

down on her lap so energetically that she cried aloud. Suddenly in a second assault of gaiety he grasped a shining lock of her hair, and against all pleading for him to let go, he held fast, gurgling and cooing oblivious of her discomfort.

In Cologne, Justin slept little that night. He left the ship's cabin and went up on deck to behold the stars. The September night was clear and chill. Restlessness hung over his spirit. His heart searched for a reason behind his feelings but found nothing. At dawn in the overhanging mist that had risen suddenly, a man who worked for Quentel was hurrying up the plank. Seeing Justin he swept off his cap and waved it frantically.

"The work is known."

Roye! Justin thought. *Or was it one of the young men working in the print shop?*

"Johann Dobneck, alias Cochlaeus, is dean of the church at Frankfurt," said the German. "He is a leading opponent of the reformation, and has learned of the work."

"But how!"

"I know not, except Quentel is also printing a work for Dobneck, an edition of the works of Rupert, a former abbot. But there is no time to waste. Dobneck has an injunction from the Senate to stop Quentel from further printing."

Justin groaned. He bolted past the man and down the plank, with Marlon quick on his heels. They ran through the still dark street as the mist swirled about them. When they reached the printer's shop a light burned in the window. They burst through the door and Quentel threw up his hands and rushed toward them.

"All your work is to be burned," he said. "And you and this 'Tyndale' with it! Go!"

"The manuscript," Justin demanded, his spirit strained but calm. "Where is it?"

Quentel glanced over his shoulder to the door. He rushed to the presses and begin grabbing the stacks of papers and piling them into Justin's arms. Marlon grabbed several bags and worked to pile the sheets into them.

"Each sheet is lettered," Quentel hissed, still looking toward the door. "We got to K, but no further."

Quentel was perspiring heavily and his hands shook as he shoved the last stack to Justin.

"You must break up the type," Justin warned him. "Destroy the forms else they will yet discover the work you did."

Quentel darted to the presses. With the manuscript safely in the bags, Marlon called to Justin. "Be on your way! I will join you soon!" He sprang to Quentel's aid as Justin ran toward the back door with Tyndale's work, not daring to risk further delay.

The alleyway was still dark but the sky lightened in the east. He darted in the shadows, taking strange cobbled streets until he came to the inn. Tyndale was up and prepared to walk to the shop, but Roye was fast asleep.

"Let us hasten to the ship. We have been betrayed."

Tyndale stood momentarily frozen. "The work! I shall not leave without it!"

"I have it all here in the bags. Come! or you will not live to see it printed."

"You are sure all of it is here?"

"All."

Justin grabbed his arm but Tyndale turned toward the bed. "Up!" he shouted, "the Philistines are upon you, O Roye!"

Roye bolted upright and sat rubbing his eyes.

"Have you spoken to anyone of the work these past few days?" Tyndale asked.

Roye was offended. "Do you take me for a traitor, Master Tyndale? I, who have labored as your clerk these long hard months, yes even in the frozen winter of Wittenberg?"

Justin exchanged glances with Tyndale. "It may have been a worker at the print shop."

Roye jumped out of bed and grabbed his clothes and shoes. " 'Twas not I!"

Marlon was waiting on the Brice ship when the three of them boarded. The sun was coming up and beginning to burn away the mist. Andrew had the ship ready to leave the harbor.

Tyndale grasped the bags, as he bent to the deck, briefly searching through them to make sure all was there. He breathed a sigh of relief. "We have this to thank God for. Nothing is lost and we have all escaped."

"What now?" Marlon whispered to Justin. "If we sail to Antwerp they may be expecting us and search the ship. It would be better if we sailed in the opposite direction."

Justin faced Tyndale. "The enemy is likely to write King Henry and Wolsey of the English New Testament. They will be on the lookout at printers and ports."

"If God means that the translation is to be printed and distributed," said Tyndale, "nothing shall ultimately destroy the work."

"There is another printer in Worms," said Justin cautiously. "But it will be more difficult to ship the New Testaments into London since Worms lies inland. But the man may help."

"What is his name?" Tyndale inquired.

"Schoeffer."

"Then by all means let us hasten to Worms. At least all is not lost," Tyndale breathed with relief. "The darkened enemy of our souls may seek to trap us in his snare, but the Lord watches our steps. To Worms, then. But what of you, my friend? With each day your involvement deepens and your life is put at risk. You must think also of your wife and son. Perhaps I and Roye should go on alone."

"I think of them much. All three of us are in His hands and purpose. If God so wills, we shall come together again in peace. Has He delivered us all and the work for nothing? Surely He is with us. Let us now have peace and assurance and proceed ever toward the goal. Regina will always be ready to cheer us on."

"At least in Worms," said Marlon, "there is sympathy for the new ways of reformation. And the printer is likely to befriend us."

In Worms they were reminded that it was here that Martin Luther had faced the Imperial Diet of Emperor Charles V. He had refused to recant and took his stand on the authority of Scripture. It was comforting to know that they bore in secret those precious words soon to spill over into England. Since Luther's stand in Worms, there were many new men who embraced the Reformational ideas, and could even walk in the open, attesting to their faith. This was because Worms was in the Hesse region where the Landgrave, Philip the Magnanimous, ruled. Philip was himself a supporter of Luther.

Schoeffer met them pleasantly enough, yet upon looking at Quentel's work he scratched his beard and shook his head with a sigh.

"I would do the work. But I cannot continue from where Herr Quentel has left off. My type, I fear, does not match nor do I possess comparable sheets. All must be done again from scratch, from Matthew to Revelation. If you will agree to that, I can begin at once. It is now October, and by winter's end you may set forth upon your journey."

Tyndale looked at Justin. Justin was thinking of the long months he must stay in Worms. "Begin at once and you shall receive full pay."

Marlon came to him in private. "I shall stay with William. Return to Antwerp."

Justin was thinking of Regina and Seth. By now the first winter winds would be blowing and the storm clouds gathering. He must go home.

"Did not William make mention of a need for learning Hebrew before embarking on the Old Testament?" Justin inquired.

"He mentioned it, but here in Worms?"

"It so happens that I was speaking with Schoeffer. There is a large Jewish settlement here. Their synagogue, it is said, dates from the destruction of their temple by Babylon. He shall be well occupied studying Hebrew during the winter. And you? . . ."

Marlon clapped a hand on his shoulder. "Never fear. I shall keep an eye on Roye. We shall expect you by spring."

As Justin returned to the house in Antwerp it seemed somber and too silent. He was met by Felix in the great hall as Justin set his bag down and threw off his hat. One look at the grieving face and Justin tensed.

" 'Tis the little one, Master Justin . . . there was no hope, so it seemed."

Seth! He tried to remain calm. "No hope? What happened?"

"He became ill. No physician could help him, nor all our prayers. 'Twas the Lord who took him home." He broke down in spite of himself.

Justin looked up the flight of darkened steps. "And Regina?"

"In her room."

"When did this happen?"

"Months ago, but she has not recovered her joy. Your return comes at a needed time, Sir."

Justin left him and climbed the steps. When he reached the door of their chamber he paused, hoping to bring his own emotions under control.

"The Lord gave, and the Lord has taken away" he kept repeating. "Blessed be the name of the Lord."

Regina sat in the chair reading. Hearing the door open, she looked up. Seeing Justin she let out a little cry, dropping the book in her haste to reach him. The moment they embraced her sobs came anew. He held her tightly, stroking her tumbling hair. They wept together.

"He is gone," she finally choked. "The only other person I have ever truly wanted besides you and he has slipped from my hands."

He held her tightly. "No," he whispered, "we have not lost him. If he is taken from our hands, then he is in Christ's. Let us comfort ourselves with that."

"But why did He take him," she wept, "why!"

"I do not know . . ."

"He was so young," she choked, "only a little baby."

He caressed her, kissing her softly as she sobbed. "I know, I know." He continued to simply hold her. "We are in a very dark place in our lives, Regina. Though we have no light at the moment, we have His Word. With it to uphold us, we can trust Him through the bewilderment of darkness."

"I do trust Him," she wept, "only, . . ." her voice broke.

"I know," he whispered, "I understand."

The spring of 1526 arrived, and the weather was good for sailing. Justin and Regina sailed for Cologne.

Schoeffer had printed six thousand copies of the English New Testament and these were bought by the English merchants and smuggled on board the ship. The merchant-adventurers who bought them were adept at avoiding the censorship of certain books at the port of London.

Regina first marveled at their skill, then with an unutterable joy threw herself with zeal into the spiritual battle. What a joy! What a privilege God had entrusted to them! English merchant-adventurers had banded together to smuggle into the darkness of England the forbidden light of the Word of God. Satan must tremble at the Sword they were about to unleash upon his spiritual garrison. He feared the Word as he feared nothing else. No human arguments, no blades of steel, no human strength could make the impact that Tyndale's English New Testament would make against his forces of blindness, darkness, and superstition.

As Tyndale joined them on board the ship, Justin, Regina, and Marlon hid the Scriptures below in the cargo hold. Cunningly, they concealed them in bales, stuffed them into crates, placed them between folded cloth, buried them with the cheese, masked them with Rhine wine, or veiled them in leather and other commodities to be brought into the London docks.

When the labor was done, Justin and Regina looked at each other somewhat dusty and perspiring, but elated, and then began to laugh. Marlon grasped Tyndale by the shoulder. It was done!

The hold of the rugged Brice ship was a cathedral of praise and joy for the victory God had wrought. For the time, all thoughts of future suffering were pushed from their minds. It was a time in profane history to celebrate, for the giant Goliath had been defeated by the sling of David. God had blessed humble men and women, and turned their feeble efforts to contest a king and a rigid religious establishment which stood against the purpose of God. Yet the war was not over. Deep in their hearts they knew their spiritual enemy would rally his darkened forces to defeat the entrance of the Scriptures, by fear, threats, and death.

As the moment passed into mellow contemplation, they joined Tyndale. "It is a great time for rejoicing, William," offered Justin. "The lost Sword has been unleashed from its scabbard."

"Yes, truly, Friend Justin! We have journeyed a long way since our youth in Cambridge. Yet there remains much still to be done. I wish you God's speed."

"And you? Will you remain awhile in Worms among the Jewish settlement, or go on to Marburg?"

In Marburg a new university was ready to open with the aid

of the Landgrave of Hesse, Philip the Magnanimous. Tyndale had been invited by certain scholars to join them.

"I know not the leading of the Lord as yet. My intentions for the time are to remain here in Worms and pursue Hebrew with the rabbis. They have been kind to me and very helpful. I have high anticipations of completing the Old Testament within the next year."

"And your clerk, Will Roye?"

"Ah, he has grown weary of my long hours at the work. Roye has parted my company."

"Be cautious. Not even Worms will remain a safe haven once the New Testaments are bought and distributed in England. When the king and Wolsey learn the name of the culprit, they will issue an edict for your arrest."

The Port of London, 1526

Justin and Marlon waited on the deck of the ship. It was night and the fog was thick. Soon their contact boarded the ship in the company of a trusted merchant. His name was Thomas Garrett, and he would head the agency for distributing the New Testaments.

He was tense, but calm.

"Is William Tyndale with you?"

"No," said Justin, "he is in Worms."

"I will see the work."

They took him down the ladder into the hold, and in the light of the lantern Justin produced a copy of the English New Testament. Thomas Garrett anxiously looked through it. He was deeply moved. "I thought mine eyes would never behold such a sight as this. How many do you have?"

"Two thousand are here. Four thousand more on the other merchant ships."

"Reform-minded merchants will buy all six thousand

copies. But they must be hidden until we can distribute them. When will the others arrive?"

"Captain Ewan Brice will arrive in ten days. Another ship, in a fortnight. We will do all we can to assist you," said Justin. "We will remain in London."

Thomas Garrett eyed them thoughtfully. "If I cannot trust friends of Tyndale, who can I trust?" He said quietly, "There are tunnels in the London Bridge where other illegal books have been stored from time to time. We could use your help to get the New Testaments there by small boats."

The fog seeped through Regina's hooded cloak as she stood on the wharf near the warehouse. It was late at night, and the quay was empty. The last small boat was loaded for the trip to London Bridge, and she joined Justin. They manned the oars, dipping them silently into the water as the small boat moved up the Thames River. Water rustled softly against the sides, and they glided like a ghost through the gray mist. Later, Marlon's boat would follow, and one by one, the others.

Regina's heart pounded. London Bridge loomed ahead. They passed through one of the arches and came to the landward side where a cluster of ramshackled houses were built on the extending walls. Steps led up to the houses, but in the wall there were several small entranceways leading into the secret tunnels that Thomas Garrett had described.

Regina felt her skin crawl with excitement as they docked the boat. She stood in the darkness and swirling mist as Justin dragged the boat onto the sandbar.

In the tunnel, Justin lit a lantern and hung it on a peg. The air was damp and stale. Working silently and swiftly they stored the New Testaments in dry kegs. They had no sooner finished unloading the boat when Marlon arrived.

They knew that as soon as the first New Testaments appeared on the streets of London, the Church would have agents out among the merchants seeking those involved. If Thomas

Garrett was discovered to be the agency for distribution, their own arrest would take place with his.

Justin whispered to Marlon, "It is needful to remain in London. Thomas Garrett will need assistance in the distribution. Are you willing to risk further danger?"

"It has been five years since my father was executed for supporting Luther and possessing his writings. But he did not die for an empty dream. Tonight, with so many New Testaments, we have proof of that. We cannot turn back now."

19

Bridewell Palace of King Henry VIII, 1527

Thy word is true from the beginning;
And every one of thy righteous
judgments endureth forever.
(Ps. 119:160).

By 1527 Tyndale's English New Testaments, along with copies of the Cologne fragments from Quentel's print shop, had swept London. The conclave of angry bishops faced King Henry VIII and Cardinal Wolsey in the great hall of Bridewell.

The bishop produced an English New Testament and with a bow, handed it to King Henry.

"Your Majesty, this is none other than a resurrection of the forbidden heresy of John Wycliffe. We urge you to issue a proclamation at once, prohibiting the importation of Tyndale's heretical work into England and ordering the arrest of those involved in the smuggling."

King Henry leafed through the New Testament with a somber face. He handed it to Cardinal Wolsey. In scarlet robe, Wolsey stepped toward the king and accepted the New Testament.

"And just who is this William Tyndale?" King Henry inquired.

"An Oxford scholar, Your Majesty," Cardinal Wolsey replied. Unlike the bishops, his voice was calm. He had read the New Testament and said privately that he found no glaring errors. He counseled tolerance. But he would soon change his mind when in early 1528 he became alarmed at its large-scale popularity among the common people. But what stung Thomas Wolsey the most was the published satire against himself, written by Tyndale's former clerk, Roye. The poetic satire called, 'Rede Me and be nott wrothe,' which was attributed to William Tyndale, infuriated Wolsey, who then moved to have Tyndale arrested at Worms.

King Henry stood and walked about the hall in thoughtful silence. The gold collar about his broad neck sported a diamond the size of a walnut, and suspended with it was a large pearl. He was a massive man who dressed to show off his size rather than minimize it. He wore with flair a French-style cap of crimson velvet, with the brim looped with gold-enameled tags, and his doublet was in the new Swiss fashion with alternate stripes of white and crimson satin. As he paced, his hand rested on the gold pouch at his hip, which covered a dagger.

"He must be silenced, Your Majesty, for the good of all England," said another bishop. "He is a known supporter of the Lutheran heresy. Where have William Tyndale's New Testaments come from but Lutheran territory?"

At once King Henry stopped and scowled. He had received the conclave of bishops half-heartedly until the mention of Luther. Was not the whole of the European continent churning like the restless sea because of this pestilent German's revolution? If William Tyndale was a colleague of Luther, then he could not be a friend to his throne.

Wherever Henry turned these days he heard talk of Reformation, and what he heard did not make him sleep securely. What of the peasant uprising in parts of Germany? Had the mobs not been against the political rulers? Luther might deny his part in instigating these mass riots and bloodshed, but as far as King Henry was concerned, he believed him responsible. Luther's works were forbidden books in England. King Henry saw the word *Lutheran* and *Reformation* as a rebellion against established authority, and he feared that it would spread throughout England, and thereby unsettle his own plans and attack the foundation of his throne.

"Sire, surely William Tyndale is no friend to England. He is no less than the mouthpiece for Luther. Tyndale is a young rebel who serves his German idol's ideas of radical reform. The Lutheran menace must be silenced before it invades England."

The bishop had struck Henry where he knew it would sting. The last thing Henry wanted was an uprising among his own peasants. And the conservative English bishops were among some of the most anti-Reform leaders in Europe, still supporting a law passed a century before prohibiting the English translation on penalty of death.

"This is no time for toleration, Your Majesty," the Archbishop of Canterbury protested to Henry. "If we do not move to condemn this work, all England will be ablaze with his teaching. Far better that the Church denounce it now, and set the books to flame."

Justin stood in the front of the crowd gathered before Saint Paul's Cross in London. The October wind harbored the omen of winter, and seeped through his rough clothing. Before him stood none other than Bishop Tunstall in a heavily furred robe addressing the large crowd. Having once embraced certain reform ideas of Erasmus, he had, nevertheless, when interviewing William Tyndale in his chamber at Westminister, refused to offer him his aid.

Tunstall lifted the English New Testament for everyone to see, and announced, "Out of obedience to the Church and the King, the work of heretics must face the wrath of fire."

He stepped forward and flung the New Testament into the

flames. A somber hush fell over the crowd. Ceremoniously, other clerics brought a large number of copies and flung them into the searing flames.

Justin felt his heart thud within his chest as the flames devoured the Scriptures. Time, energy, expenses, and the risk of life—it all went up in the intense heat.

Tunstall, having issued his injunction against Tyndale's work, now urged on pain of excommunication, the burning of all copies in London.

"Know assuredly that any rebellious soul who persists in buying, selling, or possessing the heretical work of William Tyndale, shall in the least, be excommunicated from the Church. I urge all souls to humble themselves in subjection to the will of God. Accept the guidance of your shepherds with meekness of soul, and turn from this heresy."

Several people in the crowd began to come forward and throw Tyndale's work to the fire. Justin was sure many of them had been placed in the gathering to add effect to the bishop's exhortation.

Later in the quiet of Oxford's scholastic chamber, Thomas Garrett leaned across the table to Justin. Regina warmed herself at the fire. The firelight on the chilly November evening fell on Justin's face. "The Archbishop of Canterbury has issued a mandate similar to Tunstall's. He will also personally buy up as many copies as he can find throughout the Continent to destroy them."

Justin's eyes glinted. "The work of God shall not cease. If they burn these, we shall print more. The hunger is there, and the people risk arrest to buy the Scriptures. We must not hold back now."

"We will not," said Thomas Garrett. "The substantial moneys the Archbishop of Canterbury spends to buy up the copies will be reinvested to print even more!"

The door opened and Marlon rushed in to face Justin. "The

Bishop and King Henry have released an edict for Tyndale's arrest. They know he is in Worms."

Justin was on his feet. "There is no time to lose. We must warn him."

"Go, and Regina with you. I will remain here to assist Thomas."

Tyndale was located in the respected Jewish settlement at Worms, studying Hebrew. He greeted Justin and Regina with pleasure until he heard their news.

"The bloodhounds are fast on your trail," warned Justin.

Tyndale was swiftly on his feet and tossed his few personal belongings into a bag. But when it came to his books and precious parchments, he took care to pack them into a worn old satchel he wore slung across his back.

"It so happens I have received an invitation to take up residence among the distinguished scholars at Marburg," he told them. "Men of the reformed faith have opened a new university there. Join me at Marburg, at least for a few months."

"Then we shall see you safely to Marburg," said Justin.

The ancient city of Marburg had once been a place of pilgrimage for the Teutonic knights during the era of the Crusades. Now the university was its focal point, housed in a former Dominican monastery. As students arrived from England and all over Europe, it seemed to Justin he was back at Cambridge. Soon after their arrival he met a young man whose thesis on justification by faith captured his attention.

The young man's name was Patrick Hamilton. "I am lately come from my own University of Saint Andrews. But I shall not be at Marburg for long. How can I be content when me own Scotland remains in spiritual bondage?" The dark eyes burned like coals and his voice was impassioned. "I shall go and freely proclaim the new doctrines, whatever the cost. If I be not a servant to me own kin, and me own blood, I ask you, who will? Aye, for too long hath Scotland mourned in darkness."

Their eyes held, in a strange, binding silence. The Scottish Reformer broke the spell himself with a sudden smile.

"Are you leaving Marburg soon?"

"Yes. It was good that our paths have crossed here, if only in passing. It is not oft I meet a fellow Scot."

Patrick Hamilton was gone from his life as quickly as he had come. But the brief exchange had sealed an unforgettable message upon Justin's heart. When the news came later that year announcing his death, Justin somehow expected it.

"The Scottish martyr Patrick Hamilton was burned as a heretic," Tyndale told him.

"At Saint Andrews?"

"Yes. By command of Cardinal Beaton, the archbishop."

Justin sat silently, unable to rid the ardent young face from his mind, nor the dedication Patrick Hamilton had shown to the doctrine of the Epistle of Romans.

Tyndale understood. He laid a hand on his shoulder. "He left his written thesis with me. I have not had time to translate it from Latin into English. Much like my own *The Parable of the Wicked Mammon,* the Scot wrote that faith alone in the work of Christ doth justify. Perhaps you would like to translate it into English?"

"I would," said Justin suddenly. And then was taken with his own announcement. "One day I shall bring it to Scotland and preach it from Edinburgh to Inverness, and to the furtherest regions beyond."

While at Marburg, Tyndale settled into a brief but welcome reprieve, and turned again to the work of translating the Pentateuch, and two other works, *The Parable of the Wicked Mammon* and *The Obedience of a Christian Man.* It was with joy that a young Oxford scholar, John Frith, whom he had met while at Humphrey Monmouth's in London, arrived. Tyndale thought highly of his scholarship. They had become good friends. But the news John Frith brought from Oxford was dark.

"The agency for the distribution of your New Testaments have been discovered by the bishop. Thomas Garrett was arrested."

Regina turned pale and her eyes darted to Justin.

Justin's voice was tense but steady. "Did you also hear of a Lord Marlon Redford?"

"No," hastened Frith, "and yet, I fear that many good men were also arrested."

"I must know," she told Justin. "Let us return to Antwerp."

The English House near the harbor in Antwerp was of sober mood. Captain Ewan Brice and Felix sat about the table in the company of Thomas Poynitz and the other merchants.

"At least Humphrey Monmouth was released," said one trying to bring a measure of encouragement to the room.

"Did he not recant?" declared Captain Brice somewhat shortly. "That is why he is free. He has confessed his 'error' in housing William Tyndale."

"Or so he has said. Do you blame him so much? Who wishes to be burned?"

Captain Brice spoke quietly. "But with Thomas Garrett it is different." He pushed his chair back suddenly and stood, his broad shoulders squared, his gaze sought each man at the table. "I, for one, will die if need be, before I recant. I am proud to have associated meself with the likes of a man like Tyndale. And as long as God gives me strength, the Brice ships will be used again to transport the Holy Scriptures into England."

"Hear, hear," echoed the firm voices.

"But what do we about his young lordship, Marlon?"

" 'Tis nothing we can do about Marlon. He is in the Tower like his brave father before him. And Marlon, too, will likely die before Christmas. The lad is too strong in his convictions to recant," said Captain Brice. A sense of grief fell heavily upon the room. Ewan Brice walked to the window and gazed in the direction of the harbor. The sun was setting peacefully with a shimmer of golden rays on the water. "Even if he found his emotions overwrought, and did recant, Marlon would soon loath his decision and turn himself in again. The Redfords are stalwart folk. My daughter-in-law Regina is strong enough in her dependence upon Christ to face yet another sorrow added to Seth, and her father before that."

20

Forever, O Lord, thy word is settled
in heaven. Thy faithfulness is unto all generations.
(Ps. 119:89-90).

Tyndale faced his friend John Frith, the brilliant young
scholar from Oxford and Cambridge. "Yet to expect a scholar
like yourself to behave the common scribe to me?"

"I will most gladly be your scribe, when the work needing
my labor is the Word of God."

"Then what can I say? The Lord has sent you! Most of the
translation of the Pentateuch is finished. With your able correction and transcription, the task will be done by the end of
the year."

Tyndale's optimism proved true. With the first five books of
the Old Testament now in English he was anxious to set sail
to Antwerp with cherished work in hand. Although his two
works, *The Obedience of a Christian Man* and *The Parable of the Wicked
Mammon* had been printed in Marburg by Hans Lufft, Tyndale
did not have the finances to print the Pentateuch.

John Frith was uneasy. "It is safer for you here in Marburg."

"The English merchants of Antwerp I can trust with my very
life. And the work? Without their assistance I doubt if the New
Testament would be in England this day. Besides," said Tyn-

dale, "they are too cautious with their finances to give me the money for printing before I show them the translation."

In March, William Tyndale left John Frith in Marburg to pursue his own work and set sail for Antwerp. Tyndale held no uneasiness as he boarded the ship with the Pentateuch and his notes and comments, all carefully wrapped in order to have his painstaking labors printed in Antwerp. He could imagine the satisfaction of the English merchants, and visualize the first five books of the Old Testament in English being sold in London and throughout Europe. But by nightfall the promise of spring weather suddenly and violently turned back to winter, and a great storm broke upon them with the fury of unleashed demons.

Below, clinging to his work, a ceaseless prayer upon his lips, Tyndale heard the mast break like cracking thunder. The ship reeled, the cargo crashed first from one side to the other, and the cold sea-water poured in.

No! Tyndale wildly grappled to keep the Scriptures dry while wind, water, and lurching ship mocked his feeble efforts. It seemed a thousand voices laughed at his desperate struggle. The lanterns went out with a serpent's hiss, followed by darkness, as a wave of water struck against him. *Lord! I ask not for myself—but the work, O Lord, what of the work?* The ship yawed rudderless and without a mast, and the hatch cover tore loose. Passengers screamed in terror. Madly, Tyndale continued to cling to the English translation, arguing, pleading, bewildered. Tyndale felt the leather strap tearing as the waters came against him again, the bag was torn, and he felt it slip through his clutching fingers. In a moment of utter despair he cried aloud, "My Lord! Why? Why?" He was flung like a rag doll against the bulkhead and he fell into darkness.

The Senate of Hamburg had authorized the reformational faith. And Tyndale found himself in the fair home of Mistress

Margaret von Emmerson, a highly esteemed Senator's widow. He had first met her kin in Wittenberg. Here Tyndale overcame his discouragement, encouraged by the leader of the Hamburg reformers, Johann Bugenhagen. He doggedly worked again on the translation, finishing the first two books of the Old Testament by August. After writing the English merchants of his ordeal, a letter soon returned from Justin offering any assistance. Anxious to continue the work, and needing funds, William packed his meager belongings for the trip to the English House.

"I hate to see you go now," Mistress von Emmerson said, for her husband was deceased and her sons grown. She had soon developed a motherly concern for William. "Your visit to Antwerp will prove far more dangerous to your life than to stay in reform-minded Hamburg. Here, as you know, we are Evangelical, but Antwerp is now governed by the Queen of Hungary, regent for Emperor Charles V. You know how he supports Rome. And the Senate has sent me warning that agents of Cardinal Wolsey and King Henry are searching for you in the Low Countries and in Germany."

"I must go to Antwerp, Mistress von Emmerson. There, my friends await me. With their support the Pentateuch will be printed and shipped into London. Fear not." He ventured a kind but sad smile. "With the apostle Paul, I, too, believe that I shall yet finish my course."

Justin met William Tyndale at the harbor in Antwerp and embraced him heartily. "How goes the great work?"

"I have enough of the manuscript to show to your friends for approval of funds. The Book of Genesis is ready, and Exodus. The others will follow."

"They will be glad to hear that God is giving us success in spite of our misfortune. Where Satan has worked against you, God is working all things for good. You will stay with us at the

English House. A room and all things you need will be given you, and any protection necessary."

"I am beholden to all."

"No, we are beholden to you."

The merchant-adventurers were anxious to meet William Tyndale for the first time. They waited with Thomas Poynitz and Captain Ewan Brice.

"This," said Justin quietly to the men who stood staring at the lean figure in the dark tunic, "is the man."

It was quiet. Then, all at once, they came forward with smiles and strong hands outstretched. Tyndale was soon lost among them. At the supper table they all gathered to listen with intense concentration to his tale of the shipwreck and the loss of the manuscript.

"How much is now ready?" asked Thomas Poynitz.

"Hopefully enough," said Tyndale cautiously with a glance from face to face, "to receive your financial assistance. I have incurred debt in Hamburg and cannot go on alone."

" 'Tsk," boomed Captain Ewan Brice. "If need be, I shall sell a galleon to pay all."

Stewert shifted uneasily at his place, but made no protest. He hoped it wouldn't come to that.

"Let us see your work and how much is done," said Augustine Packington.

Tyndale hastened to his bag and spread out on the long table the Books of Genesis and Exodus, and the notes and papers on the rest of the Penateuch.

Justin marveled over the portion ready for the printer, as did Regina, exchanging smiles between themselves. The others assured him of support, and that the Pentateuch could be printed in Antwerp.

"You will then stay with us?" asked Thomas Poynitz.

"Yes," said Justin firmly. "He will."

Justin and Regina led him up the steps to the small chamber

where he would stay. Weary, Tyndale set his bag down and sighed deeply. Justin built a small fire, and Regina disappeared and returned with a pot of hot cider which she hung across the hearth. In kindred spirit they sat for awhile in silence.

A window faced the harbor with its anchored ships. A swallow's nest was built in the eaves above the window and Tyndale watched the birds darting to and fro, feeding their young. *Yea, the sparrow hath found an house, and the swallow a nest for herself, where she may lay her young, even thine altars, O Lord of hosts, my King and my God*, Tyndale thought, remembering the words from Psalms.

"The vigilance of the authorities has increased against us," Justin told him. "Under threat of torture or the faggots of fire, some of our supporters have recanted," said Justin. "Henry Monmouth was arrested, but was released after he vowed to meddle no more with heretics. Thomas Garrett was arrested, and Lord Marlon."

Tyndale leaned forward, glancing at Justin and Regina.

"Marlon did not recant," said Justin.

Tyndale's breath eased from his lips and he leaned back in silence. "Then what we do, we must do quickly. If they burn me, they will do no more than I expect." He looked at them squarely. "It is my friends I fear for."

"Long ago the consequences of involvement were weighed and judged worthy of risk," said Justin. "The least we can do is to stand with you."

"I need add nothing," said Regina firmly. "I, too, have faced the cost and will not turn back. It is too late for that, Master Tyndale."

"Then we will see it through to the end," said William.

"And now," said Regina, "let us speak of pleasanter things. "Your work in England is in more demand than ever. And *The Obedience of a Christian Man* has even reached King Henry."

"Is that so, indeed?"

"It was by the hand of Lady Anne Boleyn. It is whispered rather loudly that she will one day become queen. The King has told Cardinal Wolsey to convince the pope to grant his divorce from Catherine. It seems that Lady Anne's friend was reading *The Obedience of a Christian Man.* Her suitor grudged her preoccupation and took it from her. Then he became so engrossed that he would not return it. It was discovered on him by the bishop and taken away. But when Lady Anne found out, she told the king, who demanded that it be returned to her at once. She then showed it to the king himself, who read it and was pleased."

"And what did King Henry say?" Tyndale asked, moved.

Regina smiled. "His exact words were, 'This book is for me and all kings to read'!"

By 1530 Tyndale's English translation of the Pentateuch appeared in London.

One morning while Tyndale was busy at his work, he heard footsteps rushing up the stairs. The door opened and Justin came in. "Bishop Tunstall and Thomas More are in Antwerp."

Tyndale stood, his hand still holding the quill. "They know I am here?"

"No, not yet. Venture not forth onto the street for any purpose. Trust no one. You must remain here in your chamber."

"I will, indeed. But if they do not suspect I am here. . . ."

"They have come as King Henry's commissioners. A peace treaty at Cambrai is being drawn up between King Francis and the Emperor. One of our own merchants, Augustine Packington, has been sent a message by Tunstall asking for an audience. I will go with him. And I have asked Felix to be on guard below."

"Let us hope they do not suspect the English House of keeping me."

Bishop Tunstall arrived at the warehouse on the quay. His fine clothing and crimson velvet hat were out of place among the crates and barrels. His shrewd gaze drifted over the wares. Packington hastened toward him with a discreet bow, then brought him into the small, cluttered office where Justin busied himself at a desk.

"And what might I do for you, good Bishop?" asked Packington.

Tunstall took Justin in from head to toe. "Have not I seen your face somewhere before?"

"No doubt, My Lord. My business often brings me into London, as well as other ports. But what business brings your Lordship?"

"As if you did not know?" Tunstall mocked, his lip twitching with an ironic smile. He turned back to Packington who was a master of businesslike innocence. "My Lord Bishop?"

"I seek a multitude of heretical works by one outlaw named William Tyndale. I am sure you have heard of him. Such copies of the New Testament are wretchedly translated from Greek into English. They are full of errors, and must, for the sake of honor to the Church, be destroyed. Surely you know of those Dutchmen and strangers who have bought the books here to sell?"

"My Lord, above all others, I am sure I can assist you in your endeavor."

"But these foreign merchants shall never hand them over without good price, My Lord," said Justin.

"I am quite aware of the greed of merchants. Why else would they risk bringing in the forbidden books?"

"Why else, indeed? For the singular motive of covetousness, no doubt."

"Do your best to claim every work of Tyndale's, and I vow to pay whatsoever these greedy fish shall demand."

"I shall work most diligently, My Lord."

When Tunstall had gone, Packington turned to Justin with a look of surprised pleasure. They laughed loudly. The books would be burned, but the high price paid would go directly back into Tyndale's purse.

The task was completed and the bishop weighed out the bag of gold guilders. "This is nothing less than robbery."

Packington bowed. "My humble apology, My Lord. It was not I who set the price."

Tunstall looked at Justin. His handsome face was unreadable. The bishop turned and walked from the dock to where Thomas More waited.

"You have committed a blunder, Bishop Tunstall. Surely the money will only pay for a better edition," said Thomas More with a hint of irony.

Tunstall heartily disagreed. "They shall be burned at Saint Paul's Cross. That in itself is a victory. The people, like frightened sheep, will think twice before buying any other copies."

More glanced back over his shoulder at Justin. "I do believe that you underestimate the common man."

"I am right glad, Sir Thomas, that you have been commissioned by the Church to write against this William Tyndale's heretical works. If any wit can accomplish his ruin, it is your own, Sir Thomas More."

Tyndale now found himself at odds with a far more able opponent than Bishop Tunstall. For More was not only a powerful and respected man in Henry's service he was also intelligent and a devout subscriber to the Roman Church. Before Thomas More had finished his attack on William Tyndale, he would write nine books against him and his works, filling more than a thousand pages with arguments against "heretics."

But for Tyndale, the "Pen and Ink War" carried on with Thomas More could wait until the primary work at hand was completed. By 1530 the first five books of the Old Testament were printed in Antwerp and smuggled into England.

Arriving at the English House, Justin came to Tyndale's chamber and laid a book in front of him. Tyndale set his quill down and looked up questioningly. Justin arched a brow. "Surely you will answer the man?"

Tyndale picked up the book. *Dialogue Concerning Heresies* by Sir Thomas More.

Justin explained, for he had read it aboard ship on the return from London. "He seeks to discredit you and attacks the other reformers. We are called the 'pestilent sect of Luther and Tyndale.' We are the 'children of iniquity' who translate the Scriptures into the vulgar tongue and endanger the Church by so doing."

Tyndale leafed through the book and his eyes caught snatches of arguments that provoked him. *Yet what can I do?* he thought.

"I am no match in wit with Sir Thomas More," Tyndale replied. "My ambition is not to debate theology, but to translate the Scriptures themselves. The truth, my Friend, will survive such scholarly attacks as More makes. History shall be the judge whether the Scriptures should have remained in Latin alone, and the abuses retained in the system. When More and I both have gone from this world, the Word of the Lord will abide forever."

"What you say is true, but you must answer him," Justin pressed. "If you do not, your silence will be mistaken for defeat. And good men yet in doubt will be left floundering, believing Thomas More to have been correct."

"Perhaps, but if I answer him, I shall wax hot."

"Then ease your temper with prayer, but answer him. Look what he says!" Justin grabbed the book and turned the pages. "He says the Roman Church cannot err. Has it not already erred in setting aside the authority of Scripture? What More cannot defend on the side of tradition, he simply excuses as of minor consequence. For example, the abuses of the clergy, veneration and worship of images, relics, pilgrimages, and more."

Tyndale scowled and tapped his quill. Justin slammed the book shut and his eyes glinted. "He has also attacked your scholarship. The English New Testament is 'corrupted,' so says More. And, 'above a 'thousand texts are wrong and falsely translated turning the wholesome doctrine of Christ to devilish heresies.' "

Tyndale stood abruptly. His face tense. "It seems that Sir Thomas More, keeper of the king's conscience, as Chancellor of England, is so dedicated to upholding the present erroneous traditions that he sees 'a thousand errors,' where none exist."

The so called Pen-and-Ink Wars, or Tyndale versus More, was argued by two capable men, but from two separate and distinct premises: Thomas More's assertion was the supreme authority of the Roman Church; William Tyndale appealed to Scripture as final authority. Agreement was therefore impossible.

"When the last jot and title of our arguments hath been written," said Tyndale, "the Scripture alone will remain as the final judge."

It was a pleasant surprise one day when Tyndale's friend and scholar John Frith arrived from Marburg. He had with him a lovely young lady who hastened to bow to Tyndale.

"And who is this?" Tyndale asked with pretended confusion. "Your sister, perhaps?"

John Frith smiled and cleared his throat. "My bride, Sir."

Tyndale hastened to congratulate them both. They were so obviously in love that he dare not show his sobriety. "You will live here in Antwerp, then?"

"Not far away," explained Frith. "At least close enough to continue our work together."

In Tyndale's mind he could see nothing else but the glowing fire of kindled faggots. He had always been in danger, but now that Thomas More and the bishop had vehemently attacked both him and his work, the efforts to find and capture him had mounted. The king had his spies everywhere, and men had been sent in disguise hoping to find his whereabouts in order to bring him to trial in London. He tried to smile. "So fair a bride deserves more than my claim upon your scholarship, John. Go then and enjoy the spring and summer while it shines so pleasantly."

"We will go," said Frith, "yet I will return to the work. I have already discussed the danger with her and she understands."

With the coming year the situation had changed in England. Cardinal Wolsey, in spite of efforts to please King Henry and thereby maintain his own luxuries and lands, had failed to gain papal permission for the king's divorce from Catherine as quickly as Henry wanted. He had been accused of treason and sentenced to death, but Wolsey's fear had been so great that he had died of heart failure on the way to his beheading.

It now seemed beneficial to King Henry to separate England from Rome. In doing so he no longer needed the pope's authority to divorce Catherine and marry Lady Anne Boleyn. But while some in England celebrated the break with Rome, others did not.

"Have you read Tyndale's *The Obedience of a Christian Man*?" Cromwell asked the king.

Thomas Cromwell was a new privy counselor who had replaced Thomas More and was a Protestant in his theology. He supported Tyndale and thought he would be of benefit to Henry in the court.

King Henry was ready to listen to any suggestion that might benefit his new program of propaganda to convince his dissenters that the break with Rome was right. "I have read it and think the work very excellent. What do you suggest?"

"That, Your Majesty, we seek to make amends with Tyndale who is quite popular with your subjects. We could use a man in touch with the common folk. Tyndale might be a powerful force to aid you."

"Then send an envoy to find him. Offer him safe conduct to return to England."

"The envoy, Sire, is already in Antwerp."

In April 1531 Justin accompanied Tyndale one night to meet secretly with the king's agent, Vaughan.

"And if I return as you ask, what does King Henry expect of me?"

"He offers you the honor of serving in his court."

Tyndale exchanged wary glances with Justin. "To serve the king? How so?"

"The King is much beholden to you for your work, *The Obedience of a Christian Man*. Others in the court are also pleased; his new counselor Thomas Cromwell, and Anne Boleyn. The king wishes a writer and scholar of your merit to serve him in his court."

"Does the king not have Thomas More?" Tyndale inquired dryly.

"Sir Thomas More does not capture the religious popularity of the common man, who buys your work so readily. You, Master Tyndale, will advance the king's new cause of seeking to elevate his authority over the English Church. He offers you a salary and safety."

Tyndale walked aside with Justin, who said, "He would simply use you for propaganda purposes. No matter how much we love England and wish to be free men again, how can you compromise your character and the work of the Scriptures to associate yourself with Henry's ambitions? You know the main reason why he wants your service. It would lend credence to his protest cause, that he might then have the authority to marry Anne Bolelyn"

Tyndale laid a hand on his shoulder. "I know that right well.

Yet, if we could get the king to agree to an authorized printing of the Bible?"

But two more secret meetings between Tyndale and the king's agent failed to produce an agreement. King Henry sent Vaughan a note rebuking him for "over compliance." "I order you to make no further attempt to bring Tyndale to England."

"We must be more cautious now," Justin warned. "The king will surely take a more hostile attitude toward you."

The news was not long in coming which validated Justin's warning. Frustrated, King Henry, in his typical fashion, then reached out to revile and ruin Tyndale. Tyndale's works were widely read and heeded. Since they could not be destroyed, and Tyndale himself would not cooperate and serve the selfish ambitions of the king, there was little left to do but destroy Tyndale.

The new Bishop of London after the death of Tunstall was Stokesley, one of the strongest opponents of Protestanism in England. When the King sent word to the Emperor, "I demand Tyndale's surrender on the charge of spreading sedition in England," the Emperor refused to cooperate for reasons of his own. (Catherine, whom the king had divorced, was the Emperor's aunt.) Bishop Stokesley then hired a man to search out Tyndale at any cost and betray him.

It was not news of Tyndale's arrest that reached Justin that morning in 1533 but the arrest of the young and brilliant scholar, John Frith. His wife had sought Regina.

"They will burn him," she wept.

As she sobbed in Regina's arms, Justin turned away. *How would he break the news about John Frith to Tyndale?*

"They enticed him to England," she said brokenly. "And the bishops deceived him. They sent a feigned supporter of our beliefs as if they would inquire of him something more carefully. He begged John to write it down for him that he might cherish it always. Then this wretched 'Judas' took it straight to Sir Thomas More."

"Thomas More! But he has since retired to private life," cried Regina indignantly.

"Yes," said Mrs. Frith, "but Thomas More is privately against Tyndale as much as he was in his service to King Henry. Sir Thomas then gave the evidence of John's faith to the bishops."

Regina sought to comfort her, to stroke her damp brow, and to assure her that God Himself would stand with John Frith even as He had with the martyrs before him. But Regina was ever aware of how she would feel if it were Justin in the Tower, Justin who would face the conclave of bishops on charges of heresy. Justin would not recant anymore than Marlon, or her father, or the hundreds before them. No words would come, only tears mingling with her friend's. Her whisper was a prayer for courage, strength, and peace.

"John will not recant," Mrs. Frith said at long last. "How can he?" her eyes sought Regina's. Regina shook her head, her eyes dimming. *No, he would not. He could not.*

John Frith, for aiding William Tyndale in the translation of the first English Bible and for his doctrinal belief in justification by faith in Christ apart from human effort, was burned at the stake for refusing to recant. He endured to the end by the sweet grace of the Spirit of God who indwelt him.

"The persecution in England has reached a new level of intensity," Justin told Tyndale, who sat head in hand, thinking of his friend. "A dozen more beside John Frith have died. One recanted, but then in shame turned back to his accusers, and with your New Testament in hand, . . ." Justin halted for fear his voice would break," and *The Obedience of a Christian Man* in his tunic, recanted of his first denial."

Tyndale's hands clenched into silent fists. After a moment he banged them upon his desk where the revised translation of the New Testament sat. "It is worth our sacrifice. We must always remember that we light the path for others to follow. One day the Word of God will be available for all Christians to own, and to read." He looked up, his eyes moist. "We shall, by God's grace, see that they have it."

21

Antwerp, A.D. 1534-1535

> For the commandment is a lamp,
> and the law is light,
> and reproofs of instruction
> are the way of life
> (Prov. 6:23).

The wind was soft against her face, and the fragrance of blossoms and the sweet trill of birds mingled with the early morning light. He came to her, kissing her softly.

"Are you sure?" Justin whispered. "This is what you want, Regina?"

"I will follow you anywhere. Then why not to Scotland? The Brice castle is yours, the lands, and the title. Felix has already said he wishes to come with us. But you, Justin, are you willing to give up the merchant business to Stewert?"

"And why not? The trade between us is fair enough. His half of the castle for my half of the merchant fleet. And as for my galleon, Andrew will be a worthy captain. Did I tell you? He and the Nubian are leaving for the New World."

"It suits Andrew and the Nubian well. Sometimes I think you would also like to join them."

He smiled. "Nay, I have another calling," he said thoughtfully. "We will identify with the spiritual struggle in Scotland.

Our friend Patrick Hamilton did not die in vain. There will be others to carry on the reform, and why not us? Already a man named John Knox is teaching the Scriptures in Scotland."

"Then we will go—with God's blessing and guidance."

"But we cannot leave as long as we are needed," he said. "If God continues to use us here, we must stay, whatever the cost."

"Yes, but I fear for Tyndale's life. I do not trust the new man from the university at Louvain. He may be an Englishman, and he may have made friends with the merchants, but I find something in his attitude which breeds of self-seeking. Why does he ask so many questions of William?"

Justin, too, was bothered by Henry Phillips. He had won Tyndale's compassion by claiming great zeal for the Scriptures. Having fled Flanders after robbing his father, Henry Phillips was said to have repented, and wanted nothing more than to learn as much as he could about the teaching of the reformed faith. Tyndale looked upon the young man with kindness.

"And why has he sought out Thomas Poynitz for friendship?" she continued. "Master Poynitz took him on a tour of Antwerp, and this man Phillips kept asking questions about the leaders of the town, and of the buildings and alleys."

"I will certainly speak to William again," said Justin. "But he is not a man to be harsh with a new convert. You know how patient he was with his clerk, Roye. Henry Phillips is eloquent in speech. The fact that he enrolled in Oxford a few years ago only makes him more favorable in William's eyes. Not to mention that he comes from a wealthy family in England, and is therefore assumed to be a gentleman."

"I do not trust him," Regina declared. "I have had no peace recently."

The next day Justin managed to get William Tyndale away from his desk long enough for a walk along the harbor. The May morning was fresh with promise. The walk among the ships, refreshing. The shrill call of the sea gulls pierced the morning haze and the water lapped the sleeping hulls of ships.

"You may be right, my Friend, yet what do you have against Henry Phillips?"

"In truth, I do not know. Yet he is too inquisitive of your work and your habits. He could be an agent of Bishop Stokesley. With agents hunting for you all over Europe, we cannot be too cautious of strangers. If a Judas comes, he will not appear with drawn sword but with a kiss."

Tyndale could hardly imagine that the easy manner of Henry Phillips to be a masquerade. Perhaps he missed John Frith too much to believe the gracious and mild Henry to be an enemy.

"With King Henry having set forth the 'Act of Supremacy,' putting an end to Rome's authority in England, I think he does not work for the throne," said Tyndale. "If he serves anyone, it would be the bishop."

"Perhaps he serves no one but himself, but you must be careful."

Tyndale took the words to heart. Yet his attention wavered from Henry Phillips, to the changes in England. King Henry had moved to establish himself as Head of the Church of England. Would this not mean a lessening of the stringent laws against heretics? Thomas More, who resisted this break with the pope, was himself in the Tower about to lose his own head. For a man who had not flinched from persecuting others, he was about to taste the fruit of his own convictions.

And Queen Anne Boleyn had within her keeping a gilded copy of the Scriptures printed in Antwerp. Would King Henry now move to authorize the Scriptures in the common tongue and permit them in the churches in England?

"Cromwell is in firm favor of such a move," said Justin. "But the king has made no such change in his policy. It was not for personal convictions of the truth that he broke with Rome, but to secure his own ambitions."

"True, yet God may use this to His own purpose. That which has recently transpired in the court of London may prove to be a crack in the walls of Jericho."

"It may be," said Justin. "Yet matters here in Antwerp have grown worse."

Tyndale grew silent. It was true, indeed. They knew of two reformers who had been burned in Antwerp. The emperor had told the queen regent of the Netherlands to put an end to heresy at any cost, and the bishops had been authorized to do whatever they deemed necessary to crush the Protestant movement. Even possessing books sanctioned by the doctors teaching at Louvain University was now against the law.

"I am not the only one concerned for your safety here in Antwerp," pressed Justin. "Thomas Poynitz has spoken to me of this same matter. He will be gone from the city for some time. He has urged me to warn you to take no chances, not even with those who say they favor our beliefs. There are now many spies who have infiltrated the movement."

"Fear not, I shall be on guard."

Justin then turned to him. "Regina and I are soon to try our hand in Scotland. Will you come with us!"

Tyndale smiled. "I wish your witness in Scotland to flourish as the heather itself in spring. Yet, I cannot follow. I will remain here. I am safe until Christ Himself has said, "Your work is done.'"

Still troubled, Justin walked back with him to his chamber at the English House. Tyndale at once resumed his work on the new edition of the New Testament. Justin stood watching him for a moment, then turned as a servant in the house appeared on the steps.

"It is your father, Captain Ewan Brice. I fear, Sir, that he has taken ill. He is on board Captain Stewert Brice's ship."

Justin found Regina and Stewert in the cabin. His father lay on the small bed. Felix, too, was there, and Andrew. At once, Justin knelt, taking his father's hand. " 'Tis only a little pain in me chest," he said with difficulty, pale and perspiring. " 'Twill go away. What did you feed me?" he tried to jest with Stewert.

Stewert drew near and knelt beside Justin. For the first time in his life Stewert broke down, his heavy shoulders shaking as he buried his face into his father's neck. "You must not die and leave us, my Father. 'Tis only now we began to know each other."

Ewan Brice sighed heavily, his breathing labored. He tried to solace Stewert with a squeeze of his hand, but Stewert found the usually strong grasp weak.

"How can we aid you?" Justin asked quickly. "Has a doctor been sent for?"

"He has," said Regina, "it happened so quickly. . . ."

" 'Tsk," whispered Ewan Brice. " 'Twas a long time in coming, a very long time, weep not for me, my Sons, I go to a far fairer abode than ever we have found here."

He reached now to Justin who clasped his hand. The blue eyes grew moist as they rested on Justin's face. "Yea . . . yer precious mother was right in naming you so . . . a better son I could not have been blessed with. It is for you to be strong . . . the work is only beginning . . . you must carry it to Scotland, Lad . . . she languishes."

"Yes," whispered Justin, "to Scotland."

Ewan Brice turned his eyes to Stewert. "And thou, my troubled Lion . . . thou must find peace."

"I have such peace, Father, but regrets as well."

Ewan Brice tried to shake his head but grew too weak. Stewert leaned his ear close to his father's mouth as he formed the words, "Forgetting those things which are behind—reaching

271

forth to those things which lie ahead—let us . . . press on to Christ."

"I had hoped we might have lunch together, Master Tyndale," said Henry Phillips in his gracious manner. "But the fine Dame of the House assures me you were going out this afternoon to dine elsewhere. A pity! For I wished to speak to you about a friend, a priest by the name of Gabrielle Donne. He is likely to be appointed the new abbot of Buckfastleigh in Devon. He seems inclined toward the need of reform, and I thought you might set him to the right path with your fair works."

Again, as he had in the past, Henry Phillips, a tall and handsome man, moved about the chamber admiring Tyndale's small library and speaking zealously of his work. "The light has dawned upon England, Master Tyndale, and who shall be able to put it out?"

"Yes, but it has not shone brightly enough, Henry. I shall not be content until the king authorizes the usage of the Scriptures in churches and homes."

"May God grant it to be so," sighed Henry Phillips.

Tyndale stood and smiled. "I would not think of sending you away without a hearty discourse over lunch. Surely Mistress Poynitz will be right glad to have you at her table."

"I fear not, Sir. With Thomas Poynitz out of town these weeks, I would not wish to impose. I would ask you to be my guest in town, but to my embarrassment I left my purse in my room." He shook his head and threw up his hands as if disgusted with himself. "I suppose I was only anxious to tell you of my friend."

"You shall be my guest," said Tyndale suddenly. "I will be most interested to hear of the priest."

Henry Phillips hastened to grab Tyndale's cloak from the

hook, and smiled. "You are truly a fair man, William Tyndale. I shall not forget this kindness."

The narrow, cobbled streets of Antwerp twisted and turned in many directions. Some of the streets Henry Phillips led him down were so narrow they had to walk in single file. The tall buildings overhead cast the shadows of darkness upon their path.

Henry Phillips lapsed into silence, which Tyndale found unusual. Walking beside him, Tyndale's mind turned to Justin's warning. He looked sideways at the young man who hurried forward. It seemed his breathing was rapid and his jaw tense. Tiny beads of moisture glistened on the smooth forehead.

Ahead stood several soldiers with drawn swords. Suddenly Tyndale stopped and understood. The street narrowed, affording no escape. A sigh escaped his lips, and he drew his worn cloak more tightly about his thin shoulders.

Henry Phillips stepped behind Tyndale and pointed his finger down over his head to identify the man. They came running toward him, but Tyndale made no move to turn and flee. The rope cut into his flesh as they hastened to bind him.

"Let me return for my books and papers," he pleaded.

Without a word they ushered him off to the attorney's home some twenty-four miles away from Antwerp, and then on horseback to the sullen castle of Vilvoorde, six miles from Brussels.

Justin knocked on Tyndale's door and waited. When there was no answer he opened the latch and looked in. The chamber had been ransacked.

In two strides he was at Tyndale's desk. The books and papers were gone! In a moment of helpless wrath against his own simplicity, he slammed his fist against the table with a cry. He ran to the stairs and shouted for the servant.

"I have been out this afternoon, Sir Brice, but earlier, Master Tyndale left with Henry Phillips."

Regina rushed to Justin's side. One look at his face and she knew what had happened. "Henry Phillips."

At the urgent message sent by his wife, Thomas Poynitz returned to Antwerp. Gathering with Walter Marsh, the leader of the English House, and the other English merchants, he paced the floor in anguish. The others sat stunned, shaking their heads in anger or grief.

"It is my error. I should have known better than to trust him," said Poynitz.

"We are all to blame, we should have guarded William more carefully," lamented Augustine Packington, and shook his head in disbelief.

"This is an unheard of breach of the privilege of the English merchants. They had no right to enter this house nor to search his chamber. We shall protest to the court in Brussels."

"And write to John also," said Mrs. Poynitz, speaking of her husband's brother, lord of the manor of North Ockenden in Essex. "Perhaps he can appeal to King Henry."

"We will all write, and work tirelessly to do what we can," said another sadly, "but I fear our strength is too small to aid William, now that he is out of our authority here."

"Yes, I fear the same," said Thomas Poynitz. Emperor Charles V is turning upon the Protestants with swift wrath since King Henry has torn England asunder from Rome. He wishes to convince Rome he is a 'loyal son.' Yet, I am determined to fight this with all my strength. The death of Tyndale will be a great hindrance to the gospel, and, to the enemies of it, one of the highest pleasures."

Through the entire meeting, Justin had been silent. He stood staring out the window as the last rays of daylight flickered over the harbor. William Tyndale was in a dungeon in Vilvoorde Castle, and fifty armed men could not get him out, much less the protests of Thomas Poynitz and the merchants. Regina read his expression and simply walked up beside him and slipped her cold trembling hand into his. He put his arm about her waist and drew her to his side.

Good to his word, Thomas Poynitz labored tirelessly to have Tyndale released from Vilvoorde, writing King Henry and pleading with Cromwell for their intervention. "You have never had a more loyal subject than in the translator nor a man of higher character."

Justin and Regina, in company with the other English merchants, appealed to the queen regent, Mary of Hungary, yet their efforts proved hopeless.

"I must go to Vilvoorde to try to see him," Justin told Regina.

Her heart seemed to lurch with fear. "If something ill befalls you," she pleaded, "I do not know if I can bear it."

His voice was calm and steady, and she did not like the implication of quiet resolve, nor the look of gravity in his eyes. "I will return to you," he insisted.

"If not, . . ." her voice broke.

"By the grace of God, Regina, I will. We will go to Scotland as we planned. Stewert has offered to take us there in his ship."

She was not listening. "If you must go to Vilvoorde, I too, shall go," she pleaded desperately, her hands clutching his arms. "If something happens. . . ."

He kissed her softly. "No, Regina, not this time." His voice was quiet but his determination silenced the protest on her tongue. "This time you must stay. Andrew and Felix have promised to guard you. I shall be back in a fortnight."

He embraced her and she clung to him. He kissed her, then turned and left. She watched him go. Then Felix spoke to her.

"Have peace, My Lady. Master Justin will return. He goes alone because he knows that Master Tyndale shall die and he wishes you not to see it. Yet, his own allegiance to all that William Tyndale dies for, demands that he be there."

22

Vilvoorde Castle, Brussels, 1535-1536

> All scripture is given by inspiration of God,
> and is profitable for doctrine, for reproof,
> for correction, for instruction in righteousness;
> That the man of God may be perfect,
> thoroughly furnished unto all good works
> (2 Tim. 3: 16-17).

William Tyndale rubbed his cold, stiff hands together to regain some feeling before picking up his quill. He glanced toward the dim light of the tiny window giving him a precious few hours to write. The frigid cell was dank and foul, and the sound of the lapping water of the moat drifted to his ears. The scratch of the quill was heard as in Latin he began in thoughtful deliberation.

"I believe, right Worshipful, that you are not ignorant of what has been determined concerning me by the Council of Brabant; therefore I entreat your Lordship, and that by the Lord Jesus, that if I am to remain here during the winter, you will request the Procurer to be kind enough to send me from my goods, which he has in his possession, a warmer cap, for I suffer extremely from cold in the head, being afflicted with perpetual catarrh, which is considerable in the cell.

"A warmer coat also, for that which I have is very thin; also a piece of cloth to patch my leggings: my overcoat has been worn out. He has a woolen shirt of mine, if he will be kind enough to send it. I have also with him leggings of thicker cloth for the putting on above; he also has warmer caps for wearing at night. I wish also his permission to have a candle in the evening, for it is wearisome to sit alone in the dark.

"But above all, I entreat and beseech your clemency to be urgent with the Procurer that he may kindly permit me to have my Hebrew Bible, Hebrew Grammar, and Hebrew Dictionary, that I may spend my time with that study. And in return, may you obtain your dearest wish, provided always it be consistent with the salvation of your soul. But if any other resolutions have been come to concerning me, before the conclusion of the winter, I shall be patient, abiding the will of God to the glory of the grace of my Lord Jesus Christ, whose spirit, I pray, may ever direct your heart. Amen.

W. Tyndale"

The end, Tyndale had thought would come swiftly, but he was wrong. For fifteen months in the dank dungeon, infested with rats and cold, he waited for the decision. The commission which was to judge him was appointed in the autumn by the queen regent in service to Emperor Charles V. Tyndale had one small satisfaction—his accusers had to translate from English into Latin his works for those who could not speak his tongue. As they labored over his writings he hoped the light might begin to dawn upon their own convictions.

The wet winter was over before the trial proceeded. Tyndale was sure in his own mind what the final outcome would be. But the delay in time gave him opportunity to work on the translation of the Old Testament. Late into the night he worked by the light of a candle, his quill scratching boldly on the theme of the believer's justification by faith, his soul burning with the flame of that profound truth, even though his body shivered with cold and rheumatism.

One supreme conviction held his desire captive: that King Henry VIII would permit the bare text of the English translation to be set up in the churches throughout England. To that end, he prayed, to that end he continued to labor, knowing his time was short.

For over six months he was under questioning. The prosecuting ecclesiastics visited him in his cell or called him to be brought by the guard of soldiers to the great hall where the judges were seated at a long ornate table, robed grandly in their religious garb or severely in civic robes. The oral examination was conducted in Latin and centered primarily on theological disputes. For six months the ordeal continued. In early August 1536 the judgment was rendered by the commission.

The Procurer General stood with a long scroll of written accusations. He fixed his gaze upon William Tyndale who stood silent before them. As the Procurer's ponderous voice distinctly articulated the charges, the words echoed against the stone hall where the torches blazed down upon them.

"William Tyndale, you do stand before this authorized commission as one hereby found guilty of the charges of heresy. By such evidence as we have before us in written form in your own hand, which you have also confessed as true by your own tongue; you are branded by your superiors as a wretched man, guilty of unlawfully translating the Scripture from Latin into English.

"And secondly, you are accused of doctrinal heresy in propagating the belief that faith in Jesus Christ alone justifies the sinner. At the same time you are adamant in clinging to your belief that tradition has no divine authority to bind the Christian's conscience to supreme obedience to the teachings of the Church at Rome but has set such divine traditions aside as secondary to the teaching of the Scriptures. In so doing you are in disobedience to the true Head of the Church, even His Holiness as Saint Peter's successor, and thereby your lord and master. In so propagating these heresies, in favor of the heretical beliefs of the reformational faith, you have denied the teaching of the Church by setting aside the doctrine of purgatory, the intercession of the Virgin and Saints on our behalf, and that they should not be evoked by the Christian in his soul's deliverance.

"This commission, in the month of August, and in the year of our Lord, 1536, finds you, William Tyndale supremely guilty according to the Imperial laws against heresy. Thereby you are found to be worthy of the sentence of degradation and death. Amen."

Justin rode his horse in view of Vilvoorde, which stood sullenly against the bleak fall sky. The castle had been built in 1374 by a duke of Brabant, and it was comparable to the Bastille, which had been built in Paris about that same time. Surrounded by a moat, with seven high towers and three drawbridges, the thick walls made Vilvoorde an impregnable fortress. The castle was now being used as the state prison for the Low Countries.

He rode across the drawbridge as the horse's hoofs echoed on wood. The gate was open and he rode through. A number of rugged soldiers were there, and an officer stopped him abruptly. Justin handed him the letter he had received from the Procurer in reply to his own letter. The officer handed it back and ushered him forward across the courtyard to an inner bailey. The rough-hewn steps led him up into a keep where the Procurer's guard met him.

"You are permitted a brief visit. I myself shall accompany you."

The passage down to the dungeons was lit with torches on the stone wall. Another flight of steps led down below the castle. Justin felt the cold dampness penetrate his woolen cloak.

He walked to the cell, and Tyndale looked up. At first he squinted to see who it was, thinking it might be the soldiers of the Imperial Guard to take him away. Seeing that it was Justin, Tyndale was on his feet and quickly to the bars. They grasped each other's arms in mutual affection.

"I thought I would never see a friendly face again, least of all yours," said Tyndale. "The Lord has granted me a kindness, indeed!"

"We have interceded before King Henry and Cromwell, but the matter goes ill. If England is no longer bent on your destruction, it has done little to intercede. Cromwell has written to the governor of Vilvoorde, but without success. It seems that since Charles V of Spain has failed to burn Luther, he will be satisfied to have you."

Tyndale was silent for a minute. "I have expected no better, my friend. If they shall burn me, they shall do none other thing than I looked for. There is none other way into the kingdom of life than through persecution and suffering of pain, and of very death after the example of Christ. But our enemy is not flesh and blood, but the archenemy of Christ Himself who bestires men's minds to wrath and rejection of His Truth."

"You have said it well. If ever the light is to dawn, it will come through spiritual warfare and will mean the sacrifice of many. The enemy fears nothing more than the light of the Scriptures spreading throughout the world. And so I shall go on to Edinburgh," said Justin.

Tyndale considered his statement, understanding all that it could mean. He was quiet, then slowly nodded affirmatively. "You have chosen a rocky path to tread, yet worth the momentary sacrifice."

"Thomas Poynitz was arrested but is now free."

"Praise God for that. I should loath to die knowing I have brought such a good friend to death with me."

"They speak of his banishment from the Low Countries, and

the loss of his merchant business, but he and certain of the English merchants are determined to go on. Your arrest has kindled their zeal even further. I bring you their hearty affection, their deep gratitude for your work, Master Tyndale, and their unceasing prayers for your strength and courage."

"Being of like mind, Justin, the fellowship of your own convictions is an encouragement to me now. With the fairest of apostles I can say, 'My departure is at hand.' "

The guard motioned that his time was up. Justin took off his woolen cloak, looking first to the guard for permission to give it to Tyndale. He stepped forward and checked every inch of cloth before nodding. Tyndale took it gratefully.

"Then it is here we part," said Justin.

There was a shared moment of deep silence. Then Justin gripped Tyndale's forearm. "As a lesser soldier I dare to leave you these words. The Grace of Christ will be with you and His nearness shall consume your heart with peace. And when in that moment you stand alone before those who are the lions of your flesh, remember to lean hard upon His breast for all that your soul shall tremble to face, and you will, according to His faithfulness, find it not wanting. For it is written that the death of His saints is precious in His sight. How much more a man who hath labored to suffer any price, and bear any burden these many years to bring His Word to the people of England. Yes, Master William Tyndale, your labors by the Spirit of God will not be in vain. Generations will arise to pronounce your name good; and the names of those who once stood so mighty in position to oppose you in translating the Holy Scriptures into English will be remembered for ill, as fighting not you but God."

Tyndale was moved. "Your words of solace are accepted in humble gratitude. Go, and be at peace as well. I face the future with eternal confidence. I should rather be a doorkeeper in the house of the Lord, then to dwell in the tents of wickedness, however comfortable they may be at this moment in fleeting time. No, not all of their fair robes nor their momentary glory will be worth one glimpse of His face. And I? By His finished work of redemption I shall see it forever! Farewell. Go and be faithful in the place God has put you to serve Him."

On August 10 the ritual of degradation began, that of casting Tyndale out of the Church as a heretic.

Escorted by the Imperial Guard, Tyndale was led to the town square at Vilvoorde where a crowd had gathered. His eyes flickered over the curious faces of the peasants, and the wealthier townsfolk. How many of them truly understood the reason for his ordeal? There was a din of voices, then silence, as the pageant of ecclesiastical and civil dignitaries assembled on the raised platform. As his eyes moved away, they fell on Justin below in the crowd.

Tyndale was led forth in a priest's robe. For that robe he had first entered Magdalen College in 1508 as a young boy. For eight tedious years at Oxford he had excelled in theology, the arts, and, especially in the original languages, to receive Master of Arts, then on to Cambridge for extensive studies in Greek.

But now the painful ritual in reverse began. Justin watched as they forced him to kneel. The knife in the agent's hand symbolically scraped away the benefitting oil of priestly consecration from his hands and bowed head. They hauled him to his feet. Across the platform came a priest bringing the bread and wine of the Lord's Supper. As they had requested, Tyndale accepted the bread and the cup, but as he took them, the agent abruptly struck both from his hands, and they scattered across the platform. A wince and a groan uttered from the crowd but was drowned out by the somber chant in Latin which uttered condemnation, denying him the right to partake of the Sacrament which the Church leaders thought were necessary for eternal life. The priest's vesture was then ripped from his body.

The bishop's fulmination's were heard over the echo of tolling bells.

It was October and the sunlight was crimson on the horizon of Vilvoorde. As Tyndale was led for the last time across the square to his place of death, the chill wind struck against his worn clothes, rustling the woolen cloak Justin had given him. The crowd was already in position behind a barricade of stakes, which had been hastily put up the night before in order to keep back what the authorities knew would be a large gathering. In that crowd there mingled friend, foe, and the merely curious. In the center of the square was a large wooden pole, his place of execution. A long chain hung from the pole, and a noose of hemp was laced through it.

The ecclesiastical pageantry for the second time marched in and took their elevated positions, their faces grave.

Justin interceded silently in prayer as William Tyndale raised his hands to be tied, and the executioner placed the chain about his throat, then waited silently for the command. The steadfast look of conviction on Tyndale's haggard face brought a sudden flash of unutterable emotion to Justin's heart. The purpose for which he would die, as it had always been, was firm and irrevocable. Neither the feel of the harsh rope nor the restriction of the tightening chain unnerved a soul in which the indwelling Christ was sustaining. In heaven, Christ the great High Priest made intercession for his servant, and Tyndale knew the faithfulness of the One he had served. The loud voice of his earthly accuser now shouted:

"You wretched soul, recant! Consider your destiny, O heretic. Recant now! Save yourself from the flame."

It was as if another Voice in heaven and within William Tyndale himself silenced the earthly din. Like the sound of a trumpet, and as sweetly as a dove, the Voice told Tyndale, "I am with you . . . be faithful unto death and I will give you a crown of life . . . you shall walk with Me in white . . . I will never leave you, nor forsake you."

William Tyndale took in a deep breath and his voice shouted in passionate prayer, "Lord, open the King of England's eyes!"

The faggots, brush, and wood were piled about his feet. The executioner moved at signal, and Tyndale was strangled. The attorney stepped forward and with a lighted torch set the brush to leaping flame.

Here is an exhoration from William Tyndale, taken from his prologue on the Epistle of Romans in his 1534 edition:

> I think it meet that every Christian man not only know it [Romans] by rote and without the book, but also exercise himself therein evermore continually, as with the daily bread of the soul. No man verily can read it too oft or study it too well; for the more it is studied the easier it is, the more it is chewed the pleasanter it is, and the more groundly it is searched the preciouser things are found in it, so great treasure of spiritual things lieth hid therein. . . .
>
> Now go to, Reader, and according to the order of Paul's writing, even so do thou.
>
> First, behold thyself diligently in the law of God, and see there thy just damnation. Secondarily turn thy eye to Christ, and see there the exceeding mercy of thy most kind and loving Father. Thirdly remember that Christ made not this atonement that thou shouldest anger God again: neither died he for thy sins, that thou shouldst live still in them: neither cleansed he thee, that thou shouldst return (as a swine) unto thine own puddle again: but that thou shouldst be a new creature and live a new life after the will of God and not of the flesh. And be diligent lest through thine own negligence and unthankfulness thou lose this favour and mercy again.

23

London, the Palace of Greenwich,
1537-1539

> Thy word is a lamp unto my feet,
> and a light unto my path
> (Ps. 119:105).

Thomas Cromwell waited before King Henry VIII who sat considering the gravity of the document in his hand. The king read its appointed and assigned injunctions, "Given by the authority of the King's Highness to the Clergy of this his Realm, designed for the reformation of the Church. . . .

"I, Thomas Cromwell, knight, keeper of the privy seal of our said sovereign lord the king . . . have appointed that any parson or proprietary of any parish church within this realm . . . provide a book of the Bible in . . . English, and lay the same in the choir, for every man that wills to look and read thereon, and shall discourage no man from reading of any part of the Bible, in Latin or English, but rather to comfort, exhort, and admonish every man to read the same, as the very Word of God."

King Henry hesitated, then instead of tossing the document aside in rejection, gestured his approval to Thomas Cromwell, who hastened to bow and placed the document with others, which the king had approved and merely waited his signature.

The king had just approved publication of a new English Bible published by Matthew Coverdale, a friend of William Tyndale. Little did Henry know that the new Bible was nearly 70 percent Tyndale's work. Assured that the edition was free of heresies, Henry proclaimed, "Well, if there be no heresies in it, then let it be spread abroad among all the people!" And in 1611 a new king from Scotland, James I, would authorize the *King James Version* which would contain some 90 percent of Tyndale's wordings.

Antwerp, 1536

Andrew and the Nubian had set sail for the New World. The galleon of Captain Stewert Brice moved silently from the harbor of Antwerp and out into the broader waters of the North Sea toward Edinburgh, Scotland. Felix sailed with them.

The wind was fresh on their faces as Justin stood with Regina. He drew his wife into his embrace and she smiled, holding him.

"Do you have any reservations, Regina?"

She wrinkled her nose at him. "What a baiting question! My reservations alter with the winds of persecution," she confessed wryly. "As you know very well. But my convictions are anchored to the Scriptures. And so! To Scotland," she declared firmly with a little smile. "It is onward, ever onward, knowing in whom we trust as Guide."

He gave her an enthusiastic squeeze admiring her courage and commitment to Christ. "Since the death of Patrick Hamilton, there has arisen one John Knox at the University of Saint Andrews. By the distribution of William Tyndale's New Testaments we shall soon light a torch for the Scottish reformation."

Below in the hold of the ship the New Testaments were packed in crates.

Regina smiled at Justin and softly touched the side of his

face with her hand, her mind wandering to the future and what it would bring. Justin was talking now. Thoughtfully, she noticed the intensity of his gaze as he spoke of the Scriptures and justification by faith. His voice came to her ears with the same compelling cadence that reminded her of those who had gone before, and her eyes clung to his as the wind blew against them and the ship moved forward.

Suddenly she placed her arms around him and held tightly. He said nothing, then lifted her chin and kissed her softly. "Regina, Regina, we could, if you wish, go back to London. It is safer there now."

After a moment her voice was steady, "No. At this time we must count the cost and go forward. We now hold in our hands the Word of God. We will not forget the cost so many paid that we may have it." She looked up at him. "How shall we ever forget William Tyndale?"

"We will not," Justin said firmly. "Now that the fire is kindled, we will work to make it burn even brighter by a commitment to teach the Scriptures. We will follow those who went before us, that God might use us to multiply their labors."

They held each other, then smiled.

"Come," he said cheerfully, swinging her in his arms. "For this moment we have each other. And tomorrow? It is enough that Christ and His Word will be there to sustain."

He set her firmly on her feet and she grabbed his hand. "Tonight we will gather the crew together and sing. I feel like singing one of Martin Luther's new hymns."

But their voices soon lapsed from vibrant song, to simply speaking the words ever so softly as they held to each other. The night was sinking about them and the stars appeared silver in the sky.

And tho' this world, with devils filled,
Should threaten to undo us;

We will not fear, for God hath willed
His truth to triumph through us.
The Prince of Darkness grim,
We tremble not for him;
His rage we can endure,
For lo! his doom is sure!
One little word shall fell him.

They paused, then went on. . . .

Let goods and kindred go,
This mortal life also;
The body they may kill:
God's truth abideth still.
His kingdom is forever.